APPRENTICE

Winner of the 2021 **Realm Makers Book of the Year Award**
Winner of the 2021 **Science Fiction Realm Award**
Winner of the 2021 **Young Adult Caleb Award**

"Apprentice is an intriguing story that will leave you second-guessing that new VR headset you just bought and psychoanalyzing your dreams again. Young has a flair for writing the sterile-perfect society of the haunting Love Collective that is both parts psychological thriller and science fiction adventure! Do not miss this story!"

— RONIE KENDIG, best-selling, award-winning author

APPRENTICE

APPRENTICE

COLLECTIVE UNDERGROUND | BOOK ONE

KRISTEN YOUNG

To Mum. My Eunice.

1

Welcome to the Nursery, children.
Here, you are safe.
Here, no Haters can harm you.
Here, you are never beyond our sight.
Love all.
Be all.
—Supreme Lover Midgate.

SOME THINGS SHOULD NEVER BE forgotten—at least, that's what they tell me. I can't forget anything. Not what I had for breakfast last week (regulation protein cereal). Not the Collective News broadcast from last month (Supreme Lover Midgate wanted to wish us all "a very happy Triumph of Love season."). Not even my first Hater Recognition Sign (Haters can't love. Period.).

Usually I can block most of it out, but sometimes it bubbles over, and I end up getting in trouble. Like when I recite my Dorm Leaders' exact words back to them. Or worse: when I recite what they said four years ago.

The name "Memory Freak" sticks to me like static electricity.

I've been living here in the Nursery Dorms for as long as I can remember. And that's where my head gets weird. Because as far as I can tell, my memories only start when I'm already a kid. Before that first day in the dorms? Nothing. After that day? Picture-perfect recall, all ten years of it.

I get it. In Nursery Dorm 492, every day is almost a mirror image of the day before. At precisely 0630, our stim-beds wake us up. Like drones we all file into the communal bathrooms. Then it's across the dorm campus to breakfast—hundreds of kids in regulation white jumpsuits, names embroidered on our lapels in case we forget. Not that I ever would:

Apprentice Kerr Flick
#540/187503

There's drill practice at 0830. Hater Recognition lessons at 0945. Love Collective History from 1030 until 1300. More drills. More apps. By the time 2030 kicks around, we're tired out and ready for the warm tickle of our stim-beds again. In between, it's a case of learn-as-much-as-I-can and avoid Myk, Bez, and Fedge. I call them the Three Fists because that's all they know how to use.

I don't have to worry about them for too much longer, though. I'm not going to be in the Nursery Dorm forever. No way. One day, I will get so far away they can't find me. One day, I'll get out of here and fly all the way to Elite Academy.

APPRENTICE: #540/187503

Transgression: Unnecessary information shared in Preparation for Life class.

Penalty: Three laps.

The words seem to float off the tiny slip of paper, condemning me in stark black type. I fold the demerit notice carefully and hide it underneath my dinner tray. No need for everyone to see that. Three laps aren't much, but an after-dinner penalty is always a cause for shame.

I tilt my head from side to side to check whether anyone saw. The dining room is full of noise. As usual, there's a large gap around me, as if my table is a forcefield that repels Apprentices.

Picking up my spoon, I pretend to be fascinated by scraping my dinner from the bowl. I've got the act down to a fine art now. Contented smile painted on my face. Eyes completely trained on the food. Ears listening carefully for any sound of approach. Hand carefully poised over the metal tray, as if this is my favorite thing to do in life.

Tonight's protein goop has a greenish tinge. It tastes like cardboard and smells like stale bread, but I gulp down two spoonfuls before I can blink.

"Ha ha ha *ha*!"

Seated on a bench at the other end of the dining hall, Fedge brays with laughter and slaps his leg in glee. Beside him, a figure crouches on the floor, hunched over a wide, oozing splatter of green. Fedge's foot sticks out from beneath the table, still pointing toward his victim, Koah.

The upturned tray at Koah's feet forms a shining rectangle in the middle of the mess created by her fall. A small crowd curves toward her from their places at the nearby tables. The laughter of Fedge and his cronies echoes off the white concrete ceiling.

"What's the matter, Koah? Can't walk properly?" Myk sneers from the other side of Fedge. Koah doesn't look up but scrapes the food back onto her tray with the edge of her hand. Fedge's foot gives her a little nudge from the back, and Koah overbalances into the green puddle. This sends a fresh bark of laughter up into the air.

"You'll never pass Fitness to Proceed if you keep falling over like that." The grin on Bez's wide, puffy face makes him look like a dog.

At his feet, Koah pushes herself off the floor.

"Poor Koah," mocks Fedge. "Now you'll have extra dirt with your dinner."

"She'll have to lick her uniform to get it!" Myk points to where a large green blob has spread across Koah's front.

Koah hurriedly scrapes a few more drips of food onto her tray and then stands up with as much dignity as she can muster. Her face is a mask of misery. The Fists' laughter swirls around her back, harsh and cutting. Every Apprentice's head turns away.

I watch her stumble down the aisle between tables, dripping tray quivering in her hands. Green slop oozes down her stomach. She looks around for support but meets only silence. Some people watch her back, only to turn their heads when she glances in their direction. She spots a vacant place along the metal bench at a table halfway across the room. With relief in her eyes, she dives toward it. Two Apprentices shift across, filling the empty space with their bodies. She springs back as if stung. Her bottom lip trembles.

Something in me snaps. I stand. Wait for her to notice me. Give her a smile. "You can sit here. With me," I say, not so loud it carries across to the Three Fists, but loud enough for her to hear me. "I got a whole table."

Her lip continues to tremble. She looks from side to side but meets only the backs of Apprentices and a wall of silence. Then, resigned, she nods and comes to sit in the wide space around me. Her head bends low, and her eyes are fixed on the messy remnants of her dinner. I realize that she must have left her spoon back on the ground near the "accident." She doesn't look at me.

"Are you okay?" I ask.

She doesn't answer.

"Just ignore them." I smile. "The Three Fists are always trouble." Koah stares down at the messy green tray. She keeps her eyes away from me.

"I'm sorry about your food," I sigh. She doesn't answer. The remnants of her dinner form a slimy, green streak along the aluminum surface of her tray. Her stomach growls over the table at me. I look back at my nearly full plate.

"Here," I say, pushing my tray across to her. I reach out and pull hers back to my side. "You have mine."

Koah's head comes up.

I give her a nonchalant shrug. "I have to go run laps anyway." I smile. I pick up the sliver of paper and wave it at her. Her face remains frozen. "Don't worry. It's not contaminated or anything."

She looks at me, then at the food I've just passed to her, then back to me. After a few tense moments, she picks up the spoon and starts shoveling food into her mouth. The expression on her face brings an old memory back. A first. There was a first time we sat here in the dining hall with that meal. All of us, smaller in our spotless white uniforms, moving our spoons from tray to mouth as if nothing else mattered in the universe.

"Koah, I was wondering," I say, keeping my voice low.

"What?" Koah replies, voice thick with food.

"Do . . . do you ever wonder if there was a 'before'?"

"What you talking about?"

I shrug, battling against the alarm bells going off in my head. "I haven't been able to ask anyone. But do you ever think that . . . maybe . . . there was a time before Nursery Dorm?"

"We've just always been here, Kerr." She turns back to her protein goop.

"But haven't you wondered when you learned to read?"

Koah glances up at me, enraged. "You stop talking like that right now. Or I will report you," she hisses, poking the spoon in my direction like a baton.

I shut my mouth and nod. "Forget I said anything," I say, stepping up from the bench. "Enjoy your dinner." I pick up her dripping tray and carry it back to the return pile.

Behind me, the dining room conversation returns to its normal low hum. When I glance back at Koah, her face is still rigid with shock and anger. I wink, but she keeps staring at me like I'm some kind of alien.

WHEN I STEP BACK INTO THE HALL AFTER my laps, the countdown music is already playing. Nursery Apprentices scurry forward, lining up in neat rows facing the large projection screen. I slot into my place just as the Collective theme song rings out around us with swelling melodies and proud drumbeats. We stand to attention.

The Collective flag waves across the oversized screen, then fades. A white studio swirls into focus, and Supreme Lover Midgate beams down on us from her place in her armchair. Her eyes are a piercing blue, and her steel-grey hair is trimmed in a perfect bob.

"Ah, my Lovelies," she says, smiling. "May you follow your dreams and find yourselves in the universe. I love you all, I mean it. Today, in the Collective, it is my honor and privilege to announce that, as a result of our Collective elections, the Supreme Executive have once again been voted in unopposed. I thank you for your wisdom and trust. We, your Executive, will not disappoint."

Her words filter into my memory even though I'm only half listening. Nearby, Apprentice Koah stares at the screen, looking as lifeless as a robot on standby. In the distance, Bez's shoulders sag with fatigue. His head begins to nod downward until his neighbor Fedge gives him a harsh nudge with his elbow. Bez jolts upright, looking back up to the screen with his chin pointing a little too high.

"You are all my Lovelies. Love all, be all. Good night."

Supreme Lover's smiling face disappears from the screen, and the hall's lights glow into life again. Apprentices glow into life too, slowly filtering out of the room toward the dorm rooms. All except for the privileged few who now get to enjoy app time.

"Stinkin' app monkeys," Bez mutters as he walks by.

"You're just jealous 'cos you got no minutes," Myk jeers.

Ignoring them, I wander over to the long bank of lockers against the inside wall. When I tap my Apprentice number into the screen, the lock clicks, and a locker door swings open. A dorm-issued infotab and headset rest inside. The cover is scratched and yellowing, and the headset's cord hangs in an untidy knot.

"Gah!" I look at the charging cable dangling free in the alcove. "Why do they never put them on the charger?"

A quick squeeze to the edges of the infotab tells me I've got 10 percent battery. If I'm lucky, it will last for all of my app minutes. If not . . .

"It'll have to be enough."

White beanbags have already been spread out across the floor, ready for the players. I pick one a little way away from everyone else and flop down into the soft cushion. Nestled on my knees, the infotab whirs into life. I enter my Apprentice number to log in, and the menu globe rotates invitingly in the center of the screen. A large time stamp in the corner lets me know how many app minutes I've earned today: *0:10:00.*

First stop is the entertainment precinct. *Elite Heroes* glows in the Favorites section beside a little red flag. I have a new episode waiting: "Election Mischief."

"Yes!" I select the five-minute episode and sit back for a few minutes of fun. Elite Lover Team Six is on the case again.

Elite Lover Hu gapes at the vidscreen data. "Election fraud? Who would consider such a heinous thing?"

"Who do you think?" Elite Lover Nissa snaps. They share a knowing nod.

"Haters," they say in unison.

After the overcar chases and acrobatic fight scenes, Elite

Lover Nissa signs off with my favorite line: "We're waiting for you." Her gaze is like steel as she stares straight at me.

"Working on it," I say, flicking to the little *Trivia Pavilion* icon. The game is so monotonous it's boring, but it's just about the only app I can use to clock up Love Points. I don't have the reflexes to win at *Hater Battle,* and nobody wants to friend me on *Collective Chat,* so this is it. At least I won't be disqualified from Elite Academy for not earning enough. My perfect record on *Trivia Pavilion* still shines at the top of the Nursery Dorm leaderboard.

A little pixelated Carell Hummer springs into life beside the question panel. "Question! Which Love Squad Hero holds the record for longest Pavilion service?" Fake Carell's voice squeaks into my headset.

I select the soldier's name and press Next. The screen goes dark.

"What?" I flip the infotab over and around, looking for what happened. When I squeeze the sides of the tablet, a little red empty battery sign glows briefly onscreen.

"Figures," I mutter. With a low groan I heave myself out of the beanbag and shuffle back to the lockers. It doesn't matter that I still have three app minutes left. One infotab a night is all we ever get. After making sure the infotab is plugged in, I close the locker door with a sigh and turn toward my dorm room.

"I bet Elites don't forget to charge infotabs," I grumble as I go.

2

The Love Collective is your Parent.
The Love Collective is your Friend.
The Love Collective is your Future.
Love all.
Be all.
—Supreme Lover Midgate.

DAY 237, 1430 HOURS. I STIFLE A YAWN. I'M
trapped in the all-white prison known as Preparation for Life
class with Lover Zink. Our ergonomic chairs force our backs
straight and our heads forward. Lover Zink blusters at the front
of the room—a wide-waisted man with more hair poking out of
his collar than on his head. It's hard not to feel sorry for him.
The white linen instructor's uniform is a disaster. He perspires
so much that by the end of our lesson, his sleeves are transparent
with large wet circles of sweat. Fedge calls him "Lover Stink"
behind his back, but Fedge would beat you senseless if you ever
threatened to tell. So I don't tell.

Lover Zink's beady black eyes scan over us. "So, Apprentices. Your time of graduation approaches. What do you wish
to do when you are grown?"

He beams at us all like Supreme Lover at gift-bearing time.

When nobody answers straightaway, he points a pudgy finger at Apprentice Koah.

She shrinks into her seat, and her voice comes out quivering and soft. It sounds like she's broadcasting from across the other side of the hill. "I just want to do the Love Collective's work," she whimpers. Then she shrinks even smaller. Except her eyes get really big and wide, like dinner plates.

Lover Zink smiles, mouth wide like a toad. "Good answer, Apprentice Koah. You get an extra three minutes of LC app time today. And you, Apprentice Fedge?"

"I want to do the Love Collective's work too," Fedge replies in a honey-sweet voice.

I sit in front of him, so I can't see his face, but I bet he's got that innocent expression which makes all the grown-ups love him.

"Well done, Fedge. Three extra minutes for you." Our instructor beams. I'm sure Fedge is smiling even wider now.

Zink goes around the room, getting everyone's answers.

When Bez proudly shouts, "I want to be an app monkey!" the whole room gasps.

Lover Zink shakes his head, his face looking like a disappointed beagle. "Now, now, Bez. It is not a monkey's job to do the work of the Love Collective. That's not approved lexicon. Five laps of the drill yard before mess hall."

"Sorry, Lover Zink," Bez moans. He has accumulated twenty-five laps so far today. He's going to miss dinner. I make a mental note to avoid him later. When he's hungry, he's mean.

"Apprentice Flick."

My head snaps up, and I'm looking into Lover Zink's pinched face. "Yes, Lover Zink?"

"Are you going to do the work of the Love Collective too?" A hint of sarcasm bubbles at the edge of Zink's voice.

The word explodes out of my mouth before I can stop it. "No."

There's another audible gasp around me. Lover Zink balks.

His glistening face reddens. "No?" he says, voice rising to an incredulous pitch at the end.

I swallow hard. "I'm going to be an Elite." I hold Lover Zink's stare without blinking. Silence spreads out across the room as forty openmouthed stares focus all their shock on me. I bet they're all expecting me to be running laps until next week. Or worse.

Lover Zink's mouth curls into a sneer. Then the instructor's belly begins to shake with laughter. "Kerr Flick, an Elite?" he snorts.

The whole class joins him, and I'm bombarded with raucous jeers and cackles.

"You need to be able to deal with people for that, girlie. One week at that Academy and you'll be back here on your knees begging to be an app mon—I mean, begging to do the Love Collective's work. Oh, ho ho ho! I haven't heard a joke as good as that in months!"

LOVER ZINK DOESN'T KNOW WHAT HE'S talking about. Okay, so maybe I'm shorter than most of the Apprentices here. Maybe my frizzy, black hair is never going to fit the Elite publicity photos. But I've got a memory that works better than any of them.

In our stories, Elites are the heroes. From their headquarters in Love City, they swoop in to save the Collective from the forces of Hate that threaten our empire. Elites fear nothing. They see everything. Elites also don't end up anywhere near Nursery Dorm 492 and the Three Fists.

In two weeks, we're going to be tested for our Fitness to Proceed. When that test rolls around, I'm going to be flying out of here on wings of electric silver. And no ignorant fists are going to stop me.

AS SOON AS THE BUZZER CHIMES US OUT of class, I make a dash for freedom. I'm passing the classroom door when Bez bumps me so hard my shoulder slams into the wall. The Three Fists make a move to surround me. Myk thumps his fist into the palm of his other hand.

"Trying to make us look stupid, Memory Freak?" Fedge snarls, leaning toward me. Before he can say anything else, I bolt away like a laser out of a gun.

"Hey! She's getting away!" Bez yells, about thirty seconds too late. Three sets of footsteps thunder down the hall behind me. I duck left into an open door, running through an empty lab and out the other side. The dorm facility houses hundreds of Apprentices, so there are plenty of places to lose them. I gave up asking the Lovers for help six years and five days ago, after Lover Zink asked me what I had done to provoke them. The Three Fists made sure I went to drill practice with a limp after that.

Today, the boys keep yelling for me in the distance, so I know where they are. I sprint out of the class building, weaving in and out of crowds heading for the drill yards. The covered walkway slopes downhill, curving at the last moment around a small rectangular building full of doors. I pick one door at random and slide in. The door clicks shut, and my world goes dark.

Blind and frightened, I step backward, bumping into what feels like a tall series of shelves. They erupt in a cacophony of rattles and clunks. Large round objects teeter and roll from their storage with earsplitting thunks. I take a sideways step to escape the avalanche, and startle a bunch of long-handled brooms out of their alcove. The tumbling sounds make me jump like a petrified rabbit.

Heart thumping, I freeze. After a few more tortured seconds of noise, the clattering dies away, and muffled voices from outside filter through the door. Voices rise and fall with the sound of a passing crowd.

"She went that way!" Bez yells in the distance. Myk's answering shouts thunder past my hiding place, growing quiet as they pass by. The darkness smells of fertilizer and bleach. I wait for more treacherous seconds until I'm sure they're gone. After a minute or two, the sounds of passing Apprentices fade into silence.

I should be relieved, but there's something really wrong with my head. Even though my back is against a wall, I can't shake the sense that someone is behind me. My thoughts get louder. A night bird hoots somewhere in the distance.

"Wait . . . what?"

Sweat trickles down my neck while I wait for my pulse to slow down. It doesn't. My breathing quickens to shallow puffs. Something pokes at the edges of my thoughts—a group of hazy impressions hovering just beyond reach. Fear. Darkness. A distant scream, wailing up through the night. I try to pin it down, but the images dance away, stabbing my temples with sharp, searing pain. My heart accelerates in ever increasing thuds.

"*No!*"

The cry is as vivid and real as if it had been shouted into my ear. I startle sideways, knocking another couple of brooms to the floor. More fragmented images tumble through my mind: Soft fabric swinging at my face, suffocating and unwelcome. Muffled shouts in the distance, dripping with malice. I'm held in place by bonds of steel, unable to move. Unable to see what is happening behind me.

"I gotta get out of here," I mumble. At any moment my heart is going to explode, or the walls will close in. I'll be squashed, forced to my knees in this darkness until I am entombed and forgotten forever. With blind stumbles and clunky footsteps over the fallen debris, I lunge for the door. A single fragment of sensible thought pierces my panic: I have to find the doorknob, or I will die.

I take two steps, and my arm hits solid metal. Feeling around in the darkness, my body shakes like a condemned Hater. The cool steel of the door handle is like a victory bell under my fevered hand. Yet my fingers are trembling so hard they can't turn anything. I twist the steel knob, lose my grip, and tear at it with increasing desperation. Finally the handle turns, the door swings open, and light floods my eyes. I tumble out of the supply cupboard, gasping for breath. There is a small grassy hillock off the side of the pathway. I fall upon it, sides heaving and tears streaming down my face. Relief slowly dissolves into me as the sunlight warms my limbs. A lone bird soars above the walls, circling in a silent display of winged freedom.

"What was *that* all about?" I ask myself. As if in answer, a new, unfamiliar sound reverberates through my mind. From the distant haze of darkness and confusion, a single word sobs into my thoughts. It crushes me beneath the weight of immense grief:

"Cadence."

3

Nursery Induction Manual
Catechesis volume 1, page 98.
   Q: What does the Love Collective provide to faithful
   Apprentices?
      A: A secure home. Daily food. Education in the
      ways of the Love Collective.

"CADENCE."

The unfamiliar word bounces around my head, now seared into my memory. I stare back at the open storage cupboard. A tangle of fallen brooms and buckets is all that remains of my terror. But my chest is still heaving, and my hands haven't stopped trembling.

"Two minutes to drill." The sweet, lilting announcer's voice through dorm loudspeakers snaps me out of my reverie.

"Great," I sigh. Dusting grass off my uniform, I pull myself upright and drag my feet down to the drill yard. It's a wide segment of open space beside the giant outer boundary wall, sterile and pristine with its plastic turf and unblemished concrete. The rest of my classmates are already lined up in crisp rows facing the drill platform. A conspicuous gap in one of the lines betrays my absence.

With a growing sense of dread, I jog to my place, head

hanging low and shoulders slumped. I'll have extra work now. My late arrival will be noted on the surveillance cameras. My dinner plate will arrive with another demerit slip. There's no point trying to explain. They wouldn't believe me, anyway.

Above our heads, beside the white stone platform, a series of loudspeakers points in our direction. The Love Collective theme blares through them, surrounding us with a wall of synthetic sound. We all know what's coming. It's been five years, four months, and seventeen days since the Lovers needed to supervise a drill.

MEMORY DATE: CE 2271.253 (10 YEARS AGO)
Memory location: Nursery Dorm 492, drill yard
Memory time: 0746 hours
We shiver. Four Lovers make us line up in front of the high platform. Each Lover holds a thick white stick as long as their forearm. It's only been three months, and I already hate their humming sound. Chief Lover Comb is on top of the platform high above us, eating a juicy red apple. His big belly sticks over the safety railing. He looks bored.

"Apprentices, march!" Chief Lover calls, spitting small pieces of apple into the air. The four Lovers wave us forward into one long line that snakes around the yard. We go faster this time. One of the little ones at the back (Apprentice Dev, #540/187546) falls down, tripped by his own feet. I wince when a Lover shoves a white stick into Dev's belly. There is a yucky sound and a loud yell, and Dev jumps, stung. The Lover swings the baton into the back of Dev's legs to make him walk again. Even though his whole body is shaking, Dev moves forward.

A HIGH-PITCHED SERIES OF BEEPS COUNTS us down, knocking the memory away for a moment. When the buzzer sounds, we all make a sudden left turn, slapping our hands to our sides with a loud clap. Then the march begins. Hundreds of feet move in time with the thumping beat of the music. Our voices combine as one, shouting into the sky.

"Haters can't love!"

"Lovers don't hate!"

"Love Collective children will all embrace their fate!"

"Haters can't love!"

"Lovers don't hate!"

"All of our allegiance to Supreme Lover Midgate!"

For an hour, we progress through all twenty-four Love Collective chants. Each chant has its own marching pattern, and by the time we're finished, our backs are drenched in sweat. I don't mind, though. The physical activity has flushed fear out of my system. Memories of terror and darkness have been silenced by a deep, satisfying physical exhaustion.

NURSERY DORM 492 ROOM EIGHT IS AS BIG as a factory, rows upon rows of stim-beds lined at 90 degrees against the stark-white, windowless walls. Every morning, a strip of blue light glows beside our mattresses, and our beds jolt us into wakefulness. When it's time for sleep, the strip of light bathes our floor with a calming orange hue. Fifty of us live in this space. There are ten dorm rooms in our sector. That's five hundred Apprentices, give or take a few.

Apprentice Koah is my closest neighbor. She hasn't spoken

to me since I gave her my dinner, but she hasn't reported me, either. When I get near her, she turns away from me, whispering to another Apprentice a few beds away. I could be wearing a purple Triumph Carnival mask, and she wouldn't take any notice.

Movement further down the room catches my eye, and my breath hitches in my throat. The Three Fists stroll up the aisle, determined scowls turned my way. I cast a glance around, searching for an ally to help. Then something Koah says catches Fedge's attention.

"You talking Fitness to Proceed?" Fedge stops beside her bed. His voice rises above the nightly hum.

"Yeah. So?" Koah replies.

"I heard some bigger kids talking about it." Fedge looms over Koah.

"How? They live in a different sector."

"I have my ways. Anyway, they said that some of their dorm-mates disappeared during the test and were never seen again."

Koah gasps, and Fedge's grin widens in satisfaction.

"They flush the failures down a big tube," Myk adds, nodding with the confidence of someone who knows nothing.

"Rubbish." Rip, one of our tallest dorm-mates snorts from across the aisle. He's the only one in our group brave enough to stand up to the Three Fists.

"Is not!" Fedge pouts, eyes ablaze. The look on Fedge's face would scare most kids, but not Rip.

"You're full of it." The taller Apprentice sniffs, giving a dismissive shake of his head.

"He's not," Bez jumps in. "But they don't recycle failures down a tube. They keep a rabid Hater under the testing room, and if you fail, he eats you." He lurches at Koah across the aisle so she flinches.

"No, it's a special machine that fries your brain if you don't answer the questions on time." Myk gives his friend a shove.

"That's stupid. Who would do the work of the Love Collective if they turned us all into vegetables?" Bez argues.

"The Love Collective wouldn't do that anyway. They're our family," says Fedge.

"Look who's the Executive-kisser now." Fedge bristles at Myk's verbal jab.

"Yeah. Who died and made you Dorm Instructor?" Bez chimes in.

"I'm not . . . You take that back." Seeing the fire flashing in Fedge's eyes and his clenching fists, Myk is quick to back down.

Rip holds his hand up to stop any sudden fights breaking out. "Have you ever thought that maybe they send the smart ones off to another dorm somewhere?" he suggests.

"Or the dumb ones," Bez rejoins.

"We won't see you anymore, then." Fedge elbows Bez with a harsh nudge.

Bez rolls his eyes. "Idiot."

"You first."

The Three Fists go on with their jokes, but you can see the tightness around their eyes. It's all a mask, hiding the nervous tension zinging underneath their skin. Nobody knows what we're going to face in that room. It's no surprise they're creating monsters in their heads.

I'm probably the only one of my classmates who actually wants to disappear.

MEMORY DATE: CE 2272.214 (9 YEARS AGO)

Memory location: Nursery Dorm 492, south hallway

Memory time: 1501 hours

His eyes are big, white with fear. He's standing there in the hall, his face a weird, sick-looking grey. Two linen-clad Lovers stand in front of him, their voices too quiet to hear. Their hairstyles are identical, clipped and smooth around the backs of their necks. I've seen them a lot but never know their names. I call them Justice. Apprentices flow around them, eddying like a river around a fallen tree branch.

One leans down to speak to the boy who's caught like a fish between their stares. His eyes start to leak tears, and he stumbles over his words. What hateful thing has he done? The Lover flicks his finger forward, and the boy's shoulders slump in misery. He turns and walks where he has been commanded, like a condemned prisoner to his Embracement. They vanish through a door-sized hole in the white wall, which closes behind them, leaving no trace.

I never learned his name.

SAFE FROM THE FISTS FOR THE MOMENT, I lean back on my mattress with nothing to interrupt my thoughts.

I'm doomed.

I don't know how I will survive if this is my life. Nobody wants to talk to me because my "gift" scares them away. In fact, they mostly want to stop me from being *me*.

MEMORY DATE: CE 2277.004 (3 YEARS AGO)

Memory location: Nursery Dorm 492, dining hall

Memory time: 1830 hours

Apprentice Koah isn't looking at me. She stares at her plate, pushing her food around with her fork.

"The thing is, Kerr, you shouldn't . . ." She bites her lip.

"You shouldn't always be telling us what we said ages ago. It's really weird."

I NEED TO GO TO ELITE ACADEMY. IF I CAN'T pass Fitness to Proceed, then I'm stuck here. Forever. Until today, I was pretty confident I'd get in. But now . . .

"You're too crazy to be Elite," I sigh to myself.

Shades of darkness flit across my memory again. Faraway screams, mingling with tumbling brooms and buckets. Nothing about this afternoon's nightmare makes sense. But then, how can it be a nightmare if I was awake and alert? It felt like a nightmare. A nightmare is the only logical explanation, unless . . .

Unless there's something seriously wrong with me.

I've heard stories about hallucinations. Haters who started jabbering in the middle of classes or muttering in the halls. If even half of the rumors are true, Fitness to Proceed will reveal that little incident, and I'll look like some kind of crazy Hater person.

"Am I going crazy?" I whisper. Nobody pays me any attention.

"Beauty Sleep in thirty seconds," soothes the calm voice of our announcement AI. Near the bathrooms a few students make a sudden dash to their beds. Everyone lies flat on their mattress, arms down by their sides. Even the Three Fists turn and run. I straighten my body on my stim-bed, head still full of throbbing pain and unsolved mysteries.

A soft, peaceful tone rings through the speakers. Every bed-light dims to a gentle glow. At the same moment, our beds begin to hum. The soothing ritual is so ingrained in me now that even with my new fears, I drift into unconsciousness.

4

Nursery Induction Manual
Catechesis volume 2, page 38.
  Q: What is your ultimate goal in life?
    A: To do the work of the Love Collective.
  Q: How does an Apprentice achieve their ultimate goal?
    A: By working according to the Collective Precepts,
    Manuals, Priority Statements, and Mission Goals
    handed down by the Supreme Executive.

FITNESS TO PROCEED. A WEIRD NAME FOR the test that determines the course of your life. Factory workers, office bean counters, Love Squad cadets, Executive wannabes. The Lovers keep telling us that our whole future is determined from this one test. This single hour. Or three. Or seven. No Apprentice knows how long it takes. They keep us in the dark about that and lots of other details. Like the important detail of what we're actually tested on. Nobody knows that, either.

After breakfast, we assemble in the drill yard to wait for instructions. We've practiced lining up so many times we all do it instinctively now. You can see the nerves. Everyone is standing a little taller, or jiggling their legs, or staring into the distance with haunted expressions.

"Love all."

"Be all!" We snap to attention in reply to Lover Zink's greeting.

His eyes wash past me, surveying the group. "My children, you are all a wonder. Congratulations on making it to this wonderful day. Now, are you all lined up according to your identification numbers? Good. Good. I caution you that your every action from this point will be recorded. So be on your best behavior, children. I would not want any of my class to fail."

Heads around me nod. Backs get straighter. I silently curse the fact that my Apprentice number puts me right next to Fedge. It would be just my luck that he would try to make me fail. Sure enough, he turns ever so slightly toward me.

"Gonna get you."

MEMORY DATE: CE 2280.338 (1 YEAR AGO)
Memory location: Corridor Seven
Memory time: 1145 hours
Fedge grabs my left arm, creating a small tear in the material. I will pay for that later.
"Gonna get you," he says.

MEMORY DATE: CE 2279.033 (2 YEARS AGO)
Memory location: Room 23
Memory time: 1418 hours
Sitting in my assigned seat, ready for Prep. Lover Zink is late. Fedge enters the room and detours from his usual route to his seat. He leans toward my face as he passes.

"Gonna get you," he whispers.

MEMORY DATE: . . .

"KEEP PACE BEHIND ME, APPRENTICES!"
Lover Zink's crisp command shuts off the vidscreen display
running through my brain. Like robots we march, our feet
making a drumbeat along the path.

The testing center gleams at the top of the hill, white concrete
walls almost blinding in the early-morning sun. Neat rows of
perfect hedge surround it, softening the hard, geometric lines
of Love Collective architecture with wavelike patterns. Glass
windows reflect light in all directions. A brightly colored Love
Collective flag flutters proudly from the rooftop flagpole. Every
surface is pristine, unstained. Nervous, I reach up to smooth
my dark, frizzy, untamable hair.

We follow Lover Zink into a grey-tiled atrium that looks like
a concrete box. The air is cool but stale. To my right, a concrete
fountain provides the constant sound of trickling water. I'm not
sure if it's supposed to be soothing or irritating. A faint smell of
lemon disinfectant wafts through the air around us.

Zink brings us to a halt in an open space to the left of the
entrance. The only decoration on the stark grey wall is a single
analog clock. There's a thin rectangular outline of two large
doors, almost invisible in the grey walls. Framed by the door's
outline, Zink arranges us into six parallel lines facing the closed
door. He pulls me to the front of one line, dragging Fedge to
stand within arm's reach beside me. My misery grows.

"Attention!" Zink commands. The sound of us snapping upright is like a thunderclap. Zink gives us all one last brief smile. He nods stiffly, salutes, and then leaves. A small ball of fear forms in the pit of my stomach.

Minutes tick by. Any moment now, another Lover will arrive to take us to our test. I don't allow my shoulders to relax. An Elite knows how to follow orders. Until someone tells me to stand at ease, I have to remain still.

More minutes pass. With no Lovers arriving to direct us, time is beginning to wear on some of my dorm-mates. A few rows away, someone makes soft cracking noises as they twitch their head from left to right. More than one Apprentice shuffles their feet. The constant trickle of water makes me need to visit a bathroom. But I hold myself as still as I can, letting my chest rise and fall in calm, regular rhythm.

A sneering whisper wafts into my hearing, barely audible above the fountain's gurgle.

"You're going to fail, Memory Freak."

I lift my chin a fraction higher, force my shoulders to straighten. I try to pretend that there is a void beside me instead of a menacing, glowering Apprentice. Unfortunately, my memory burns Fedge's every word permanently into my brain.

"You can't do drills, Memory Freak. Remember last week?"

MEMORY DATE: CE 2281.195 (THIS YEAR)
Memory location: Nursery Dorm 492, drill yard
Memory time: 1545 hours
Drill practice. Routine change. Two lines of marchers intersect, crossing through each other. Fedge sticks his foot out as he passes, sending me crashing to the floor.

"DID YOU THINK THEY'D ASK YOU LOTS OF questions so you'd show them your big brain? This is a fitness test. You got none of that."

Shut up.

"You're going to be shoveling dirt on the highway, Memory Freak. Not even good enough to be an app monkey."

I glance at the clock. Half an hour has passed, and there is still no sign of a Dorm Instructor anywhere. The shuffling noises behind me are joined by the occasional cough. My ankles are beginning to burn with the pain of standing still. Someone finally loses patience.

"Oh, come on!" calls an exasperated voice from the far corner of the room. A ripple of nervous giggles follows the exclamation. I let my mind run back over the Elite Axioms: *Elites focus on the goal, not the game. Elites put performance ahead of pleasure. Elites are always on duty. Elites are never sloppy. Elites—*

"Memory Freak thinks she's too good for us," Fedge says, louder. There are more giggles behind me. I glance at the clock again. Another five minutes. I risk a glance toward Fedge out of the corner of my eye, careful to keep my face forward. His mouth breaks into a cruel smirk.

"Gotcha."

I snap my eyes forward again, willing the door in front of me to open. Words begin to tumble out of Fedge's mouth, as incessant as the trickling fountain behind us.

"You failed, Memory Freak. You're never going to be an Elite, Memory Freak. Give up now, Memory Freak. Let the big boys take it from here. You should have been Embraced at birth, Memory Freak."

He doesn't let up, not even as the clock ticks toward the

hour. *What if he's right?* I think. *What if I'm not cut out to be an Elite? Maybe he knows more than I do.*

I focus on my breathing, counting the seconds as my lungs fill and then empty. *Breathe in . . . two . . . three . . . four. Breathe out . . . two . . . three . . .* A sharp sting to my ear pierces my concentration. My first instinct is to turn to the source of the pain, to stare daggers at Fedge in response to the painful flick of his fingernails. But I refuse to give him satisfaction. He leans in so close that his breath tickles my ear. It reeks of stale vitamin juice. His whisper is barely audible: "You've failed, Memory Freak."

When I don't respond, he hovers behind me, circling his whispers from my left ear to my right. The sting in my ear keeps on throbbing. Something trickles down my earlobe and between my neck and collar. It takes every ounce of willpower I have to stop my hand from wiping the trickle away. But Lover Zink commanded us to stand at attention. So I stand.

The crack in the door widens at exactly one and a half hours after we arrive. Behind and around me there's a sudden burst of activity, and even Fedge returns to his place in a flurry of panic. My heart begins to beat faster. A man I have never seen before steps out of the doorway. He stands before us, clasping his hands behind his back.

"Good morning, Apprentices. My name is Lover Peers and I am your chief examiner today. When I call your number, proceed to my left to line up in front the clock. If I do not call your number, remain where you are."

Tension ripples over the group. Lover Peers pulls out a miniature infotab from his belt and begins to recite numbers. My heart is thudding wildly now. The group begins to thin, separating Apprentice from Apprentice.

"Apprentice #540/187502."

Fedge straightens and marches quickly to join the new line. Finally Lover Peers folds his infotab back into his belt. I resist the urge to look backward. From the corner of my eye, it looks like almost everyone is lined against the other wall. A large door slides open in front of them, and they march away down a long white hall.

Fedge's mouth curls into a sneer before he passes out of view. He mouths one final insult: *"You failed, Memory Freak."*

When the door slides back into place, it's as if the entire group no longer exists. Lover Peers looks at me, unsmiling. I feel lightheaded.

"This way." He beckons, and we march forward. I take the opportunity to wipe the side of my ear. A clear, sticky liquid shines on my fingertips. Fedge spat on me. What kind of idiot does that in a Fitness to Proceed test?

Beyond the door is another long hallway, white and sterile. I risk a glance to see how many Apprentices remain. Apprentice Koah gives me a nervous grimace and flicks her eyes to Lover Peers's back. There are four others. Apprentice Rip is one of them.

We follow Lover Peers down the hall lit by cold white LEDs that make my skin color pale from a warm olive to a dull grey. Lover Peers walks to another large door at the far end of the hallway. He waves his wrist in front of an ID panel set halfway up the wall, and the door glides open. I gasp.

The room beyond the door is better than my wildest dreams. VR stations line grey, metallic walls. Two instructors sit at a long console table at the far end of the room. Their hands glide over the glass, and 3D visual displays rise above the table. It looks exactly like the one Elite Lover Nissa uses to stalk criminals.

"It's Elite Lover Team Six!" I say, eyes wide.

"This isn't infotab entertainment." Lover Peers's tone is dry.

Nobody talks as Lover Peers leads each of us to a VR station. We each step up onto a circular platform at the center of our own booth. A single vidscreen hangs on the wall in front of me. When the screen winks into life, I see myself from behind.

I bounce from foot to foot while the two attendants hand out special gloves to each of us. They stretch across my fingers in sleek grey fabric.

I am trying to play it cool, but I can't hide the grin that breaks out across my face when Lover Peers hands me a streamlined helmet, sleek and grey. As I pull the helmet over my head, a black visor descends past my eyes, and my ears are cocooned from the outside world.

It doesn't matter if the helmet is more clunky than Nissa's slim glasses. Doesn't matter if this is an exam. If I could spend my life in this kind of space, I'd be happy forever.

5

Nursery Dorm Mission Goal Document 4.581
Statement 7: Memory and Loss.
Never forget, dear Apprentices.
Never forget that we are too close to the days of evil.

THROUGH THE VR HELMET, ALL I CAN HEAR is the sound of a rushing hurricane. When the wind shuts off, a quiet, authoritative voice drones through the speakers:

"Welcome to the Fitness to Proceed test . . ."

A keyboard appears in the air below my face, hovering in darkness. I raise my hands, and my fingers appear in virtual form, poised above the keys. When I wiggle my fingers, the virtual fingers wiggle too. The gloves gently prod my fingertips every time I press down on a key, simulating the real thing.

Seconds later, a giant red countdown fills my visor: *03 . . . 02 . . . 01.* A series of glowing questions flashes across the screen. In answer, my fingers begin to fly over the keys.

Q: What are the five Hater Recognition Signs?

A: The Five Hater Recognition Signs are 1. Doubt, 2. Chaos, 3. Language, 4. Appearance, 5. Allegiance.

1. Doubt.

Haters question what they are given.

*Haters do not understand the privilege they have to live in the
Love Collective.*
Haters doubt the testimony of their superiors.
Lovers do not doubt their Supreme Leader's affection.
Lovers do not doubt the truth of the Love Collective.
Lovers do not doubt.
2. Chaos . . .

I have just completed question two hundred and fifty-two
when my headset plays an alarm. Shortly afterward, the visor
rises away from my face. I stagger a little, disoriented by the
sudden return to the real world.

I twist around in my spot. Apprentice Koah gives me a
timid thumbs-up from her booth beside me. Apprentice Rip
stares around the room, looking confused. Two Apprentices
are missing.

The instructors crowd together over the console table, heads
together in low conversation. Screenshots of us in the VR room
hover side by side above the table. When Lover Peers glances
up at me, his brows knit together.

"Apprentices dismount," drones an artificial voice in my
helmet. I obey with reluctance. My first experience of VR, and
all I get to do is type stuff? I thought there were flight simulators
and quests. It seems a waste to use all that tech when I could
have sat in front of an infotab.

I drag the helmet up off my head, securing it under one
arm while I pull off the gloves. Then with shaking legs I take
a careful step off the platform. The other Apprentices do the
same. Koah catches my eye, and I mouth the words, "Is that
it?" to her. She shrugs. A slim instructor with close-cropped
blonde hair approaches and collects the helmets and gloves
from everyone except me.

"Thank you, students," Lover Peers says to the other
Apprentices. "Please follow Lover Argos to your next
assignment. Apprentice Flick, you will remain."

Rip frowns at me like I've disappointed him somehow. Koah gives me a quick, apologetic smile. They head out of a door at the back of the room. After they leave, Lover Peers returns to his intense discussion at the console table. I hover beside my VR station, holding my helmet and gloves awkwardly. Have I failed? I think back over the questions, running the test through my head again. I answered exactly as they taught me. Everything. Even some extra things that I researched via infotab. Was that the problem? Too much?

Stupid memory.

Taking great care, I begin to smooth out the folds of my gloves, laying one on top of the other. I must have entered information that I wasn't supposed to know. That must be it. I never should have done that extra research. The Love Collective wants me to be obedient, not wild. Fedge was right. I was always going to fail.

"Apprentice Flick."

My head snaps up, and I realize by the sting at the corners of my eyes that I've nearly been crying. "Yes, Lover Peers?"

"My apologies. We have been organizing the final examination for you. It seems . . ." He coughs somewhat nervously. "It seems we have never had to provide the Elite test to any of our students before. We were looking for the correct protocols."

My eyes widen at the same time my panic evaporates. *The Elite test?*

"Sorry, Lover Peers." I'm trying to play it cool, but a smile forces its way onto my face and into my voice. My whole world makes a sudden upside-down shift.

"Do not apologize. I have summoned Chief Lover Comb. If you pass, you will bring great honor upon us all here at Nursery Dorm 492." Lover Peers beams at me.

"I will do my best, Lover Peers."

"You have already done more than any of your dorm-mates.

The VR experience is disorienting, and we usually lose most of them before the test starts. But you—well, we will see."

"What happened to them?" I ask. "The others."

"Strictly speaking, that is not your concern, but—"

"Thanks be to the great minds of you all!" booms a loud voice behind me. I jump in fright.

"Love abounds and abides," replies Lover Peers in the well-rehearsed formal greeting.

"May we all reach for our dreams and find ourselves in the universe!" chortles Chief Lover Comb, his booming voice filling the VR room. The chief of our Nursery Dorm strides up to me, his rounded face cracked in a wide smile. The white linen of his uniform is marred by a large sauce stain on top of his bulging stomach. A pair of eyeglasses rests on top of his shiny bald head, and a large napkin still hangs from his collar.

"Ah, this must be Apprentice Flick, our academic wonder," Chief Comb says, wiping at his mouth with the corner of his napkin. "I hope you don't make me regret leaving my morning coffee break for this." He wags a fat finger at me in mock disapproval.

I salute and stand to attention. "I will do my best, Chief Lover Comb."

"That's all we can ask for, Apprentice." He turns to the small gathering of instructors, clapping his hands together. "Well, let's get this show on the road."

"As you wish, Chief Lover Comb." Lover Peers salutes. "Apprentice Flick, please return to your testing position."

As Chief Lover Comb and Peers huddle at the instructors' console, I step back up to my platform. Gloves safely on, the black visor descends over my face once more, and I am thrown off balance by a sudden rush of images. I battle against a wave of nausea and disorientation. Images flash past me faster than my brain can process them. It takes all my effort just to remain upright.

The rush of images fades, replaced by a lush country landscape. Like a drone, I hover above the ground. When I point my head forward, I begin to fly over sunny green fields. The roar of wind sounds in my ears. Fields recede beneath suburban homes, which give way to dense high-rise towers. My flight carries me over a large city that straddles a gently flowing river. A wide avenue decorated with brightly colored flags leads over a bridge and up a large hill. At the top of the hill is a palace, a fortress of gleaming white stone lit by white beams of light. The gigantic Love Collective flag waves majestically from the top of the building.

As I drop toward the golden gates, a soothing female voice croons in my ear. "Welcome to Love City, jewel in the crown of the Love Collective nation. The Hall of Love welcomes you."

The Hall of Love. Awe nearly buckles my knees. These hallowed halls are the home of only the best of the best. Golden gates gleam and twinkle in the virtual light. The filigree motto spelled out across the gate arch sparkles so much it hurts my eyes:

LOVE ALL. BE ALL.

My nerves zing, waiting for the gates to open. Nothing happens. Beyond the gates lies a wide paved courtyard. Far across the courtyard is a set of broad stairs, climbing up to shimmering glass doors. Tentatively, I lift my knee. The platform beneath me moves like a treadmill. I step up to the latch on the gate for a better look. When my special gloves touch the lock, an electric shock zaps me so hard I snatch my hand back in pain.

Taking care with the treadmill platform beneath me, I walk first to one side of the gate, then another. Golden bars meet smooth, unbroken white stone. There are no doors or intercom buzzers or keys. Apart from the gate, there is no way in.

I walk back to where I started, thinking over all my lessons. I learned about the Hall of Love, that's true. But what did they tell me? It's where the Supreme Executive live and work. It's where the Love Broadcasts happen. It's where, each year, a lucky ten couples selected during the Triumph of Love festival get to go on an all-expenses paid tour. But none of the infotab movies I saw showed me how to get inside if the gates were locked.

I walk up to the lock again and put my hand on the latch. The gates send me a painful electric shock. Again. I shake my injured hand in frustration.

"I'm here for the test!" I yell, cradling my pained fingers. "Helloooo? Is anyone there?" Nobody answers. Nothing moves beyond the gates, and the city street behind me is silent and empty. It's creepy.

"I love the Love Collective!" I say to the gates. When there's no reply, I start reciting one of my Love Collective drills.

"Haters can't love! Lovers don't hate!" I shout, marching back and forth across the gates. They don't even twitch.

"Love all. Be all!" I yell.

I go through everything I can remember from Supreme Lover Midgate's evening lectures. I'm soon reciting axioms and slogans and even an entire Triumph of Love speech. The gates remain closed and silent.

Elites focus on the goal, not the game. Elites put performance ahead of pleasure. Elites are always on duty. Elites are never sloppy. Elites—

Performance ahead of pleasure. That's it! I step as close to the gates as I can. A series of filigree roses on a thorny golden vine wrap around the lock in an infinite mobius-style loop. The thorns are razor sharp, and no doubt the gloves would punish me well for attempting to touch them. But there's a thin line around the base of each rose that gives me an idea.

With trembling fingers, I reach out and press the center of one rose. The electric shock this time isn't a harsh pain but a gentle buzz that is almost bearable. Even better, the rose clicks down into the vine and rotates in a clockwise direction. Elated, I press down on the center of the next rose, and receive a harsh zap. With a whir and click, both roses rotate backward and return to their original positions.

"Gah!"

Frustrated, I press the first rose once more and then choose a different one. For the second time the roses click and whir back into position, and I am left nursing a painfully zapped hand. I try again, moving from the first rose to a flower that almost disappears around the back of the lock. I only receive a slight buzz, and the two roses remain still. I hop from foot to foot in excitement. Unfortunately, I'm so excited that I don't think, and the third rose zaps me hard, whirring back into place along with the first two.

It takes a few tries and more than a few painful zaps, but eventually I work out the first six roses in sequence. Only three roses remain. By this time, I've received so many painful zaps through my gloves that I have to swap hands each time I press a rose. My fingers burn.

"Thirty seconds remaining," croons the artificial voice through my speakers. Panic thrills through me. My hands shake. I repeat the sequence, but I fumble around the fourth rose and receive another unwanted, painful zap.

"Focus, girl," I growl through gritted teeth. This time, I get the sequence of six right, leaving only three. They're located along the top of the gates, left, right, and center. I press the right one, and all seven roses click back into their starting positions. The zap brings tears to my eyes.

"Not the right one, then," I huff. I press the rose sequence again. When I reach the final three, I try the left one, and miraculously it works. That leaves only the center and right roses to go.

"Ten seconds," croons the voice.

Panic rising even higher, I take a deep breath and press the rose on the right again. It zaps me, and all the roses click back into their unopened positions. My mouth is dry and my hands tremble. But I can't stop. With a burst of focused speed and anger, I press every rose in the sequence I can remember.

"Five," counts down the voice as I reach the fifth rose.

"Four," the voice says. I press the sixth rose, watching it click into place.

"Three," I move to the top of the lock, pressing the left rose.

"Two," I press the center rose, and it clicks into place.

"One," I reach for the final rose, feeling the gentle buzz of the shock as I press down. The whole scene goes dark. I scream with frustration.

"I was so close!"

A pinpoint of white light appears in the center of my vision. Slowly it grows into a wider and wider circle, bright enough to make me squint. White light envelops me.

"What—?" I stammer. I am deposited in a large white room, empty except for a single wingback armchair. The white cushions are sleek, and the high back of the chair faces away from me. It hits me in that moment that I can see someone's feet through the gap under the chair. Someone wearing white linen pants and white patent-leather shoes.

I take a deep breath and step forward. The scene whirls, and I am standing in front of the chair, staring straight into the piercing blue eyes of Supreme Lover Midgate. She smiles at me, regal and patient. I throw myself onto the floor, pressing my forehead onto the tiles.

I have disgraced myself. I didn't bow fast enough. If they threw me into the Haters' Pavilion right now, I would get what I deserved.

"Welcome, child," Supreme Lover Midgate purrs. I'm too scared to even glance at her shoes. "Let me be the first to extend my congratulations to you on successfully passing the Elite entrance test. You have chosen a great and glorious journey. But I must warn you that the path ahead is not easy. Only the best of the best join us here in the Hall of Love. Work hard, train well, and remember: love all, be all."

6

Haters fail. The Love Collective can only rise.
—Supreme Lover Midgate.

A ROUND OF APPLAUSE STARTLES ME. AT the command console, Lover Peers and the other instructors clap and cheer. The vision of my prostrate figure on the floor of the white room is frozen in 3D above the console.

I lift my head from the VR platform and scramble to my feet. Chief Lover Comb bustles down the center aisle toward me, beaming and holding his arms out wide.

"You have done it! My dear Apprentice Flick, well done! Well done, child!" Chief Lover Comb crows. He grabs my pained fingers, pumping my arm up and down until it feels like it might fall off. I wince. The smile widens in his face, and his beady eyes shine at me. "My dear, we were afraid you were going to fail at that last second. You certainly gave us a bit of a thrill, I can tell you! But well done. Well done. Nursery Dorm 492 has finally arrived!"

"Thank you, Chief Lover Comb," I manage to say between vigorous arm pumps. Smiling adults crowd around me, slapping me on the back.

"An Elite cadet! Just think of it!" Chief Lover Comb waggles his finger at me. "We expect great things from you, young lady!"

"I will do my best, Chief Lover." I wobble on my feet.

Lover Peers steps forward. "Right. Apprentice Flick, we have half an hour before the transport arrives. So let's get you some food before your journey. If you don't mind, Chief?"

"Yes, yes, good, good. Take her to my mansion, Peers. I want to record this occasion with the pomp and ceremony it deserves."

"As you wish, Chief Lover, but we may not have time to get her to your quarters and back in time for the transport. Perhaps we could arrange something here in the instructors' dining hall instead?"

Comb gives a disappointed sigh. "All right. It's not as opulent, but it will have to do. Good. Good. Yes. Send her in. Make sure the publicity department is informed. We want this on the next local newsfeed ASAP. Nothing but the best for our little Elite, eh?" The Chief Lover rubs his hands together in glee.

"As you wish, Chief Lover."

The attendants snap to attention and then bustle away. Lover Peers holds his hand out toward me.

"This way, young lady," he smiles. "Let's get you some food before you fall over."

I drag my weary legs behind him, a mixture of excitement and exhaustion warring for control over my body. The next few minutes pass in a blur. We stop near a bathroom so I can freshen up. Then Peers leads me to a sleek silver elevator. We rise to the top of the building, where a wide, window-lit space on the top floor forms the staff dining hall.

For a few precious moments of peace I stand at the window, surveying the dorms below. My own dormitory wing stretches out in front of me, surrounded on two sides by walls like the spokes of a wheel. Other dormitory wings lie on either side of it. The drill yards form the boundary, hemmed in by a large circular wall that blocks off all vision of the outside world.

This is all I've ever known. Does life even exist outside these walls?

I don't get to wonder for long. News travels fast, and a crowd gathers around my table. Surrounded by the uncomfortable gazes of my old teachers—including the rather shamefaced grimace of Lover Zink—I scoff down a plate of the best food I have ever tasted.

When the plate is empty, I smile for cameras and handshakes and publicity shots until my cheeks ache. Then just as quickly, I am whisked away. Chief Lover Comb accompanies Peers and me into the elevator. When the leader waves his wrist over the scanner, a new row of buttons appears on the elevator console. A crowd of Lovers waves and cheers as the silver doors glide shut.

The lift descends into the lowest reaches of the building. When the elevator doors open, a stale gust of air buffets us. We step out onto a subterranean platform, gleaming white and grey tiles arching over my head. The tiled floor ends at a sharp drop. Beyond the drop, a tunnel disappears into darkness. I'm still wondering what I'm looking at when another burst of stale air pushes at my clothes. A squealing metallic sound erupts from one side of the tunnel, and then a long train bursts into the black space. It glides to a stop in front of the platform, a sleek grey-and-white bullet.

"Your transport awaits, my dear!" Chief Lover Comb says.

"Where are my things?"

"Oh, forget about that. You'll get new things at Elite Academy!" He laughs, arms out wide. I open my mouth to protest, but a quick nudge from Lover Peers stops me.

The train doors glide open, revealing a carriage full of rows and rows of empty seats. I take a deep breath and step in, enveloped by a hum of artificial light. A gentle gust of air swirls around me, cooling after the hot stuffiness of the platform.

Two steps in, the carriage lurches forward. I scramble for a place, grasping hold of the cushioned tops. My seat is plush and comfortable. Within minutes, aided by the rhythmic clack of the train over tracks, I fall into a deep sleep.

LOVE. PURE LOVE. I'VE NEVER FELT SO warm and comforted and . . . held.

My eyes flutter open. He stands in front of me, but I cannot tell how tall he is. His face is kind and caring, wrapped in beams of glorious light. He reaches out for me, and when he speaks, I want to cry with the joy of the love that pours from his words.

"I am calling you. Cadence."

Lyric.

An image flashes across my mind. A room full of glass that lets the sun stream through tall windows. A wall of bookshelves, full of real books. Soft carpet leading to a wide oak desk. At the desk, a woman sits. Her hair is swept back from her face in tiny black braids. She is wearing the formal Love Collective uniform of someone important, but her face is sad. The man wrapped in light stands behind me, urging me toward the desk.

"Come find me," he says again.

THE HIGH-PITCHED SQUEAL OF BRAKES pierces through my dreams, dragging me into groggy wakefulness. I blink away a strange, dizzy sense of disconnection. I had hoped my little delusion in the supply cupboard was the only time. But now I'm dreaming of voices? Trust my brain to have the bad sense of timing to go crazy just as all my Elite wishes are about to come true.

My body lurches forward, and the train slows to a stop. Doors roll open, sending my nerves zinging. Seconds later, a girl bounds onto the train, followed by a tall boy with deep olive skin. The girl's hair sits in tight curls around her head, bouncing with each skipping footstep she makes. She stops, turns, and waves brightly at someone outside the door. Then she bounces down the aisle toward me. Still a little groggy from my sleep, I stare stupidly back at them. The girl walks past all the rows of seats and comes to a stop beside me.

"Sif Grohns," she says, holding out her hand. Her skin is a deep brown, and her dark eyes twinkle.

"Kerr Flick." I give her hand a tentative shake. She plonks herself in the seat beside me, oblivious to the shimmer of annoyance on my face. This entire carriage is empty, and she has to sit *there*? After the noise and crowds of the Nursery Dorms, I was having a nice time to myself. Me and my crazy dreams. Now she's sitting so close she might even hear them.

The boy sits across the aisle from us.

"That's Cam." Sif cocks her finger at the boy, oblivious to my mental grumbles. "He's super smart, but don't let that bother you. We all are, aren't we, Cam? Where are you from, Kerr?"

"Nursery Dorm 492," I reply in as gruff a voice as I can manage. She doesn't take the hint.

"Serious? I never even knew there were that many Nursery Dorms. Crazy. We're from 57, aren't we Cam? You heading to the Elite program too?"

"Yep."

"We can all be buddies, then." Out of the corner of my eye, I see Cam nod. I stare down at my knees.

"K."

"What was your test like?"

I shrug.

Sif goes on as if I needed explanation. "You know—Fitness to Proceed. We had to stand around for hours, and I thought I was going to faint, and then a whole bunch of people were taken away. They sent us into this big room where we—"

"Yeah, I had that too."

"Did you do VR?"

"Yep."

"With electric shocks?"

"Yep."

"Crazy."

I don't answer. We sit in silence for a few minutes. Nothing changes outside the darkened windows. Nothing changes inside, either.

I let out a quiet sigh. I should probably be nice to these guys. If the Elite Dorms are anything like Nursery Dorm 492, I could use a friend or two.

"Have you always lived at 57?" I ask.

"Yep," Cam replies. His voice sounds warm and gentle. Nothing like the Three Fists at all.

"What was your dorm like?" I ask.

Sif grins widely and runs off into a long description of their dorm, which sounds exactly like 492. Occasionally Cam interrupts to add a few details.

"Who were your favorite instructors?" I ask.

"They were all nice, but Lover Pinnow was my favorite. She let us research the Elite test before we went, even though we weren't supposed to. If it wasn't for what she said about problem solving, I'd never have opened that lock in time."

Sif gives a little frown, her eyebrows furrowing. Seeing her crestfallen expression, Cam leans forward and pats her on the wrist.

"She'll be okay," he says, giving her a sympathetic look. "Remember what Lover Pinnow said? She'll make Dorm Instructor, easy."

"Who?" I ask.

"Myf," Sif replies shortly. "Friend."

Her face twists, and she turns her head away from me for a moment. I can't tell whether she's trying not to cry or whether she's angry. When she turns back, a determined smile is plastered across her cheeks. I get a small pang of envy. What would it be like to miss someone from the dorms as much as Sif seems to?

"I wonder how long we'll be on the train," Sif says, staring brightly around the carriage. "We could set up forts and pretend to be Elite Lover Team Six."

"What? You like them too?" I gasp.

Sif gives me a withering look. "It's only the best show ever," she says, arms folded.

"I'll be Elite Lover Hu," Cam volunteers. "You get to be the first lot of bad guys."

"Sounds good. I need to move." I nod.

The next hour descends into a squealing riot. Two of us play Haters, trying to reach the end of the carriage while the other tries to tackle and stop them. When it's his turn to be Hater, Cam is brilliant. He creeps and sneers, and when Sif catches him, he transforms instantly into a blubbering heap of fear.

"No! Don't Embrace me! I didn't do anything!" he says before lunging forward to escape Sif's clutches. Sif has the best imagination, and she puts on a great imitation of the Haters' Pavilion Show commentators. Every time she roars "They're *goooone!*" exactly like Carell Hummer, I laugh so hard that tears end up streaming down my face.

No one has ever made me laugh like that before. My stomach muscles hurt.

The high-pitched whine of the brakes jolts us out of our games, and we race to our seats. Sif toys nervously with the back of her hair. Cam sits as still as a person can when they're out of breath. I try to get my own breathing under control, but it isn't easy when my nerves take off again. The train stops. The doors open, and a tall linen-clad woman with dark braids steps in. She raises her eyebrows when she sees us clustered together.

"Apprentice Sif Grohns? Apprentice Kerr Flick? Apprentice Cam Pervous? I am Lover Herz. Welcome to Elite Academy."

7

Elite Axioms Volume I
  Axiom 45: An Elite is master of the Five Skills:
    Conformity
    Regulation
    Obedience
    Observation
    Leadership

BUTTERFLIES SOAR AND TUMBLE IN MY stomach as we step from the carriage onto a wide concrete platform. A second train sits idle, parallel to ours on the other side. Groups of Apprentices alight from it. I glance to my left, startled. The ceiling above us is low, tiled in square white tiles. Four black plastic bubbles of surveillance cameras stand out vividly against the white porcelain.

"There were others on our train too!" I hiss to Sif, watching the groups step out from carriages behind us. She nods, her eyes wide.

"You thought we'd be the only Elites?" Cam winks.

"I didn't know what to think."

Linen-clad instructors corral us into neat lines, three abreast. It doesn't take long to realize that Sif and I are among the smallest Apprentices in this crowd. Two bulky-looking boys march toward us behind an even bulkier instructor. The man is like a walking muscle. They walk to the front of the group, and nobody is game to argue.

Beside an elevator tube that cuts the platform from ceiling to floor stands a high marble plinth. A woman stands on it. She has the physique of a warrior, regal and still. Her face is stern, and her hands are clasped carefully in front of her waist. Her braided black hair is pulled back into a severe, tight bun. Out of habit, I stand to attention, but inside I am screaming.

It's the woman from my dream.

"Welcome to Elite training," the regal woman's voice rings out. "My name is Dorm Leader Akela. Congratulations on being selected for this program. You have already succeeded where many of your contemporaries have failed. But I must remind you: this is only the beginning. Your training will be harder than you ever thought possible. You must perform at the highest level all day, every day. The Love Collective expects nothing less."

For the first time I notice an older Elite Apprentice beside her, clad in a grey uniform with indigo trim. His hair is a warm gold, and his eyes are the most piercing shade of green. His figure is athletic and shoulders broad. He passes a small infotab to the Dorm Leader's waiting hands. She nods to him and flicks her hand along the screen with graceful, practiced movements.

"You are Freshman Group K. We have already assigned you sleeping quarters. For the first year, you will be bunking with students who are at higher levels than you to help you settle in."

Akela nods to the instructors beside her, and they ferry us into the elevator. We crowd into the sterile grey interior and wait in awkward silence while the lift rises up through the dorm. I'm not quite sure what I'm expecting to see, but the view I get when the doors open is way beyond anything I've seen before.

"Whoa," Sif breathes.

"Exactly what I was thinking," I agree in awe.

"Yeah," whispers Cam.

I always imagined Elite Academy would be military barracks, marching drills, and uniforms. But this is nothing like it at all. The ceiling far, far above us is decorated with glittering and swirling mobiles. They are agile and intricate like origami, and they turn and swoop and soar on an invisible breeze. Below them, polished concrete walls laser-carved with interlinked designs look like a waterfall. To my right, high windows fill the space with golden light from the street lamps beyond. The lamps illuminate an avenue of tall green trees, lush even in the artificial light. A sliver of moon glows high in the night sky.

Inside, a collection of bright orange lounges scatters across the polished concrete floor. Small groups of people gather on these seats. A few of them turn to us, curious.

"This way," my instructor directs, pointing to a large glass door on my left. Our small group marches through it into a sparse white passage. At the end of this hall, a large set of double doors leads into a large indoor space.

"This looks more like it," I mutter.

"Just like home," Sif agrees.

We're in a cafeteria, much bigger than my Nursery one. At the far end from where we stand is a window into a large commercial kitchen with open servery. Next to the kitchen lies an ocean of mess hall benches: stainless steel and sterile. Lover Herz guides us toward the kitchen. Black surveillance camera bubbles are spread out across the ceiling. There's more here in this one area than I remember seeing in my entire Nursery Dorm.

"Evening meal is at 1800," Lover Herz says. "Since you arrived at 2130, we have set aside a supper for you all. From tomorrow, you will be dining with the general population. Breakfast at 0700. Lunch 1230," Lover Herz explains.

I nod, barely listening. My brain will remember everything

anyway. I'm too distracted by all of the cameras. If the Three Fists were here, I'd never have to worry again.

We gather our own protein broth, and before long we're sitting down at a clean steel table together. My tablemates cast sly glances around at each other between mouthfuls. When I do the same, my heart sinks. Everyone around this table is taller and broader than me.

At the far end, two boys with identical sandy hair and mirror-image faces tower over their plates. They already look five years older than my fifteen years, broad shoulders and arms corded with muscle. Beside the twins sit four statuesque girls, one of whom could probably beat the twins in an arm wrestle. Three others line the bench beside Sif: two boys and a girl, all with black hair and almond-shaped, hazel eyes. Sif and I are the odd ones out, but even Sif's head towers over mine.

After supper, Lover Herz steps forward.

"Time to get to your rooms," she says. "I'll show you where you will be living for the next few months."

We rise from the tables, placing our bowls on a separate bench, then follow her through a distant set of doors. She strides along a series of disorienting hallways, identical in shape and color. I'm completely lost by the time she stops at a pristine white door, no different from hundreds we've already passed. A quick wave of her wrist over the ID panel, and the door slides open. We peer into a tubelike space lined with bunks set into the wall. Herz leads us in, stopping at the rear of the room in front of a steel door. A black camera bubble hangs from the ceiling above her head. Oblivious, she pulls out an infotab and begins to read off names.

"Apprentices Lee and Pim," she says, directing two of the black-haired Apprentices to a rear set of bunks. "Your bunks are here. Opposite are Apprentices Cam and Chu. Apprentices Rook and Arah, you're here." The hulking twins move into the narrow space beside Lee and Pim. "You're opposite Apprentices Zin and Farr."

"Why are we in with them?" Farr lifts her chin toward the boys.

"Problem?" Lover Herz raises a single eyebrow at her.

Farr crosses her arms. "I've never bunked with boys, that's all."

"Well, that's a strange anomaly. By now you should know that the Love Collective always makes the right decision." The Lover's tone carries a strong warning. "Always."

Farr's face pales. She gives a faint nod and steps back beside her new bunk. "Yes, Lover Herz," she mumbles, eyes directed at her feet.

Lover Herz looks back at her infotab and continues, "Apprentices Sif and Kerr, you're in this space. That just leaves Apprentices Dona and Buff."

Sif gives me a grinning thumbs-up, and we stand beside the wall alcoves that will be our homes for now. We smile and nod at the two girls opposite us. They nod back, unsmiling. Buff is tall, with regulation-cut blonde hair. Dona already looks like a Love Squad officer, even though she can't be any older than me. She cracks her knuckles and stares at Lover Herz. The sound makes my skin crawl.

Lover Herz smiles when we're all standing beside our bunks.

"Right. Tomorrow you will receive your provisional IDs, which will enable you to enter and leave this room at will. The bathroom is through that door at the back. We will collect you at 0600 sharp for your first day. Get some sleep."

Lover Herz salutes us, and we return it. Chatter erupts as soon as the door closes.

"You don't mind if I take the top bunk, do you?" Sif leaps up before I can answer. "Didn't think so. Thanks."

I shrug, watching her scamper up. She can have the ladder if she wants. The bottom bunk is like a cave where my head can hide behind a narrow wall of shelves. There is nothing to unpack, but a small bag of bathroom supplies and a towel sit in each of our alcoves.

"Do we get clothes?" I ask, looking down at my crumpled uniform.

Sif shrugs. "I don't know."

Dona gives a harsh snort. "The Love Collective always does what is best."

"I know. It wasn't a complaint or anything," I say, feeling a little panicked. It would be my kind of bad luck to bunk right near someone with a Hater-reporting hair trigger.

"I'm sure they'll tell us when the time is right." Buff smiles. "We're blessed to even be here."

"You're right about that." I nod. "This is everything I've ever wanted."

I give Cam a little wave, but he's busy chatting to Chu. Zin and Farr waste no time introducing themselves to the hulking twins, who mostly ignore them. Rejected, the statuesque girls turn their attention to Lee, who answers their questions politely. The girls act as if Pim isn't there. When I catch Pim's stormy frown, I stifle a giggle. The petite Apprentice unzips her toothbrush case with such force I am surprised it doesn't break.

"Excuse. Me," she snaps, forcing her way between the girls and Lee before disappearing into the bathroom. The girls roll their eyes. They continue drilling Lee for information about his dormitory (16), his Fitness to Proceed test (exactly the same as ours), and his plans for Elite training ("As long as I don't fail, I'm good.").

With a tired sigh, I sink down onto the edge of my bunk. There are four sets of empty bunks at the front of the room. Judging by the fullness of their shelves, it seems we already have roommates. I wonder who they are. I wonder where they are too. I wonder what tomorrow will bring and what Elite training is going to be like. Do we get new uniforms? Will I get along with my new roomies? Will my instructors be nice?

Whatever happens, this is where I want to be. It would be perfect if I didn't have the constant echo of delusional images floating around in the back of my mind. They're going to wreck everything. I just know it.

SOMEWHERE BEYOND MY SPLINTERING skull, a distant siren wails. I wake, trembling and covered in sweat. The roof of the bunk hangs above my head, cocooning me in darkness.

"Are you okay?"

I jump, frightened. Sif is staring at me from outside my bunk. It's too dark to see her face, but her hair makes a fuzzy dark halo against the dim light.

"What?" I reply, drawing back toward the wall and pulling my blanket closer to my chin. "Why wouldn't I be okay?"

"You were crying."

Embarrassment radiates over me. I stare down at my hands, now picking absently at the blanket. "Sorry."

"Don't be. We all miss home." Sif reaches down to pat my hand.

I look down at my hand, confounded by the strange sensation.

"Nobody's ever done that before," I say, staring.

"Move," Sif hisses. I shift my legs sideways, letting her sit down on the edge of my mattress. She sighs, glancing out toward the other beds along our tube of a room. Pim is lying like a starfish, an arm and leg hanging over the edge of her bed. Buff and Dona are both snoring loudly. We're the only ones awake.

"What do you miss about home?" I ask.

"Myf, mostly."

I bite back the stab of jealousy. "You were good friends?"

"Yeah. She was an outsider, like me. Neither of us fit with anyone else. We would have been in trouble more, except our marks were always too good. But she always used to—" Sif pauses. "Never mind. You and me are Elite now, and that's all there is to it. It's good. It'll be good. We'll be good."

She turns a forced smile upon me, so obviously fake that I don't believe anything she's just said.

"You don't have to pretend, Sif."

For a few seconds, Sif doesn't answer. She stares down at her own hands, frowning.

"What's Cadence?" she asks suddenly, eyes alight in the dim room.

"Wha-at?" I pretend that I don't know what she's talking about.

"You were saying that word over and over a minute ago."

"Was I?"

"It sounded like it meant something to you."

"Must have been a nightmare. You telling me you never had a bad dream?"

"None that made me cry in my sleep."

"Lucky you."

I'd been so caught up in my own worries that I didn't notice the tall, bulky figure standing just beyond my bunk. When he coughs, I jump so high my head nearly hits the bunk above me.

"Back in your bunk," the boy says in a deep, menacing voice.

Sif stiffens. "But I was just . . ."

"No excuses. Stay in your bunk or get sent to Realignment."

A long, puckered scar on the boy's face is illuminated by a flashing orange glow that I didn't notice before. It seems to be coming from Sif's bed. My new friend scrambles up the ladder with an agility and speed that surprise me. The orange glow shuts off as soon as her weight settles on her bunk, and the taller boy fades into the darkness. I lie in my own space for ages, listening to the quiet sounds of breathing. I can tell by the pattern of her breathing that Sif is still awake too.

8

Love Collective
Guide to Care and Protection of Identity Markers
  Congratulations!
   *As the new owner of an Identity Denominator (ID), you
are now free to enjoy all the benefits the Love Collective
provides its faithful citizens. Payment for goods and services,
free travel, access to employment are all yours, thanks to your
ID. Check in everywhere to earn Triumph of Love Rewards
and glittering Executive Benefits. The world is your playroom,
thanks to your Collective ID.*
   Love all. Be all.

AT PRECISELY 0530 THE LIGHT ABOVE MY
head switches on. An irritating buzzer emits a long, sharp tone,
and my mattress transforms from comfortable cushion to rock-
hard dining table. Then it tilts so that my natural movement is
to roll out of bed, bleary-eyed and yawning.

Sif lands on the floor beside me, groaning.

"Top bunk wasn't such a good idea after all," I tease.

"Shut up," she growls, rubbing her back. I'm about to
respond when eight taller, stronger students push their
way past me.

I exchange a look with Sif.

"Not going to argue," she says, eyes wide.

"Me neither," I reply.

Watching our roommates muscle their way into the bathroom, Dona's face is clouded with fury. Pim glares toward the bathroom door, her arms crossed and face a picture of angry resentment.

"Bet they think they're better than us too." Pim snorts.

By the time the older roommates emerge from the bathroom, we have five minutes until Lover Herz's arrival. Rook and Arah naturally elbow their way into the bathroom first, and the rest of us follow meekly. We find individual cubicles in which to wash and then pull on our old uniforms. I finger the embroidery of my Nursery ID, wondering what Koah and the others are doing today.

At exactly 0600 the door slides open. Lover Herz steps back to allow the older students a chance to leave. Then she smiles at us.

"Good morning, Apprentices," she says, her glance sweeping over us all. "I trust you slept well."

"Yes, thank you Lover Herz," replies Zin with a dazzling smile. Out of the corner of my eye, I can see Pim's expression darken.

"Good. Let's be off, then."

She sets off at a brisk pace through the crowded corridor. Conversation flows out of open doorways. There must be a hundred identical tubes of windowless sleeping quarters on this floor. Unlike us, the Apprentices are all donning grey Elite uniforms, crisp and streamlined. We stand out in Nursery white.

Cam jogs up beside us, Chu with him.

"How did you sleep?" Cam asks.

"Fine until that last bit," mutters Sif.

"How about you?" I return Cam's smile.

"Don't remember anything, so it must have been good." He grins, showing a row of perfect teeth.

Herz guides us to a broad staircase, wide enough for ten people to ascend side by side. At the top of the stairs, we arrive in another glass-lined atrium. Sunlight beams through the windows with the brightness of a clear, cloudless morning.

"Well, this is awesome!" Cam's eyes shine as he stares up and around us.

"I never thought it would look like this." Sif smiles back. "It's so . . . so shiny."

"I've seen better," Chu says, and I notice that he's looking straight at Sif. She catches him looking, and dimples appear in her cheeks.

A great stream of grey-uniformed bodies emerges from the stairwells below. As if by some unseen signal, they assemble in neat drill lines, parallel to a solid wall at one end. Lover Herz leads us to the outer edge of the gathering, beside the windows. She stops at a curving steel beam that arches up over our heads. When we amble to a stop in front of her, she frowns.

"You can do better than that, Apprentices," she says.

We hurriedly arrange ourselves in a neat line and snap to attention. She gives a satisfied nod.

A few moments later, more white-clad Apprentices join us. There are thirty-six of us in all—three crews of twelve. One crew is led by the muscle-bound instructor I remember from last night's arrival. The other group marches behind a tall, slender woman with red hair. The instructors all stand in front of their groups, casting shrewd glances over the rest of us.

In the distance, Dorm Leader Akela appears at the top of an escalator leading down from the upper level. As she descends, a drill sergeant begins a team chant.

"Love all!"

"BE ALL!" boom the students in the room. The chant is deafening.

"Love all!"

"BE ALL!"

Dorm Leader Akela glides through the rows of students, nodding with approval as she passes by. Her linen robe flutters with her footsteps. When she passes our group, her gaze hesitates on me. Is it my imagination, or does she wink? She is gone before I can smile, exiting the large assembly space on a wave of chants.

"Love all!"

"BE ALL!"

"Love all!"

"BE ALL!"

AFTER BREAKFAST, OUR INSTRUCTORS take us to the infirmary, which sits deep below our accommodation. As soon as the elevator doors open, we're greeted by a cold rush of air that carries a strong smell of disinfectant. I rub at the goosebumps prickling along my arms.

"Brrr, who'd work down here?" Sif mutters. "It's like an ice cube."

"Forget the cold. I'd go crazy without the sunshine," Chu replies. He makes a funny face at her and she giggles. The sound draws a harsh look from the muscle-bound Lover nearby. There's something about the Lover's gaze that sends a shiver down my spine.

Following Lover Herz, we pass through the lobby doors into a hallway full of glass panels. Behind the panels are a series of treatment rooms. Most rooms are sparsely furnished with rows of clinical beds and medical monitors. Only a few are occupied.

Lover Herz travels past the treatment rooms and makes a sudden left turn at the end of the hall. We enter a long glass-fronted room containing a small console and a hulking machine. The machine looks a bit like a tall shower cubicle with a keyboard protruding from its outer left wall. Instead of taps, two black sleeves hang out from the wall at chest height.

"What's that?" Cam asks. I open my mouth to reply but catch Sif's exaggerated eye roll and close my mouth again.

Lover Herz waits in silence for the whole group to enter. She is joined by muscle-man and redhead, who form a kind of guard beside her.

"Welcome to the Identity Denominator. I am Lover Herz. This is Lover Fuschious," she indicates the thick, nuggety man who stands to her right with his arms folded. "And this is Lover Kalis." She waves her other hand to the redheaded woman on her left. Lover Kalis stands to attention and looks somewhere above our heads, as if none of us exist.

"This morning, you will all receive your provisional ID marks," Lover Herz begins. Lover Fuschious steps in front of her, and I notice the flash of displeasure that passes over Herz's face.

"Don't think you can go out into the big, wide world straight away," he warns. I'm sure his neck is as thick as my waist. "The provisional ID will let you into your room and some—only some—Elite facilities. You only get your full ID when you graduate."

"Or end up demoted," Lover Kalis adds. She takes her seat at the only other item of furniture in the room, a small desk with an infotab console.

"Which some of you are no doubt destined for," Lover Fuschious informs us. It's hard not to take his words personally, especially since he's staring straight at me.

Well, you'll prove him wrong, won't you? I say to myself. I stare right back until he looks away. So what if I'm the shortest recruit here? Height isn't everything.

They line us up in alphabetical order, so of course I can't see what's happening. I lean out to get a better look. Apprentice Arah strides forward, his arms held up toward the machine with quiet confidence. Lover Fuschious grasps his wrists, guiding them into the black sleeves. When Fuschious steps away, Arah is elbow deep in the machine, his back toward us. The machine lets out a quiet whir, followed by an electric whine, and Arah flinches. The whine intensifies, and he lets out a loud gasp. A few seconds later the whine shuts off, and then Arah rips his arms away from the sleeves as if they are burned. He sets his shoulders and walks to where Lover Kalis waits. Although his mouth is set in a grim line, he cradles his left wrist with care.

Lover Fuschious summons Rook forward. Over at the desk, Lover Kalis inspects some vivid black marks that have appeared on Arah's wrist. Then she runs his arm under a scanner. When the scanner makes a loud beep and a green light blinks, Arah is released. At Lover Kalis's signal, he slinks over to a distant corner of the infirmary.

Rook's performance is almost exactly the same as his brother's, except that he lets out a sharper grunt of pain. When he goes over to the corner to meet his twin, Arah gives him a subtle nudge, smiling in triumph. Rook frowns back.

Apprentice Buff is next. As the machine begins to whine, she lets out a loud shriek and tries to pull away, but can't. Whatever is inside that black sleeve has her caught in an iron grip. By the time the machine releases her, she is sobbing. Lover Fuschious shakes his head.

"Pathetic," he snaps. "To be an Elite, you need to put up with worse than that, girlie."

"But I thought it was just supposed to be a tattoo!" Buff wails.

"If it was just a tattoo, it wouldn't hurt like that, now would it?" snorts Fuschious.

Contempt for the taller, stronger-looking Buff is almost violent. I vow that no matter how bad the ID branding is, I won't scream. I will rise above. I will be strong. I will stand tall. I will . . .

I will cry like a little baby.

When my turn arrives, I don't wait to be guided to the machine. I smile at Lover Fuschious's arrogant scowl and thrust my hands into the soft, velvety sleeves. My arms disappear almost to my shoulders. The machine makes a quiet whir. Thick cuffs wind around my arms, holding me in place so tightly that I can't even rotate my wrists. The electric whine whirls into action, and a burning needle of fire rips into my arm. It's like my hand is being torn off with a laser blade. I clamp my eyes shut. A small sound erupts from my closed lips, but that's all I let go.

Finally, the cuffs retract, and my arms are free. Throbbing with pain, I stumble toward Lover Kalis. Tears slide down my cheeks. Like a robot I display the sleek black bars of my newly stamped ID for scanning. Then I join my place at the back of the line, trying to hide my sniffles.

Sif casts an anxious glance toward me before putting her arms in the machine. She jolts in shock when the ID is carved, but apart from the initial jump, she does even better than me. When the machine releases her arms, she strides to Lover Kalis. She looks confident, pushing a forced smile out across her cheeks.

"Was that it?" she jokes, holding her wrist out for inspection. "I thought there was supposed to be some pain up in there."

"That's the spirit." Lover Kalis smiles.

My admiration for Sif grows a few notches. We might be the smallest of our class, but I know neither of us is going to go out without a fight.

9

Nursery Induction Manual
Catechesis volume 2, page 39.

Q: What dreams are open to faithful and hardworking Apprentices?

A: The Love Collective offers unimaginable rewards for those who conform closely to Collective Precepts.

"IF YOUR WRIST AIN'T UP TO THE JOB, DON'T think y'all gonna get sympathy from me," bellows Fuschious, inches from my face. He's so close I can see the bead of sweat forming beneath his hairline. "Twenty squats. Now!"

It's nearly midday, and the sun beats hot on our heads. We've been drilling for almost two hours now, and most of us are nearing drop-dead exhaustion.

"Yes, Lover Fuschious!" I shout, easing down into a squat. Back straight. Hands clasped behind my head, it takes every ounce of my fast-evaporating energy not to collapse. By the time I'm done, my muscles are shaking like a Hater about to lose the Haters' Pavilion Show.

Our instructor struts up and down our line. Every so often he leans down close to someone's ear, screaming so loud they flinch. "You're a waste of space, Apprentice Lee!"

"Yes, Lover Fuschious!"

"I seen better squats from an old street hag, Apprentice Dona!"

"Yes, Lover Fuschious!"

"Cam Pervous! You are wasting my time!"

I risk a glance sideways, just in time to see Lover Fuschious's boot connect with Cam's back. Cam crashes to the ground with a loud moan of pain. I jolt forward, then force myself back in line. Clashing with Lovers never does anyone any good.

MEMORY DATE: CE 2272.127 (9 YEARS AGO)

Memory location: Nursery Dorm 492, drill yard

Memory time: 0739 hours

We have a new drill routine. It's much harder than the old one. Apprentice #540/187469 doesn't like it. Every time we have to wheel right on the downswing, he wheels left. The Lover beside him has to deliver the baton to his legs five times. Just as the Lover is about to deliver baton strike number six, Apprentice #540/187469 stops in his tracks, fists down by his side.

"No! I won't do it anymore! You made it too hard!" he yells at the top of his voice. I miss a step in shock and have to race to catch up. We all keep marching, but every eye is glued to that one spot on the drill field.

Two Lovers join the other to surround Apprentice #540/187469. Ignoring his kicking and screaming, they lift him off the ground and carry him away. He is whisked away from the yard and out of our sight forever.

The beats of the drill music go on, undisturbed.

"ATTENTION!"

"Yes, Lover Fuschious!"

At the sudden command, twenty-four Apprentices snap upright, eyes front, hands rigid by our sides.

"What did I say to you? What did I say?" he snarls, pacing along our line like a lion hunting for his lunch.

Don't do it. Just don't, squeaks the sensible part of my brain. Of course I remember what Lover Fuschious said. Every inflection, every drop of spittle shooting from his lips, every mangled syllable, every eye twitch.

Nobody else answers. Mainly because nobody knows what Fuschious wants them to say.

"You pathetic bunch of losers!" he screams, face as red as a tomato. "How do you expect to make it through Elite training when you can't even answer a simple question? *What did I say?*"

Don't. Do. It, screams the increasingly desperate voice in my head, but for some reason my mouth doesn't listen. It just opens and words tumble out before I can stop it.

"Lover Fuschious, sir! You said—sir!—'This is Elite physical training. Nobody passes Elite Academy without bein' the utmost physical peak condition. If you think Nursery drills are where it's at, then you got a serious lesson train comin' right at ya between the eyes. Far as I see it, less than four of ya deserve to be here, and I ain't gonna to say who'—then you looked at Arah and Rook, sir—and you said 'Unless you pass my class, y'all gonna be app monkeys before next semester, so you better snap to it and work those flabby butts until they harder than steel.' Then you said, 'Fifty laps!' and we ran, sir! We were on lap seven when you yelled at Apprentice Buff, and you called her a 'pathetic piece of swamp weed' until she cried again, and then you called Apprentice Pim 'a Hater who wouldn't last five minutes on the Pavilion show,' and then—"

"Thank you, Apprentice Flick. That will be enough."

"Yes, Lover Fuschious!" I yell.

The cold, quiet way Lover Fuschious speaks sends a jolt of fear down into my gut. He's even speaking more correctly and carefully than usual. I guess he wasn't happy about the way my memory produced an exact copy of his accent. Sure enough, he stalks up to me until his mouth is an inch away from my nose. His hot, angry breath blasts over my face like the fumes of a furnace. It even reeks of sulfur.

"For that elegant piece of mockery, Apprentice Flick, you can give me twenty more push-ups."

"Yes, Lover Fuschious!"

See? I told you to shut up! my brain screams at my mouth. I lower myself down to the ground again while the whole class watches on. My arms are still shaky, so my first attempt is slow and tentative.

"One," Lover Fuschious counts, enmity dripping from his lips. When I go back for a second try, his boot lands on my backside, just hard enough to push me down.

"Keep your spine straight, worm. Two."

Panting with the effort, I keep going, enduring the constant drip of insults coming from my instructor. He starts to circle me, spitting negative comments about my posture, my lack of fitness, my short height, and even my frizzy, black hair. By the time I reach halfway, my newly ID'd wrist is burning, and every muscle in my back is on fire. But there's no way I'm going to let Fuschious win. When I'm done, I collapse heavily on the ground. Lover Fuschious scans the class with a gaze of steel.

"For the record, the correct answer to my question was: work or die. I said 'work or die.' Now get up."

My rise from the ground is slow and painful, but I get there. Finally on my feet, I raise my chin toward my instructor, keeping my eyes down and hoping I don't pass out. He waits for me to look at him. I don't. He leans in close to my face again, speaking in a tone not quite loud enough for my classmates to hear.

"You just made an enemy you can't afford, Apprentice. Nobody talks to me like that. Ever. Especially not upstart little girls who think they're too clever to need physical training. You hear me?" His voice is a low hiss.

"Yes, Lover Fuschious."

"You're on my radar now, Flick. Every drill. Every obstacle course. Every training session. I'll be watching you closer than a Sweepstakes winner at a Pavilion show. Just give me one excuse, and I'll have you in Realignment so fast you won't even have time to squeak."

"Yes, Lover Fuschious. It won't happen again, Lover Fuschious." Miserable, I stare at my shoes. The heavily muscled trainer takes a step away from me.

"You can all thank Apprentice Flick that you're late for lunch. Dismissed!" he yells at the group. As one, we jog away toward the dining hall. We're halfway across the field when Sif and Cam jog up beside me.

"What was that about?" Sif hisses. "You *trying* to get yourself demoted?"

"He . . . asked us . . . to tell him what he said." I shrug, panting.

"So you read off a transcript?" Cam says, incredulous.

"It's how my head works."

"Remind me to sit next to you in our exams." Sif's voice is full of grudging admiration.

"Thought you already were." I grin.

She gives me a gentle nudge, and we go down the stairs toward the mess hall. The wall of sound hits us as we walk into the large dining room, conversation mingled with the clinking of glasses and plates. We stumble into the crowded dining hall, red-faced and glistening. A hush ripples across the room.

"New blood on deck!" yells a deep voice somewhere from the back.

"Whomp!" the whole room shouts. Everyone gives us a salute I've never seen before: left fist smacking right shoulder, then raised in a straight line up in the air. In spite of my exhaustion, a warm, happy pride creeps over me. I bite back a goofy grin, straighten my aching shoulders, and walk tall to the food window. Even the green slop that drips over the side of my plate can't dent my joy. Lover Fuschious might do his worst, but I'm an Elite Apprentice now.

Right where I always wanted to be.

AT THE END OF OUR FIRST DAY, WE HEAD for the assembly atrium, waiting for our next instructions from Lover Herz. Surprisingly, the older Elite Apprentices are already there, lined up in the same drill lines as they were in the morning. Everyone stands to attention. I lean in to whisper to Cam, who's standing beside me.

"What's going on?"

"Drill practice?" His eyes rove around the crowd as if he might find some clues.

"We already did that." Sif stifles a yawn.

"Maybe they do more at Elite Academy," I wonder.

Just then, the large concrete wall at one end of the atrium bursts into light, startling all three of us. As the white rectangle begins to swirl with color, the familiar strains of the Love Collective anthem echo around the cavernous space. Colored swirls sharpen into an image of the giant Love Collective flag billowing above the Tower of Love. Then the image of the flag dissolves, and the smiling face of Supreme Lover Midgate solidifies before us. She sits with prim poise at her desk, hands neatly resting in front of her. When she smiles at the camera, small crinkles appear at the corners of her blue eyes. Her silky hair is styled in a perfect silver bob, not a single hair out of place.

"Good evening, my Lovelies. May you live your dreams and reach for the universe. I love you all. No really, I mean it," she begins, opening her hands wide as if she wanted nothing more than to give us a hug. "Tonight, across this great Collective of ours, it warms my heart to know that we are all contending as one for the glory of our Collective and for the loyalty that the Supreme Executive so rightly deserve. I am so encouraged that you are working hard to help us seek out enemies and Haters. They want to shatter our hard-won peace. But we will not lose, will we? No. We will continue to triumph. The Love Collective will always win, no matter how many Haters wish to break us down. Remember this, my Lovelies: we can only be free to love when all threats to our loveliness have been eliminated. Sleep well, my Lovelies. And remember: love all, be all."

The vision winks out.

"Should have known we'd have to see the nightly lecture," Sif mutters.

MEMORY DATE: CE 2275.089 (6 YEARS AGO)

Memory location: Hater Embracement practice, Nursery Dorm 492, assembly auditorium, Row 18, Seat 27

Memory time: 1457 hours

We are all smiling, heads bowed low as she glows into our vision, and then her face is really there for the first time. Head almost as big as the vidscreen on the front wall behind the stage. She has specially come to visit us here and now. Nursery Dorm 492 has been graced with the presence of Supreme Lover Midgate herself. I would like to look as polished as her one day. My unkempt hair won't obey, though. It makes me sad that I might never be as lovely as our Supreme Lover.

"Love all," she says in a crisp, correct accent.

"Be all," we chant back.

"I am so pleased to be here with you children. You have done so well this year. Let me be the first to congratulate you. No Haters found in an entire term. Well done."

We beam proudly at the compliment.

"Thanks to your stellar performance, you are privileged to witness a small glimpse of our Triumph of Love festival. One day you will attend for yourselves, which is an even greater privilege." Her smile evaporates, and she regards us with earnest sincerity. "But the road ahead is long and hard. We can only be free to love when hate has been eliminated from our midst. So keep watch. Even now there are secret followers of the Haterman who want to destroy this beautiful Collective we live in."

Her expression becomes so sad that I would do anything to make her happy again.

As if she has heard my thoughts, a smile returns across Supreme Lover Midgate's face. She holds out both her hands toward us. "But, even though we must be ever vigilant, tonight is time for celebration. I hope you all enjoy this special presentation. You are all my Lovelies. May you follow your dreams and find yourselves in our universe."

We wave and cheer wildly as Supreme Lover Midgate's face fades from view. Even the excitement of the Triumph of Love festival is weak by comparison. We have been noticed by the Supreme Lover. Our lives are now complete.

"IT USED TO BE WAY MORE EXCITING,"

I sigh, then get a bit panicked. "I mean, I love Supreme Lover more than anything, and I know it's important to watch, and—"

"Relax," Sif says. "I know what you mean."

I look at her, searching for any signs she might be off to report my less-than-enthusiastic response to a Lover.

She winks. "I'm not the reporting type," Sif says with an impish grin.

A group of Elites marches around us. I catch sight of a small group heading down toward the gym. Another group marches past us, infotabs clasped under their arms.

"Hey, do you think they give us app time here?" I ask. "I haven't seen any infotab lockers anywhere."

"Don't know. This place is already different. Good, but different." Sif stares up at the atrium ceiling high above us. I nod, following her gaze to where the stars are winking into view outside the darkened windows.

"Life here is going to be awesome," I reply.

10

Elite Regulations, Behavior Standards and Protocol.
47b. Fraternization
    i. While resident at Elite Academy, Elite Apprentices must be single-minded, focused only on training and improvement.
    ii. Fraternization of any kind is an unnecessary impediment to training and must be avoided.
    iii. Fraternization rules may be suspended for the duration of Triumph of Love season only.
    iv. Any Apprentice who engages in fraternization outside these guidelines may be sanctioned.

OUR LITTLE GROUP STUMBLES BACK TO THE bunk room, hunched and limping. The day has passed in a whirlwind. Our silver tube of a bunk room has never been such a welcome sight.

"Right now I'm really glad you chose that top bunk," I say to Sif.

"Can you lift me up there?" she moans.

I'm too tired to even laugh.

The bigger boys muscle their way to be the first into the bathroom, and I just let them. With weary shuffles, I reach my new bunk home and stop, shocked. My shelves are now full of neatly folded Elite uniforms. I can't stop my smile when I see the embroidery on the gold-trimmed lapel:

Elite Apprentice Kerr Flick
#540/187503

Sif lifts her uniform as if it were a precious jewel. Her hand caresses the grey cloth with slow care. When she catches me watching, a joyful grin spreads across her face.

"Is this really real?" she breathes, eyes alight.

"Oh man, I hope so." Forgetting our bone-weariness, we jump up and down together, giggling like little kids.

"How can you still have energy?" Cam groans. He has already collapsed onto his bed, arm draped across his face in exhaustion.

Sif raises one eyebrow, and we both break into giggles again.

Lee drags his exhausted feet to Pim's bunk, flopping down on her mattress. Pim gives him a shove. "Oi. Off."

Moaning, Lee collapses onto the floor.

"But it's too high up there," he complains. "I'll never get to bed."

"You better, or you'll regret it," says a deep voice from the entrance. Every head turns toward the speaker. A tall Apprentice steps into our room, face grim. I can see his olive skin and curly, black hair better in the light. It's the same muscular Apprentice who found us in the middle of the night. Behind him, a group of older Apprentices filter into the room.

"Who are you, and why should I listen?" Lee groans with a bravery I can only admire as he pulls himself upright. The big guy could possibly snap Lee's neck without breaking a sweat.

"Hodge. Your bunk room leader. If you're not in bed on time, you're marked absent. If you're marked absent, you get Realignment, and I get a black mark. So you're going to sleep in your bunk if I have to throw you up there myself."

"That would be good. At least I wouldn't have to climb," Lee quips.

"You'd regret it."

He shrugs at the deep menace in Hodge's tone. "Whatever."

Zin flicks her hair and turns away from Lee. She holds her hand out toward Hodge.

"I'm Zin." She smiles, fluttering her eyelashes at him. "This is my friend Farr. We only just met him, by the way. But you could throw us into our bunks any time."

Lee looks displeased at Zin's sudden flirtation. I can't help noticing the triumphant grin that flashes across Pim's face. A statuesque blonde senior sidles up behind Hodge, draping her arm across the back of his neck.

"Hodge isn't into Nursery tots." She looks haughtily down at Zin.

Zin drops her hand, propping it against her hip as if she intended it to be there all along. "And who are you?" Zin raises her nose into the air.

"Mill. Trying to save you from wasting your time," replies the blonde. She turns her back on Zin with a sinuous twist of her hips.

Lee's mouth drops open ever so slightly.

"Ugh," Sif intones under her breath.

"I think I want to throw up," I mutter back to her.

"Since we're all sharing for the next term, you better learn our names," Hodge says to the rest of us. "Me and Mill you know now. But these two guys"—he points to two slender, sandy-haired boys who are even taller than he is — "are Freb and Rosh. They're training to be Engine Roomers. Those meat-wagons over there are Loa and Yip." He points to a boy and a girl who are slowly removing white athletic tape from their wrists. Their short hair looks like a dark fuzz over their otherwise bald heads. "They're about to graduate into the Love Squad program. The last two are with Mill heading for Pleasure Tribe: Josam and Jimoway."

The seniors nod at us, polite expressions hiding their real

thoughts. Josam and Jimoway are the most beautiful people I've ever seen. Long tresses of red hair cascade in perfect waves down behind their shoulders. They aren't as muscular or stocky as Loa or Yip, nor as tall as Freb or Rosh. But there is something in the way that they walk and move that is almost mesmerizing.

"What's the Pleasure Tribe?" Sif asks. She stares wide-eyed at the redheaded Apprentices before giving herself a little shake. "Sorry, my name is Sif. I don't know what all those . . . things are."

"You will," Freb says, crinkles appearing at the corners of his blue eyes. "You're going to end up in one of them."

"What?" Sif replies.

"One of the five cadres."

"You lost me." Sif shakes her head.

"Elites are divided into five operational categories called cadres," explains Freb.

Rosh nods. "Engine Roomers manage Love Collective logistics—troop movements and supplies, health centers, all the mechanics and stuff," Rosh goes on, smiling at the mention of the word *logistics*. "None of us are Coders, but they do the techie app-writing stuff."

"We do the fighting and shooting." Yip grins, rubbing her stubby fingers over the black remnants of her hair.

"Pleasure Tribe . . . well, the name speaks for itself, doesn't it?" Jimoway smirks, licking his lips in a way that makes all the hairs stand up on the back of my neck.

"We are the beating heart of the Love Collective," Mill adds with a proud toss of her hair. "We run the Triumph of Love festival, fill the apps with love and joy, and bring peace and harmony to citizens everywhere."

"Sounds like fun," Farr replies, a look of eager anticipation in her eyes.

"It's a pleasure." Josam smiles with a seductive curl to her lips.

Lee lets out an involuntary squeak.

"You said there were five groups," Pim interrupts. "I only heard four."

"Forget the last one. It's too hard to get into," Hodge says.

"What's too hard to get into?" Rook asks, emerging from the bathroom, rubbing a towel over his wet hair.

"The Watchers. They're kind of the secret workers high up in the Hall of Love. But nobody's made Watcher in five years."

Sounds like a challenge, I think. I make a mental note to find out everything I can about the Watchers, and more importantly, how I get to be one of them.

Why bother? You'll never get there, whispers a small voice of doubt in the back of my mind. Unbidden, the echoes of screaming and darkness waft back into my memory.

LATER THAT NIGHT, THE SOUND OF scuffling wakes me. I squint sleep away from my eyes. A bright amber light pulses over Zin's empty pillow. Near the front of the room, two shadowy figures stand beneath the dim green glow of the exit sign. Zin's willowy silhouette leans against a hulking shadow that can only be Hodge.

"I thought you'd be more fun than this." I can hear the pout in Zin's voice. "Isn't that a part of being Elite? More fun?" She reaches up with her free hand, pressing it against Hodge's chest. It's impossible to miss the invitation in her voice.

Hodge lifts her hand away, grasping both of her wrists in one chunky fist. "You need to memorize the fraternization rules, girl," Hodge rumbles.

"I didn't mean anything by it," she says in a plaintive whine.

The larger, bulkier shadow looms over her. "If you knew

what they could do to you, you wouldn't even think about this. Now get back to that bunk before the big guns arrive."

With gentle but determined strength, he propels her down the walkway. She saunters away from him with as much dignity as she can muster. Then she pauses, one hand on the rungs of her bunk ladder.

"You're going to regret that, boy-oh," she says.

"I sincerely doubt that." Something about the way Hodge replies is so funny that I can't help it. I let out a snort.

Zin's head whips toward me, and even in the dim light I can see her face is livid with fury.

"What are you gawping at?" she snarls. I shrink back into the shadows of my bunk. It's a good thing, too, because her claws are suddenly raking at the air where my face had been, and she's spitting words at me. "You're dead, Hater witch."

"Stop. Now," Hodge commands from his end of the room.

At the same time, the door to our bunk room slides open, and two darkened figures fill the doorway. Zin pulls back from my bunk and goes deathly still. Hodge flattens his body against his bunk, and a guard steps into the room. The man is dressed like a Love Squad soldier, his inky black uniform all carbon fiber armor and tight, muscular padding. His sleek black helmet throws a nightmarish red glow across his face. As he approaches Zin, she juts her hip sideways and pushes her shoulders back. I can tell she's freaked out by the way her hands have started to shake.

"What seems to be the problem, office—" Before she can finish, the officer places his hand over her mouth, flips her 180 degrees, and then drags her backward out of the room. Shocked, I can only watch. Shortly afterward, the flashing orange light on Zin's bunk winks out.

"You okay?" Hodge mumbles at me.

"Fine. Sorry," I say.

"Not your fault." He sighs. "Get some sleep."

It takes a long time for my heart to slow to a normal pace after that. I've never seen a Love Squad officer up close before. They're always lined up on Carell Hummer's show, standing in the background as a decoration. But up close, they look . . . scary. Hodge said that being absent would lead to bad things. They must be pretty harsh if the Love Squad is removing people in the middle of the night.

IN THE MORNING, THE ALARM SPITS US out of bed again. This time I'm ready. As soon as the harsh tone sounds, I spring up, vaulting out of the way before Sif can fall on me. But she's more prepared too. She lands on her toes with a graceful leap, stretching her arms high above her head. We both yawn, then giggle when we realize we've done it in sync.

I cast a quick glance toward Zin's bunk. The empty space is confirmation that last night wasn't just some kind of vivid dream. Hodge's bed is also vacant. I hope he isn't in trouble too.

Farr lands on the floor, thanks to her rolling mattress, and glances around with bleary eyes while she scratches her back. When she notices Zin's empty bed, her eyes harden. She snaps her head around from one side to another, suspicion thick in her gaze. I fuss with my sheets, avoiding eye contact.

"How did you sleep?" Sif asks. Oblivious to the little drama unfolding beside us, she drops onto my bunk, bouncing up as if stung. "Wow, that's not comfortable at all."

"I slept fine," I say.

"You seem pretty tired for someone who slept fine."

"Bad dreams."

"You want to talk about it?"

My eyes stray to Zin's empty bunk. "Maybe later."

"Oh. Okay. Hey, let's try and get to the showers before the big kids."

She darts for the bathroom, grasping her towel and gear in her fists. I scramble to catch up. Josam and Jimoway are already ahead of me, and Mill isn't far behind. Feeling a small thrill of fear, I lock myself into a cubicle beside Sif. I hope we don't cop it later.

I'M BRUSHING MY TEETH WHEN A VOICE screeches into my brain.

"Cadence!"

I jump, startled. The voice is so loud and so close it sounds like someone shouted behind me. A thousand needles of pain stab through my temple.

"What?" Sif swivels toward me, a toothbrush still hanging out of the side of her mouth. Toothpaste lines her lips like a tiny moustache.

I squint into the mirrored wall above the sinks in front of us. Apart from Sif, me, and a random towel someone left hanging over a cubicle door, we're alone.

My mouth goes dry.

"Nothing," I mutter. I rattle my own toothbrush against the sink and I bolt away. The bathroom door glides open, and I rush out so fast I crash heavily into a chest as solid as stone. I feel my face warming with embarrassment.

"Sorry," I mutter.

"No harm done," Hodge grunts. I risk a glance upward and meet his light-brown eyes. He smiles.

I duck my head and squeeze past him.

Nothing to see here. Just me and my crazy voices, I think to myself.

11

Nursery Induction Manual
   Catechesis volume 2, page 40.
   Q: What is the fate of Haters?
      A: Haters can never understand the truth. They
      are never able to learn the way of the Collective.
      The only fate we can accept is to expel them
      from among us.
   Q: Why must Haters be removed?
      A: Hate is a cancer that destroys everything in its
      path. We must use any necessary means to protect
      our way of life.

THE QUIET HUM OF CONVERSATION HOVERS
above me while I do my best to pretend I'm normal. All the
new arrivals sit in a semicircular lecture theatre, looking down
at a platform that stands in front of a high white screen. A row
of windows behind us all casts beams of morning sunlight over
the front lectern. It smells like everything else here: bleach,
metal, and lemon-scented cleaner.

When a linen-clad instructor strides in through large
double doors down below, the hum dies into silence. Everyone
straightens in their seats. Light from the screen behind the man
reflects off his bald head, and he squints up at the high windows

beaming sunlight into his eyes. With a quick press of a button on his console, the daylight is shuttered out.

"Love all," he says with a perfunctory wave of his hand.

"Be all!" we chant in reply.

"Right. My name is Lover Weekes. I'm here to take you through Elite Orientation. No doubt you've all been researching Elite Academy for years from your Nursery bunks. But I'm supposed to make sure you know everything you need to know to actually live here. So here we go."

He holds his clasped hands out in front of his chest. Then with a quick wave, he pulls his hands wide apart, and a display rises from his lectern. He turns and thrusts his hands in the direction of the screen. The display flies from his console through the air to land on it. I gasp, amazed at the show of light and sound. Nursery Dorm never had anything that advanced.

A virtual tour of the campus begins to play.

"Welcome to a day in the life of an Elite Apprentice," says the narrator in bright, chirpy tones. The movie flies through the halls, and the narrator explains meal times, classes, drills, and rules. I gasp when I see the study room, a large space full of cozy booths where we can sit with our infotabs and research.

It looks as if Elite Academy is a giant donut of a building that encircles green drill yards, gardens, and even forests. The large atrium we walked into this morning is only one of six separate wings. We're in the Introductory and Accommodation wing, but there are other wings for each of the five Elite specialties. Final year Apprentices get to live in their specialty wings. For now, we're all lumped in together.

When the glowing images and flyovers fade away, Lover Weekes steps back to his space at the lectern. He scans our group with practiced boredom.

"Right. Time for questions. Who wants to go first?"

A room full of hands shoots up. Lover Weekes's shoulders slump. Then he nods toward a redheaded Apprentice to his left.

"When do we get into VR?" she asks, eyes bright. Lover Weekes's eye roll is so exaggerated I can almost hear it.

"Twenty years of this, and that's the first question. Every. Time." He turns the full force of his withering stare at the redhead, who visibly wilts. "The vision explained it. You should have listened. You start normal classes tomorrow. They will be your classes every week until you're filtered into a cadre. Okay? Elite Axioms, Physical Training, Loyalty Drills, Brain Focus, Coding, and yes, VR practice. Happy?"

A frisson of excitement shivers over the class, despite Lover Weekes's scowls. More hands shoot up. Every question receives a sarcastic response until only a few hands remain.

"What are the cadres?" asks a skinny boy toward the back.

"How many of you even watched the information documentary I just showed you? Somebody else answer this one. I don't have time for this."

MEMORY DATE: CE 2279.013 (1 YEAR AGO)

Memory location: Hater Recognition lesson, Nursery Dorm 492, Room 37, Row 5, Seat 4

Memory time: 1622 hours

"How many of you watched the vision I just showed you?" Lover Beresfield demands, hands on hips. I wave my hand as high as I can, uttering little squeaks with the effort.

"Thank you, Apprentice Flick. I want to see if anyone else can remember the details of the Hater Recognition Signs as well as you." There's a small snort from Myk, who is sitting directly behind me. Lover Beresfield appears not to notice. "Any other students want to tell me what the Hater Recognition Sign 'Doubt' means? Somebody else answer this one. I don't have time for this."

A few timid hands slowly creep into the air. Lover Beresfield nods at Apprentice Koah, who makes a nervous little shift in her seat.

"Lover Beresfield, 'Doubt' refers to the following things." Koah begins to count the information on her fingers. "Haters question what they are given. Haters do not understand their privilege. Haters doubt the testimony of their superiors. Lovers do not doubt."

She finishes the last one with a broad, proud smile and is rewarded with an answering grin from our instructor.

"Very good, Apprentice Koah. You will do well in our Love Collective."

MY HAND SHOOTS UP. LOVER WEEKES WAVES his hand for me to speak.

"Lover Weekes, sir, there are five cadres . . ." I begin to recite the information video word for word as my memory recorded it.

Lover Weekes nods, face an expressionless mask. "Well. At least one of you watched the video. Are there any other questions?" Weekes turns his head from side to side, daring one of us to respond. I ignore a hard nudge from Sif's elbow beside me. When I glance toward her, she gives me a wink and mouths, "That was amazing!"

I grin.

"How do we get into the cadres?" asks Chu from the front row.

"You're tested at the end of this semester," Weekes says. "The tests will reveal your abilities, and you'll be assigned accordingly. Next?"

"What if we fail the tests?" Chu persists.

"You get the privilege of being sent away to be an app monkey, son. Now, anybody got a question that isn't a colossal waste of my time?" When he sees my hand raised, he stops. "This better not be something we've already covered," he warns.

"How do we get into the Watchers?" I ask.

Lover Weekes lets out a loud bark of laughter that echoes around the room. "Oh, sweetheart, you've got guts. I'll give you that." He shakes his head. "We don't have control over that one. The Hall of Love decides when it needs new Watchers. Sends us a shopping list. Sometimes they even pick the specific kids, based on testing transcripts. We don't always know who or what they want. But they're never below the top 1 percent. On everything. So unless you like disappointment, I wouldn't make that a lifelong goal if I were you."

"I want to try," I say, stubbornness thick in my voice. Lover Weekes looks at me as if I just said I'm a doorknob.

"Why in the love would you want to do that?"

"Because it's the Elite of the Elite."

"You are either the bravest or stupidest girl I've ever met here at Academy. Guess time will tell which one." Weekes sighs.

I want to keep asking questions, but we're interrupted. The doors at both sides of the lecture room slam open, and half of the class jumps in fright. Two large carts wheel in, pushed by uniformed attendants. Lover Weekes rubs his hands together.

"Right. Here are your class supplies," he says to us all. "When your name is called, you will receive a bag containing your infotab, VR headset, and activity tracker. You are fully responsible for maintaining your equipment at all times. Infotabs must be completely charged in the morning. We'll go through the study app in a moment. Make sure you pay attention because you have lots of reading to do. Activity trackers must remain on your right wrists at all times."

"What happens if we don't wear it?" Rook calls out, a cocky grin on his face.

"You want to be demoted? Just give it a try." Lover Weekes's expression could kill a small animal. In response, the tall, bulky

Rook shrinks in his seat, and Arah shakes his head in disgust at his twin.

Nobody asks any more questions after that. Lover Weekes calls out our names, and we step forward to receive our new equipment bags.

THE NEAT, WHITE BAG RESTS ON MY LAP, silver zippers shining. Sif strokes her bag like it's a pet. Beside her, Cam rips the zipper open so fast that a small bundle of items falls onto the floor, and he bends down with gangly arms to try and retrieve it from under his seat. I smooth down the canvas on the front of the bag, feeling the solid lumps inside, then I unzip the bag to find my presents. The sleek white rectangle sits at the top of the bundle, gleaming.

"My own infotab," I whisper. "I never owned anything like this before."

Sif grins. "I guess I'll actually have to look after this." She waves her own infotab at me. "My Nursery Dorm ones were scratched and old."

"Mine too. Always sticky."

I scan the surface of my new acquisition. Smooth white metal forms a slate with rounded edges. It's slimmer than the Nursery Dorm tabs, but slightly taller. I squeeze the sides, and the face lights up in greeting:

Welcome, Apprentice Flick.

"Shiny," Chu purrs, turning his own infotab over and over in his hands. Cam pops up with a cry of triumph and holds aloft a thin white strip. With a quick flick of his wrist, the strip folds out to reveal a neat pair of VR goggles attached to a headband.

"Ha! Look what I've got!" he exclaims with a wide smile.

"Wha-at? VR headset!" Chu ducks his head down into his

own bag and emerges a second or two later holding his own set of glasses. In his other hand he holds a pair of grey gloves. The two boys don their VR headsets and gloves and start to mime a mock VR battle against each other.

"Pew pew pew!" Cam shoots Chu. "You're dead!"

"Missed me," Chu taunts.

"Hey!" Cam complains. "That was a fair shot!"

"You two are idiots." Sif shakes her head.

Chu whips his headset off, looking embarrassed.

12

The Love Collective is not limited by time and space.
It is everywhere.
It sees everything.
  —*Supreme Lover Midgate,* Intimate Diaries of a
  Loving Leader, *page 418*

ENTERING THE VR CHAMBER IS LIKE finally winning the Love Collective Jackpot.

"Ooh," breathes Buff as we step into a wide aisle down the middle of the room.

Black metallic walls curve seamlessly into a vaulted ceiling. Intricate laser-cut holes and designs curl across every surface, surrounded by thin blue pinstripe lights. Fifty VR stations line the walls.

"That screen is as tall as me!" Lee hurries over to investigate one of the stations. He plonks himself into one of the chairs that hangs from the ceiling and bounces in circles.

"Not yet, Apprentice," Lover Herz warns. "Everyone to a station. We need to do a quick equipment check."

I flex my hand, feeling the snug fit of the new gloves. My new suit is the most comfortable thing I've ever worn. The grey, metallic material might be ugly, but it's flexible and warm. My sensor-equipped sneakers rebound over the floor. The VR headset perches on top of my head, ready to slip it down when it's time to go.

"Eyes front!"

A majestic figure in white linen strides into the room, and my breath catches in my throat. Dorm Leader Akela's eyes sweep over us, cool and evaluating. Hundreds of tiny grey braids weave down from her scalp, gathered behind her head by a simple gold band. I resist the urge to smooth my hair flat. Lover Herz rises from her seat to give her leader a crisp salute. Akela nods to her, then turns to us.

Why were you in my dream? I shake the thought away. It's just a coincidence. I must have glanced at her photo somewhere in my research. My memory-freak brain must have inserted her into my travel fears. There's no other explanation. I mean, I never forget a face, and I can't remember any research that showed me the Dorm Leader's photo, but still. It's the only explanation that makes sense.

We chant the regular Love Collective greeting, and Dorm Leader Akela nods, satisfied.

"Good morning, Apprentices. It is good to see you have survived your first few days in Elite training," she says with a smile. "I trust you are all handling the new lessons well."

"Yes, Dorm Leader," we reply.

"Enjoy your introduction to VR training today. I just wanted to step in and remind you that if at any time you are struggling with your lessons, my door is always open. The learning curve from Nursery Dorm to Elite Academy is steep. At the Elite Academy we hold to the highest standard. But that doesn't mean we are without compassion. Understood?"

Again, I am not sure I imagine that her gaze rests on me for a second longer than the others.

"Understood, Dorm Leader," chants our whole class.

"Good. Remember, your first year is about finding your

niche. You will adapt to some lessons more easily than others. This is all part of the process. Are you ready?"

"Yes, Dorm Leader!" we chant.

Our leader's smile is brief and tight-lipped. She nods to Lover Herz.

"Apprentices mount," says Lover Herz.

As one, we step up to our platforms and lean back into the suspended chairs. My chair naturally lowers to my height so my feet rest comfortably on the ground. It's like I am being scooped up by a large spoon.

I flex my fingers again, letting the gloves move with me, then I lower the visor over my eyes. My world descends into black. A flutter of nerves circles around my stomach. Seconds later, searingly bright white letters flash across the screen.

State your name.

"Apprentice Kerr Flick."

State your apprentice number.

"Apprentice #540/187503"

Prepare for retinal calibration scan.

A line of light passes over my eye, and I try really hard not to blink. It's a huge relief when my screen goes dark for a few seconds. Then a scene fades into view, as if the sun has just risen. We're on the drill fields. My whole class stands in a circle. Lover Herz stares directly at me from her position in the center.

"Welcome to our training program," she says. Her eyes never leave my face. "This morning, I want you to become familiar with the physical controls of your VR kit. We have set up a scavenger hunt as an exercise. Thirty-five red stars have been hidden in various locations around the Academy."

Lover Herz holds up her right hand, and a glittering star appears in the air above her palm. It shimmers and rotates, ruby red and slightly transparent. Excitement thrills through me. I wish all my lessons were games like this.

"You have an hour to find as many stars as you can," Lover

Herz continues. "If anyone is able to find all thirty-five, they will receive a bonus prize, though that is hardly possible. We have included a few tricks. Whenever someone finds a star, it will take thirty seconds for a new one to regenerate. Your visual display will include a map of the Academy, which will display your classmates' locations at all times. Go."

A starter siren sounds. At the signal, everyone runs away. I nod to Lover Herz, noticing that the star is still hovering over her hand. When I reach out and my hand passes through the star, there's a loud *ding*, and a tally lights up in the top right corner of my vision, right next to the countdown clock: ★=1

"Well done, Apprentice Flick." Lover Herz smiles. "Your intuition is on target today."

"Thank you." I smile back and take off at a run, searching my heads-up display for everyone else. Rook, Arah, and a group of seven others have gathered at one end of the athletics field. Their avatars hover in a tight circle, unmoving. If they want to waste time, that's fine with me. I'm not going to stand around for half the hunt, waiting for one star to regenerate.

A lot of my classmates want to wait, so they give away the location of half the stars. Pim and Lee freeze in the middle of the drill yard. Chu and Cam hover nearby. Back in the kitchen, Farr, Zin, and Buff wait near the servery. Dona and a few others pause in the large reception lobby. I file all of their locations into my memory and move into a section of the Academy where no other students have run. Sif seems to have the same idea. Her icon is nowhere near any of the others either.

Running in VR is weird. The scene blurs at the periphery of my vision. When I want to turn my head, I have to take it slowly, or else my whole world disappears for a split second. Too fast, and I get dizzy.

A second star waits in a large lecture theatre, frozen behind the lectern. When I swipe it, my headset dings, and the display lights up: ★=2. I make a quick check of the heads-up display.

Frozen classmates give away another four stars, which I store for later. One glows beneath the back row of our Elite Theory classroom, but most of them seem to twinkle at the tops of various stairwells. A lone star rotates on the Academy roof.

On the top floor of our classroom wing, Sif finds me. She waves from the other end of the hallway. "There's one in the west wing bathroom!" she shouts. I let her know where I found the others, not stopping long enough to give our location any meaning. "Can't stop!" I say.

"Good plan!" she replies, heading for the lecture hall where I've already been.

The jackpot comes when I find a small cluster of stars in the VR lab, one for each class member. I run down the aisle, grabbing stars as I go. By the time I leave, my tally is reading ★=30.

After running far enough away from the VR room, I take a moment to scan the Academy map. In a distant corner of the classroom wing, a group of four dots hovers in a room that I haven't seen yet.

"Gotcha!" I say to myself, then head back to the kitchen, picking up two before I get there. The fourth is way out across the drill fields. By the time I collect it, only five minutes remain. I break into a sprint.

My virtual footsteps take me back across the drill fields, up stairs, and through winding corridors. Synthetic sound effects pound down the floor in sync with my real-life steps. Seconds tick away.

"Kerr! Hey!" calls a familiar voice behind me. Sif jogs up, a crisp and neat avatar of herself. Her face looks as if a photo of her has been stretched over a 3D model of a head. I have to stifle a laugh when she starts to speak, because I've never seen anything so unnatural. Instead of a moving mouth, a black circle appears and disappears not quite in sync with her words.

"What?" she says. I can tell from the sound of her voice

that she's annoyed. Her face maintains its serene, artificial expression.

"Have you seen yourself?" I laugh.

"Shut up. You look just as dumb. Anyway, I'm still missing a bunch of stars. Can you help?"

"Did you find the VR room?"

"Yeah. Just. Lee tried to snatch the last one before I could get it, but I was too quick. They're still down there now, waiting for them all to regenerate. How many do you have?"

"I know where the last one is," I say. "Wanna come? We can compare where we found them on the way."

Sif shrugs. "Sure."

We take off, flying down the hall as fast as our legs can carry us. The final hiding place seems to be a supply closet of some sort. The walls are narrow, and it's tucked between two Engine Room labs.

"You found the lecture hall?" I ask.

"Yeah." Sif's voice sounds breathless, but her avatar glides smoothly over the tiled floor.

"Drill yard?"

"No."

"Elite Theory room?"

"No. Didn't even look in there."

"Kitchen?"

"Nope. I'll have to go fast after we find this one."

"Okay. You get this star first, then."

"You sure?"

"Of course. We've still got two minutes. Plenty of time for me."

"Wow, thanks."

"No problem."

"I knew I did the smart thing picking you as my friend." Sif gives me a virtual pat. The sensors on my suit press in on my upper arm where her hand has been.

We bound up one more flight of stairs and enter an unfamiliar corridor. Synthetic echoes bounce around us, a convincing imitation of a deserted hallway. I smile. Only one star left. If I catch this last star, I'll win, and then I'll be one step closer to Watcher.

Sif rips the door open, and we peer into a dark space, illuminated only by the faint glow of the rotating red star. I can vaguely make out the shape of shelves lining one side of the room from floor to ceiling. The other side is a coat rack. An irrational prickle of fear tugs at my senses.

It's just a closet. Why would I be scared? Okay, so the last time I entered a dark, enclosed space I had a major crazy episode, but that doesn't mean it's going to happen now. This is VR, not real life.

"Want a lab coat?" Sif asks, grinning. She leaps forward, arms outstretched, aiming past the coats at the star. Just before she reaches it, she turns back to me. Her strangely stretched avatar face looks blankly at me.

"You sure you're okay with me taking this?" she asks.

"Go! Do it! I don't want to run out of time."

Her voice sounds hesitant. "All right then. But only because you made me."

There's a faint *ding*, and Sif jumps back out into the light of the corridor. She grabs my hand, and the sensors on my glove respond with the painful pressure of a tight handshake.

"Thanks. I owe you one."

"Go."

Sif nods, releases my hand, and bounds away down the corridor.

"Don't get stuck in there!" she yells back over her shoulder.

"Ha!" I reply with sarcasm, though deep down I've been worrying about exactly that.

I peer uncertainly into the closet, holding onto the doorknob for reassurance. Time counts down on my headset display:

1:15 . . . 1:13 . . . 1:11 . . . There will only be seconds to grab the star once it regenerates, but it's not the time limit that's making my heart beat faster.

I try and talk myself out of a panic. Less than thirty seconds to wait. Not long. That cupboard might be creepy, but it's not forever. I'll just step in, grab the star, and get out. Easy.

My body won't listen, though. Both palms are clammy, and my breath is coming in shallow gulps. I jump from foot to foot, trying to calm my nerves. That star should have regenerated by now. Why is the room so hot? My knees are wobbly. I will be fine. Of course I will. Elites aren't afraid of confined spaces. I mean, come on.

"Hey!" yells a loud voice from the end of the corridor, followed by the sound of heavy footsteps. I turn. Rook and Arah sprint toward me, determination etched across their faces. Taking a quick, shaky breath, I step into the closet and pull the door closed, shrouding myself in utter darkness. I fumble at the lock, clicking it into place just as the pounding of heavy fists erupts on solid metal.

"Open this door!" Arah screams.

"You're dead!" adds Rook, his voice crackling through my headset. I shrink further back into the closet, letting the soft fabric wrap around my face. Just then, the star winks into life again, casting the room in a dull red glow. A sudden stabbing pain attacks my forehead.

"Not again," I gasp as my world collapses around me.

13

Haterman, Haterman,
Don't hate me.
Haterman, Haterman,
Let me be.
I'm in the Collective
Can't you see?
Haterman, Haterman,
Don't hate me.

DARKNESS. FLASHES OF ORANGE AND red light. Screams in the distance. So many screams.

I am dissolving. Evaporating into a thousand tiny fragments of agony. My head is a cacophony of pain.

"Cadence!"

Red light paints everything, like a neon sign glowing through fog. Somewhere here there was a virtual star. Or was there? Lover Herz must be waiting for me, but I can't find the way out. I flail around blindly, and everything goes dark again.

The sound of distant shouting comes closer. I wave my arms around and find nothing. The door has gone. So have the shelves. This feels too real to be VR. I'm kicking and fighting against darkness, as if I've been bundled up into a sack by the

Haterman. Something is covering my arms and my legs, holding them against my body. I'm rocking . . . rocking . . .

Shaky breathing behind me. Whispers almost too low to hear.

"Don't forget . . ."

I shut my eyes tight.

A scream splits the darkness, echoing around me like a blaring siren. Bonds of steel snake around my arms, clenching them against my sides. The more I writhe, the tighter they get. A scream erupts behind me, pain radiating from every agonized breath.

"Cadence! No!"

I am the one who is screaming.

I WAKE UP, COVERED BY A THIN BLUE blanket. I'm lying on a raised bed in the middle of a glass-walled room. Quiet, rhythmic beeps emanate from an infotab console nearby. The pain is gone, but my brain feels like it's packed full of marshmallows.

I reach up to touch my throbbing forehead, and my fingers nudge a small headset circling my skull like a halo. This seems to create a small hiccup in the machine's rhythm. Not long afterward, the glass door in front of me slides open, and a smiling Lover glides to the console. She is tall, with black hair as fine as silk, cropped in regulation Love Collective fashion. Her white linen collar is marked with an embroidered red scalpel. She reaches for the console, her elegant fingers flying across the screen.

"How are you feeling, Apprentice Flick?" she asks without looking up.

"Where am I?"

The medic gives a slightly condescending smile. "You're in the infirmary."

"What happened?"

"A small episode in the VR chamber. Don't worry."

Snatches of memory pierce my head like poison-tipped arrows. After the incident in the Nursery Dorm, I was hoping that I'd never have to go through that again. Guess I was wrong.

"I failed," I whisper, breath hitching in sorrow. Lover Zink was sure I wouldn't last a week in this place. I guess he was right. I'll be demoted now, for sure.

Tears sting at the corners of my eyes. The attendant pats my hand, reassuring.

"Now, now, it was your first VR day. We had another ten in here earlier with dizzy spells and nausea. Small setbacks are normal for the first entry into VR classes," the medic coos.

"This wasn't a small setback."

My medical attendant frowns. "Setbacks are what you make of them, Apprentice."

With a sharp turn, my only companion strides out of the room, leaving me alone with nothing but my thoughts for company. I try to sit up. Dizziness attacks me in a sickening wave. I close my eyes against it, forcing myself to remain upright. Whatever they've given me is potent. Every sound and sight comes to me as if wrapped in fog. I could happily sink back into bed and sleep for a month.

"Elite Lover Team Six would be disgusted with you," I tell myself.

With determined grunts, I swivel my uncooperative legs over the edge of the bed. I'll never be a Watcher if I lie around in bed all afternoon. Visions and delusions be Embraced.

Agony erupts across my temples, so painful I let out a shocked gasp. The machine beside me hiccups again, and my medical attendant glides back into the room.

"What are you doing?" she cries, dashing toward me with eyes ablaze. "You need to rest."

"I'll be fine," I grumble. "I need to get back to class." I lean forward, ignoring her disbelieving frown. She rests her hands on my shoulders, immovable. It's like fighting against a concrete pylon.

"You are not going anywhere until I say so," she states, laying me back on the bed. I'm too weak to resist. When she presses something on her infotab, the fog in my head gets thicker.

"What are you doing?" I mumble. My tongue feels like it's wrapped in cotton wool. Slumber falls on me like an avalanche, and I am buried beneath it.

MEMORY DATE: CE 2276.142 (5 YEARS AGO)

Memory location: Hater History lesson, Nursery Dorm 492, Room 37, Row 5, Seat 4

Memory time: 1627 hours

Lover Zink wears a non-regulation yellow sash around his waist, which seems to be losing the battle to hold up his linen trousers. There is a small sweat stain spreading underneath his left arm. I know this because he swipes his hair across his forehead with his left hand every few minutes, even though it is already pasted across his skin like a greasy cartoon smile. He takes a gulping breath.

"Love all," he stammers.

"Be all," we reply in polite, obedient tones.

"Thanks be to Supreme Lover Midgate," he says.

"May we find ourselves in her universe," we reply.

"Right, lesson eight should be appearing on your infotabs. 'Who is the Haterman?' Read the paragraph, and then answer the

questions. Does anyone not understand these easy instructions? Yes, Apprentice Bez."

When I glance to my right, the pudgy Apprentice has his arm straight in the air. He leans up into it as if he's trying to make himself taller.

"Why do we need to know about the Haterman?" Bez asks. "I thought we weren't supposed to talk about him."

It's impossible to miss the contempt in Lover Zink's exaggerated eye roll, but there's something else beneath it too. Something most of the others can't see.

Lover Zink is afraid.

"Why does the Executive keep sending me these rejects?" he mutters to himself. Then he turns the full, withering force of his stare on the hapless Bez. "Do you not remember lesson seven? Know your enemy. We cannot be free to 'love all, be all' if we are taken captive by the enemy's lies. Did you listen to nothing?"

In my head, the transcript of lesson seven begins to play like a vidscreen recording. Can't stop it. The memory weaves itself into lesson eight, embroidering my infotab readings. By the end of the lesson I am in a room full of mirrors—memories playing and replaying into the present, extending into infinity.

BY THE TIME MY EYES FLICKER OPEN AGAIN, a face is staring at me that shocks me wide awake. I flinch away from Dorm Leader Akela, who smiles as she sees my eyes open. If the Elite Academy boss is here, my situation must be really bad.

"How are you, Apprentice?" Akela asks. Her warm brown eyes twinkle, and small creases appear around her eyelids. Behind her, my dark-haired medical attendant stands to attention, looking a little displeased.

I do a mental check of my system. All the pain has gone, and so has the sensation of trying to think through a wall of marshmallow.

"Much better, thank you," I reply with as much politeness as I can muster. *"Why were you in my dream?"* I almost ask.

"Are you well enough to stand?"

"I think so," I reply. With the speed of a glacier, I raise myself up from my bed. This time, I actually manage to swivel my legs out of bed without wanting to throw up. Medical attendant lady in the corner crosses her arms and sniffs in disgust. She might want me to stay lying down, but whatever she did with that headset has worked.

Dorm Leader Akela nods, satisfied with my progress. "Good," she says. She turns to the medical attendant and indicates the door. "You may leave us now."

Disapproval etches deeper into the medic's face, but she obeys without a word. The glass door swishes closed, and then I am alone with the Elite Dorm Leader. My skin prickles.

"You have had quite an episode." Her smile fades.

Infotab research flutters across my memory. *Elite Axiom four: Elites are never sloppy. Elite Axiom nine: Elites show no weakness.*

I lift my chin. "It was nothing, Dorm Leader. I will do better next time."

"They found you on the floor. Can you tell me what you remember about the test?"

Darkness and stars. Pain has left such a vivid memory that I flinch.

Elites show no weakness.

"No, Dorm Leader."

Akela's frown deepens. "Pity."

"I am sorry, Dorm Leader."

"I know you are upset. Let me reassure you that you are not facing censure for this. We just need to know what happened."

Her expression almost gets me, and I fight a strong urge to open my mouth and spew words until I lose my voice. But the Elite Axioms won't fade. I have to be strong. If I tell her about my dreams, she'll think I'm crazy. The only future I'll have then will be app monkey. Or worse.

"I lost my footing," I say. "I can't tell you any more than that."

Akela leans toward me, patting my hand. "Child, I know what you want to be. A Watcher is a supreme . . . aspiration. But if you are susceptible to fits, then we cannot let you back into VR. Now is the time to tell me whether there is anything else going on."

The blood drains from my face. Without VR, my Elite career is finished. Every cadre needs it. Even Engine Roomers.

"It wasn't a fit, Dorm Leader. I slipped in the simulation of the storage room, and I must have hit my head and blacked out for a second. I'm sorry. It won't happen again."

For a long, painful moment, Dorm Leader Akela searches my face, her mouth compressed into a thin line. Then her face gets sad, just the way it did in my dream.

"Very well. Because of your stellar results so far, I shall give you one more chance. But if you black out again, then your case will be out of my hands. Do you understand?"

I nod. "Thank you, Dorm Leader. I promise I won't disappoint you."

"Lies disappoint me more than failure, Apprentice. Remember that."

With those words, she turns and glides smoothly from the room.

Nursery Dorm Mission Goal Document 4.581
Remain vigilant. Always.

AS SOON AS THE BUNKROOM DOOR OPENS, Sif flies at me like a stun net from a Love Squad utility belt. I can't even step inside before I'm engulfed in a suffocating hug.

"What the love happened to you?" she cries, pushing me back to arm's length so she can glare into my face. Worry creases the edges of her eyelids.

Chu comes up beside her. His smile is a nice antidote to the anxious frown Sif is giving me right now.

"Great to see you too." I give her a weary smile, inwardly pleased that someone noticed.

"I'm serious. I've been freaking out that you were abducted by Haters or something."

"Nope."

I walk to my bunk, mostly ignored by the older Apprentices. When I collapse onto the mattress, Chu and Sif flop down beside me. Safely settled and hidden from some of the passing crew, Sif turns to me.

"Spill."

"What do you want me to say?"

"You left me alone for four hours. Lover Fuschious's drill

class was in the middle of that. He screamed his lungs out the whole time."

"That guy has serious anger issues," Chu adds.

"What happened to you?" Sif slaps my knee in frustration.

"You okay, Kerr?" interrupts a quiet voice from outside our little den. Lee and Pim hesitate beside the bunk. For once, Pim's usual petulant expression is absent. Cam joins them.

"We saw you in the infirmary," Lee continues. "You looked pretty bad."

"And that's coming from the guy who needed the puke bucket," adds Pim, gesturing toward him.

"So did you!" Lee shoots back, flushing bright red.

"Not as much as you. You were like this all afternoon." Pim grasps her stomach and heaves.

Lee scowls. "Next time I'll aim for you."

"I'm okay." I smile, not wanting them to descend into a rumble. "Nothing a good night's sleep won't fix."

"They said you went down pretty hard. Are they going to let you back into VR?" Pim asks.

"Yeah. But I'm on probation. If I fall over again, I might be out for a while." The thought brings a stab of anxiety to my heart.

"Serious? But almost everything Elites do has to be in VR." Disbelief is written in Sif's eyes.

"I know." I can't say anything else, too busy biting back the sudden rush of tears. *Elites show no weakness. Elites show no weakness.*

"You were the only one to get all the stars. Did you know that?" Cam leans against the shelving at the head of my bed, his arms folded.

"They didn't tell me anything."

"Well, you were. Well done." Pim gives me a surprising thumbs-up.

"We all decided. Next time we're teaming up with you," Lee says.

Sif glares at him. "I saw her first."

"If we're going to split hairs," interjects Cam. "I saw her before you did, so . . ."

Sif gives Cam a little shove. I lean back, resting my head on the wall behind my bunk. It's nice they're fighting over me, but right now it kinda feels like a flock of vultures arguing over a corpse.

"After today, I'm going to have to slow down a little, you know?" I tell them.

"Slowing down isn't such a bad thing. Maybe you'll give us half a chance to win." Chu forces out a little laugh, but I can tell he's not really joking. There's too much envy in his eyes.

"You don't need me," I protest.

Sif's response is swift and sharp. "Of course we do!"

"Yeah," says Lee. "Who's gonna find all those stars for us if you don't?"

MY UNWANTED CELEBRITY STATUS FADES after a few days, and after a few more weeks, the spectacular collapse of Kerr Flick in the VR lab is almost forgotten. Which is probably a good thing, since the Academy keeps throwing new curve balls at us that leave me exhausted.

"What even is the Pleasure Tribe, anyway?" Sif asks, shoes squeaking on the tiles. We spread out across the hallway, bags slung over our shoulders. Although we share a bunkroom with Pleasure Tribe Apprentices, it's taken three whole months for the Academy to let us into the secretive training rooms.

Pim wrinkles her nose. "I don't know. But if Farr is so

desperate to be in it, I'm pretty sure I'll pick a different cadre," she says.

Lee rolls his eyes at her. "Come on. It's Elite. It must be good."

"I wouldn't bet on that," Dona counters from behind us. "Have you seen the way Josam and Jimoway walk around in our bunk room? Like they're too good for us? Flicking their red hair everywhere. And Mill . . ."

"Mill. Oh yeah." Seeing Lee's enthusiastic nods, Pim's look of disgust deepens.

"Put your tongue back in your head before you drool all over the floor."

"You're just jealous."

"It takes more than looking good in uniform to make someone Elite, Lee," Dona says.

"Nothing wrong with looking good." Lee's grin broadens wickedly. Chu and Cam laugh.

"Ugh. Why did I end up with you as a training partner?" Pim turns away from him.

"You needed someone to fix your mistakes." Lee chuckles. Pim shoves him sideways, but they're both smiling.

I shake my head. "I'll never get you two," I say.

"We're late." Sif dashes ahead through the classroom door. We follow her into a space that smells like chalk, sweat, and dust. The room looks like a cross between a theatre and a gym. Everyone is already lined up in front of Lover Weekes, the bored instructor from our first lesson. He sits on a weight bench, resting his elbows on his knees. As we enter, he raises his head with effort and waves a lazy hand to direct us into a semicircle around a circular performance space.

We mill around, jostling to be closer to the front. Buff is the last to arrive, and she gently closes the door behind her. All sound from outside the room shuts off as the door clicks into place. We're cocooned in a strange, silent gymnasium.

"All here?" Lover Weekes says, eyelids hooded. "Finally. Right, let's get started."

Lover Weekes leaps toward a long silk curtain that drapes down from the ceiling beside him. Before I can blink, he has curled the silk around his wrist and pulled himself up into the air. He climbs, wrapping himself in silk as he goes. Three-quarters of the way up he pauses to stare down on us with his now-familiar boredom. His muscles strain beneath a tightly fitting white shirt.

"Welcome to the Pleasure Tribe training room," he says from high above our heads. "Although most of you won't cut it here, I have to show everyone what makes up the Elite's best cadre."

With an amazing elegance and poise, Lover Weekes twists, and he is suddenly flying high above our heads with only the silk to hold him. Then he somersaults upward, wrapping the silk around his foot as he goes. The class gasps as he seems to fall, but then he is twirling faster and faster upside down, silk flowing behind him like a waterfall. Another twist, and he spins horizontally, his two hands grasping the line. Then he slides downward, stopping inches above the floor. The class erupts into applause.

"Thank you," Lover Weekes says, stepping away from the silk. A small smile curls at his lips. "Entertainment is not all we do here. But it is the most visible aspect. All right, over to the learning circle, and we'll get on with it."

He raises his arm toward the back of the room, indicating a series of cube-shaped gym blocks. Farr dances on her toes over to Lover Weekes. She opens her mouth but then seems to think better of it and falls into a quiet, sashaying walk beside him.

"Who's she trying to be? Mill?" Sif grumbles.

Ignoring them both, I plonk myself down on one of the cube seats. It shifts beneath me, unsettling my balance. It's like sitting on a bag of marbles.

"All right, future citizens. What keeps the Love Collective working smoothly?" Lover Weekes asks, strolling to the middle of our learning circle.

Rook's hand shoots up. "The Engine Room, Lover Weekes. Without the supplies—"

"No," Lover Weekes snaps, his eyes half-lidded.

Farr sits up straight in her seat, raising her arm high above her head.

"Yes, Apprentice?"

"We do?"

"Close." Lover Weekes gives her a half smile. He picks up an infotab from a table, waving it slowly through the air.

"A happy populace is a pliable populace, Elites. Remember that," he says. "No amount of food or medicine is going to keep you out of trouble if you have nothing to look forward to after work. That's where we come in."

He sits down cross-legged on one of the cubic seats without the slightest wobble. The infotab rests easily across his lap.

"Whether it's making content for the LC app, or entertaining at the Triumph of Love, or providing"—his mouth quirks—"*personal* services for our clients, the Pleasure Tribe is vital to the ongoing health of our Collective. We are the glue that holds our nation together. By the time we are finished with the app monkeys, they're exhausted and happy and ready to go back to work. Pliable."

He flicks his hand upward, and the LC app menu appears on the wall behind him. We're all familiar with the display. But this globe has far more options. Every rotation brings different icons and more continents into view. Lover Weekes begins to play with it, shifting the globe around so that we can all see.

MEMORY DATE: CE 2271.210 (10 YEARS AGO)

Memory location: Preparation for Life class, Nursery Dorm 492, Room 14, Row 2, Seat 3

Memory time: 0947 hours

"The Love Collective is a beautiful place for those who do the will of the Love Collective. Let me show you something special."

Lover Zink pulls a shiny white rectangle from a drawer below his desk. He holds it up for the whole class, and as if by magic, the screen blooms into life. Five people in the class gasp. Three people make an "ooh!" sound.

"This is an infotab," Lover Zink explains. "If you work hard here in Nursery Dorm, you will be rewarded with app time. The better your behavior, the more app time you will be given."

A shimmering globe rotates on the screen with little satellite images. Lover Zink smiles and presses one of the satellites. The tiny box expands to fill the screen, and a funny cartoon starts to play. We laugh.

"But mark this, Apprentices. If you fail to do the will of the Love Collective, you will find this kind of love beyond your reach."

With a dramatic flourish, Lover Zink presses a button, and the white rectangle goes blank. Apprentice Koah lets out a little whine.

I decide I will do anything Lover Zink wants if it means I can hold one of those white rectangles.

LOVER WEEKES'S FACE REMAINS IMPASSIVE. Like he's seen it all before.

"The Pleasure Tribe is divided into several departments. Creatives think up the content. They're the artists, the writers, the imagination behind your favorite shows."

"Like *Elite Heroes*?" Sif asks.

Lover Weekes nods. "That's one of many. When the Creatives create, the Entertainers fill the content. Crews work behind it all to make it happen. Should you be allowed into Pleasure Tribe, you will eventually be assigned to one of these three departments, depending on your skills."

Farr's hand shoots up. "Lover Weekes, how soon can we specialize as an Entertainer?" she asks, eyes wide.

Lover Weekes rolls his eyes up toward the ceiling and sighs heavily. "You need to prove yourself first, Apprentice." Lover Weekes stares at her for a second too long before returning to his characteristic boredom.

Farr nods, pleased.

"Right, I need to get a picture of your abilities," he says. "I've set up a rotation of dexterity tests. Two Apprentices at each station, please."

Obediently we spread out into the gymnasium. Sif drags me over to an impossibly high balance beam stretched across a gym mat. She bounces on her toes, stretching her arms above her head.

"You're eager," I say.

"Why not? This looks like fun."

A small purple cardboard square gives us our instructions. My heart sinks as I read them:

Step one: Mount the balance beam.
Step two: Walk to the end. Turn.
Step three: Hop back. Turn.
Step four: Cartwheel or skip. Turn.
Step five: Handstand walk. Turn.
Step six: Dismount.

"I don't like the look of this," I gulp.

A whistle blows.

"If you're so scared, I'll go first." Sif smiles. With a graceful leap, she pulls herself up.

A little trickle of envy curls into my thoughts. How does she make it look so effortless?

She bounces along the beam to the end, swiveling around on one foot to face me. "Easy. See?" she crows, hopping back to the other end like she's not standing on a knife-thin edge.

"Can you handstand?" I ask, voice trembling.

She gives me a wink for an answer and then catapults herself forward, landing on her hands. She edges along the beam sideways. When she reaches the end, she turns slightly, then throws herself down, landing with a thump on the mat. Although she's out of breath, her face is split into a wide, pleased grin.

"Woo, that was amazing!" I clap.

She grins at me. "Your turn."

With trepidation, I reach my clammy hands up to the bar, hefting myself upward until my stomach rests on the beam. The next step seems impossible. Slowly, I lean forward, bringing my feet up behind me. Then I am kneeling. With one last heave, I push myself upward, shaking and wobbling into place.

"What's the next step?" I call out, even though I know what it is.

"You know that already. Get going!" Sif yells.

She knows exactly what I'm doing. Heart thumping in my chest, I wobble slowly to the other end of the beam. "Now what?"

"Get on with it. You're not going to make it, though!" Sif laughs.

Sure enough, I haven't even finished my first hop before I'm plunging to the mats. I somehow avoid landing on my butt, but it's a close call.

Sif rushes over. "Anything hurt?"

"Just my pride."

The whistle blows.

"Next station!" calls Lover Weekes.

I give a sigh of relief. "Whew. Saved by the bell."

"You might not say that if you knew what we have to do next." Sif is looking past me at something behind my shoulder.

When I see what she's looking at, my heart sinks.

"No way am I ever going to be Pleasure Tribe," I groan.

15

The Haterman.
An essay by Kerr Flick, Apprentice #540/187503. Age: six.
> *The Haterman is a very bad person. The Haterman wants to kill our way of life and every good thing, like food. Without our Supreme Lover, the Haterman would invade our dorms and take us all away to his factory where he makes guns and bombs and tries to kill people all the time. We are very happy in the Love Collective. Supreme Lover Midgate is our friend.*
> THE END

MOST OF THE CLASS HAD ALMOST ASSUMED Zin was gone forever. But then she is back. One minute we are all walking to our Coding lesson, and the next she's gliding along beside me, quiet and serious. I have no idea where she has come from. The old sway of her hips is gone, and so is the flirtatious way she used to lean all over the twins. Something is off.

"Are you okay?" I ask, leaning toward her.

Fury flashes in Zin's eyes when she turns toward me, but she doesn't get a chance to say anything. Farr, who's been walking ahead, turns around and sees who I'm talking to.

"*Zin!* Ohmylove, ohmylove, ohmylove, I'm so glad you're

back," she cries, leaping at Zin. "Where have you been? It's been weeks! Months! Are you okay? What is going on?"

Zin stares away into the distance while Farr clasps her in an embrace and excitedly prattles on. Zin looks slightly dazed, as if she's just woken out of a sleepwalking dream. Our group travels the length of three whole corridors before Farr finally realizes that her friend isn't talking.

Hands on hips, she plants herself in Zin's way. "What's wrong with you? You look like you swallowed a stun grenade."

"I'm fine, Farr. Just don't ask, okay?" Zin replies, flinging her hands up like a shield.

Farr takes a tiny step backward. But it seems she just can't help herself. "I'm your friend. Am I not allowed to worry? Where were you?"

Zin sighs in resignation. "Realignment."

"Re-a-what-ment?" Farr's face is all quizzical confusion.

"Forget it. Just don't break any rules. You don't want to be there." A violent shudder ripples across Zin's shoulders.

"Whatever." Farr shrugs, the moment forgotten as quickly as it appeared. She loops her arm through Zin's elbow and pulls her forward.

Walking behind them, quiet as I can be, I lean close enough to eavesdrop. What has happened to her? I've almost plucked up the courage to ask when Zin suddenly turns and the words evaporate from my lips. Something dark glitters in her eyes. She raises her hand, an accusing finger pointing at my head. With slow, graceful precision she cocks her thumb. Her hand becomes a gun, miming a slow-motion shot headed straight at me. The corners of her lips curl into a cruel smile as she finishes off the threatening pantomime, blowing imaginary gun smoke away from the end of the barrel. Then with a flick of her hair, she is striding ahead, Farr still prattling into the air beside her.

Sif wanders up beside me. "I'd be careful of that one," she warns, watching Zin's back recede into the distance.

TWO MONTHS PASS. I MAKE IT THROUGH VR
without passing out, but I still have to talk myself back into it
every time. Maybe it's the little white scrape marks at the back of
my headset. Maybe it's the memories that won't fade. Whatever
the reason, whenever I step up to that training station I have to
chomp back nerves that flutter in the back of my throat.

"Not going to pass out this time," I say under my breath. It's
more of a command than a prophecy. No way am I going to be
that person again. Not ever.

At her desk, Lover Herz's fingers fly over her console. She
keeps glancing at me from the corner of her eye. I decide to
ignore her.

"Apprentices mount," she commands. We step up to our
chair rigs. There's a slight hum at my fingertips from the gloves.
I pull the visor down, and with a whirl and a flash I'm back in
the circle out on the open drill field. Lover Herz waits for us,
hands clasped.

"Welcome, students," she says. "Today's lesson will be
another step forward in your Elite training. You have one goal:
to find the Haterman."

Arah laughs and jabs Rook. Makes sense. The Love
Collective defeated the real Haterman long before we were
born. Now the Haterman is a child's game, a nightmare cartoon
we all gave up believing in years ago.

A stern look silences the giggles, and Lover Herz continues.
"You will be transported to a practice scenario. The Haterman
will be hiding in plain sight. But be warned, this task is
deceptively easy. You may end up losing points—or worse—if
you fail to find your target. Be alert. Be ready."

We launch into the air, spreading out in different directions.
I watch the landscape pass beneath me. Too soon, I descend

down over Love City, flying along the wide brown river that cuts through the city center. The electric whine of traffic begins to hum in the distance. Overcars and transports glide across a large arching bridge. They head along a broad avenue that rises up the hill toward the Hall of Love—a distant white square on the horizon.

I land in a neatly coiffured riverside park. Green hedges line the paths, trimmed into wavelike patterns. A large crowd strolls along the wide boulevard that runs parallel to the water's edge. Wandering to the shade of a tree, I scan the scene. Sif has landed nearby. Like me, the VR program has her clad in a Love Squad uniform, and her VR face glows red beneath the helmet's display. Also like me, a large rifle hangs from a strap around her shoulders. She nods and then turns away to scan the passing crowd.

"Where's Cam?" I ask.

Sif shrugs. "Even if he was here, how could you see? There must be thousands of them."

"A black uniform would stand out in that." I survey the business classes, a sea of white linen flowing through the park. A splash of color catches my eye, and adrenaline bursts into my system. But it's just a street worker, clad in the rainbow-colored uniform of the menial class. He meanders along the edge of the path, picking litter with a long-handled claw.

"Maybe," Sif says. "But unless the Haterman's wearing a neon helmet and setting off flares, I don't think we're going to find him." A small gaggle of maids in navy tunics passes, heading to their hotels for the morning shift.

"Herz did say this would be deceptively easy."

"When she says 'deceptively easy,' I think she means 'completely impossible.'" Sif continues to watch the crowd movement. "Do you see his cape anywhere?"

"I don't think he's going to be in uniform." In my memories, the Haterman has an oversized, cruel face. He wears a turquoise-and-black suit with a cape.

"Well, it's going to take all day to stop and search everyone." Sif sighs.

A young girl walks toward me, clutching an infotab tightly to her chest. She glances at me and then away. She seems to be accompanied by a taller woman. As they pass by, the woman places her hand on the girl's neck. I can't explain why, but something about the woman's expression gets me curious.

Sif looks at me. "Where you going?"

"Just a sec." I push myself off from my resting place and start to stroll along with the crowd. A group of three men provides cover so that I can follow the girl unobtrusively. As soon as I do, I am smacked from behind. My VR suit can't apply too much pressure, but it's enough to startle me. I spin around, scanning for any blue in the crowd. Nothing. When I turn back, the girl and her companion have disappeared.

Swept along with the crowd, I feel oddly peaceful. To my left flows the river—a long brown ribbon embroidered with boats. A pleasure cruiser floats by, dull electronic beats thumping mindlessly while revelers sway and dance. The distraction is nearly fatal. Another solid thump hits me, sending my body headlong toward the fast-flowing water. At the last moment I grab a bollard, grasping it with both hands. Pulling myself away from the water, I spin around, trying to see who pushed me. Vast crowds of white linen walk past.

I bound back to Sif.

"Did you see anything just then?" I ask.

"Nope."

"Someone hit me."

"Really? Sorry. I didn't see it."

"Huh."

Her eyes never leave the flowing crowd. I follow her gaze. A group of maids is passing in their navy tunics, eager and hurried. With a start, I realize they're the same group that passed earlier. Which means . . .

"They're repeating the pattern!"

I dash forward. Sure enough, the young girl comes around, still clasping the infotab. The tall woman places her hand on the back of the girl's neck. Again. This time, though, I don't follow her. I scan back through the crowd. The trio of men is walking toward me now. I search behind them for any rage-filled, crumpled face that looks like the Haterman pictures from my childhood.

Behind the three men, another group of six linen-clad workers hustles along. Two women laugh together. They are followed by a wrinkled old woman, her shoulders hunched but her hair carefully coiffed in Supreme Lover Midgate's style. Next to her, two men argue into their infotabs, waving their free hands in wild gestures. An overweight man puffs along behind them, red-faced and sweating.

I step into the crowd behind them, keeping my distance. When I spot that backward glance, I raise my rifle, doing my best imitation of a Love Squad officer.

"Freeze!" I yell. The old woman flinches, then breaks into a run that is far more agile than I thought possible.

I push my way through, hopping and skipping around citizens to get closer to her.

She grabs the young girl by the neck, swiveling her around like a shield. "Don't come any further," the old woman says in a deep, threatening voice. She peers at me from behind the terrified girl's left shoulder, face twisted in the Haterman's ugly scowl. A knife glitters at the young girl's throat.

The girl whimpers—a soft, wet sound that stirs a long-repressed memory. For an agonizing moment I hesitate, until a glaringly obvious thought tumbles into my head.

These people aren't real.

I squeeze the trigger.

"Well done, Apprentice," Lover Herz crows in my earpiece as the virtual crowd around me cheers and celebrates. The images of blood and the prone bodies of woman and child fade away, replaced by the walls of the VR lab. I rip my headset off and lurch out of the seat as if burned.

"First to find him." Lover Herz gives me a thumbs-up from her seat at the console. "I knew you had it in you."

I nod, numbness giving way to a cold, creeping dread. My mind is reeling. If I've won, why do I feel like I've failed?

"They weren't real," I whisper to myself. "The girl was just a program. They weren't real."

I MANAGE TO HOLD BACK THE MEMORIES of blood and death during the busy time of the day, but at night there's nothing to stop them. By the time I finally give up trying to forget, soft, sleeping whispers of breath fill the bunk room.

"Sif!" I whisper. "Sif! Are you awake?"

There's a soft groan from the top bunk. "Whuhuh?" The slats creak. "What?" Sif says with a snap, sleepiness giving way to irritation.

"Sorry. Go back to sleep."

"I'm awake now. What's up?"

"It's nothing. Sorry to bother you."

My friend's head appears over the edge of the bed, looking down at me. I can't see her face, but I'm sure it's frowning.

"You can't do that to me," she hisses. "Something's up. What is it?"

"What's your earliest memory?"

Sif's head goes very still. "Can't remember, exactly. Think I was five. Why?"

"Me too."

MEMORY DATE: CE 2271.298 (10 YEARS AGO)
Memory location: Nursery Dorm 492, Dorm Room Eight
Memory time: Indeterminate. Night.

A soft sound wakes me. Where am I? I'm in a sea of identical beds, stretching away from me in both directions. Small lumps of human lie below sheets. Their arms are straight by their sides. They lie on their backs, asleep.

Except for one. About five beds away, a small figure wriggles. She rolls toward me, and her face is wet with tears. She keeps moaning a weird word, over and over again.

"Mumma . . . Mumma . . . Mumma . . ."

I wish she would be quiet. The word makes my head hurt. Her bottom lip quivers, eyes scrunched in grief. When the doors sigh open behind me, I shut my eyes tight.

Some bigger people come into the room. I can tell they're big because of the way their shoes squeak. They pass my bed going one way and then pass going back again. When I open my eyes, the girl's bed is empty.

"DON'T YOU THINK IT'S WEIRD THAT WE can't remember anything before we were five?" I whisper.

Sif rubs a hand across her face and yawns. "Never thought about it before. Wait." She looks at me. "I thought you remembered everything."

"Not before then."

"What?!" Even in the dim light, surprise is visible all over her face.

I persist. "Have you ever tried to think back before then?"

"Nope. It is what it is."

"Try."

"Why?"

"Try to think back earlier than five."

"What—now?"

"Humor me."

"Fine."

Sif's head disappears back into her bunk. For a few seconds there's no sound, and then she lets out a gasp of surprise and pain.

"Ow!" The silhouette of her head appears again over the edge. "What. Was. That?!" she gasps.

I can't help the triumphant feeling. It's not just me, after all.

"That was what happens when you try to remember before five."

"Wait. You get that too? That pain like your head is going to crack open and your brains are gonna fall out?"

"Every time."

"That's weird."

"Yup."

Sif lies back on her bed again, and for another few moments there's silence, followed by another pained grunt. I listen to the pattern. Silence, then grunt. Silence, then "Unh!" Silence, then "Ow!"

Her head appears back over the edge again. "What the love is going on?"

"I wish I knew," I reply uneasily.

16

Elite Curriculum 1.72
Goal 7: Seamless operations
  Elite work is most effective when it is invisible.

A FEW DAYS PASS WITHOUT ANY MORE nightmares. I think I must be getting better, but something is up with Sif. When we wander down to breakfast she scowls at everyone, wrenching her food tray along the metal shelf of the servery with a loud bang. The man who usually ladles oatmeal into our bowls blinks at her in surprise. She just stomps away, shoulders hunched in gloom.

I hurry to catch up with her, and we navigate the narrow aisles to reach our usual place. At our table, Sif drops her tray on the steel surface with a loud clatter and sits heavily on the bench next to Chu. Cam gives me a look full of questions. I just shake my head back, hoping he gets the "not now" message.

"I don't get it." Sif pushes her tray away from her and slumps her elbows onto the table. "Why only five? Why both of us?"

"Both of you what?" Chu's words are muffled through a mouthful of cereal.

Sif looks up as if she's only just noticed we're not alone. A thoughtful expression passes across her face. "What's your earliest memory?" She includes Lee, Pim, and Cam in the question.

Pim looks startled. "Never thought about it."

"Me neither," adds Lee, his spoon frozen halfway to his mouth.

"That's easy," Cam replies. "Nursery Dorms, obviously."

"Try to remember a time before you were five," Sif challenges them.

"Why?" Cam's eyes narrow in suspicion.

"Just humor me." Sif's expression is so earnest that Pim gives a little shrug and then closes her eyes in concentration.

"Ow!" Lee interrupts, grasping at his head in surprise.

Pim's yell is not far behind him.

"What did you do?" Pain etches across Chu's face.

"Ha!" Sif crows, almost jumping out of her seat. "You get it too!"

"Get what? A splitting headache?" Pim grumbles, holding her head.

"How old were you in your memory when that pain hit?" Sif asks.

"Um . . ." Pim squints, her eyes focused somewhere above us. "I dunno. I was just a little kid."

"You can't remember earlier than five years old, can you? There's this thing that stops you from trying to go back before it, isn't there?"

"Whatever you're doing, stop it," Cam growls at her, hands clutching his forehead.

"She's not doing anything," I tell him. "Trust me."

Pim frowns. She closes her eyes again but quickly winces in pain.

Lee shakes his head, grasping his temples. "You saying you get the head stabs when you try too?"

"Even Kerr gets them, and you know what a memory wizard she is," Sif says.

Lee's and Pim's mouths both drop open in shock.

"No. Way." Lee stares at me like I've grown two heads.

I nod.

"When is your earliest memory?" Pim asks me.

I tell them about waking up in the dorms, and the Lovers who came to take away the girl.

Disbelief replaces the pain in Pim's eyes. "That doesn't sound right," she says. "Are you sure that wasn't just a bad dream?"

I give her a scowl.

She throws her hands up in defense. "Okay, okay. I just had to ask, is all."

Lee bites his lip. "I'm trying to think back to then, but it's like trying to climb a hill covered in soap. It's weird."

"What's weird?" From the other side of Lee, Rook leans his head over his bowl, trying to hear our conversation.

Lee turns toward him. "How far back can you remember?"

Rook frowns. "Dunno," he says. "Just Nursery Dorms. Every day was the same there."

"Aw, c'mon. Surely you remember something?" Sif cajoles him.

He shrugs and turns back to his breakfast.

Pim shakes her head. "I don't think he cares."

"I was five too," Farr interrupts from the other side of Sif. I didn't even realize she was listening.

Lee looks at her. "Have you ever tried remembering before five?"

"No. The Love Collective is our future, remember? Who wants to bother wasting time over the past?" Farr's voice drips with contempt.

"Well you're a walking Midgate lecture, aren't you?" Pim says with exasperation.

I can't see Farr's face, but everyone can hear her mutter, "Hater."

Lee turns to me. "Kerr, have you ever tried to remember before that first memory?"

I shake my head.

"You have, haven't you?" Pim points her spoon across the table at me. "You *must* remember something."

"I woke up when I was five," I say, hoping it's enough to avoid more probing questions.

Pim raises a single eyebrow and fixes me with a hard stare. I suddenly get really interested in my oatmeal.

"Don't you all think it's weird, though?" Sif asks. "Kerr, our memory wizard, can't remember before five. I can't remember before five. None of you can either. Our brains try and stop us from going back, and when we do, we get zapped."

"I just thought all kids didn't start remembering stuff until they were older." Lee shrugs.

"Maybe." I can tell by Sif's suspicious tone she's not even nearly convinced.

"Lee's right," Farr adds. "We're in the Elite Academy, for crying out loud. Who cares what happened before we were old enough to remember anything?"

"Doesn't explain the head zaps." There's a stubborn set to Sif's shoulders.

"Whatever," Farr says with a dismissive roll of her eyes.

Lee and Pim exchange a look and then turn worried glances toward Sif and me.

"Is there something going on?" Pim asks in a low voice.

I don't say anything.

Sif leans back. "If it was just one of us, I could explain it away."

"But it's all of us, isn't it?" Cam's eyes look haunted.

Sif nods.

"Which means . . ." Lee pinches at his lip, deep in thought.

Pim finishes his sentence for him. "Which means we're all crazy." She makes a silly face and shoves Lee sideways. He retaliates with laughter, and they're quickly joking and teasing each other.

Sif frowns at me, ignoring the jokes flying across the table around her. "I've just got one question."

"What?" I ask.

Sif's brow is furrowed. "What did they do to us?" she finally asks.

I wish I could give her a rational response, but all I can hear in my head is imaginary screams.

MEMORY DATE: CE 2273.099 (8 YEARS AGO)
Memory location: Nursery Dorm 492, Dorm Room Eight
Memory time: Approx. 0500 (uncertain)

My eyes open slowly, blinking against sleep. Dim dawn light glows beyond the door at the distant entrance to the sleeping quarters.

I had a dream. A nice one. My groggy mind wants to go back to sleep and erase any stories, but my memory won't let them fade.

I was flying. Someone's hands were holding me up so that I circled high above a wide grassy hilltop. My voice rang with laughter. Around and around I flew in tighter and tighter circles. Below me, words I can't recall were spoken by a deep, warm voice that added to the delight of summer sunshine. The aftertaste of the dream is delicious. I try to recall the details, but every time I command my mind to go back, tendrils of pain curl around my thoughts.

LOVER TINKS IS ALREADY WAITING FOR US in the Coding lab, her fingers a blur over her control console. Columns of code scroll upward from the display. I've remembered the entire contents before I'm seated. Zin scowls at me from her place beside Lover Tinks. Like every other day, I pretend to ignore her, but she still weirds me out. A couple of times she's tried to get me in trouble, so I just keep my distance now.

"Love all." Lover Tinks waves, keeping her eyes fixed on her console.

"Be all," we chant back.

"Right. Your Coding assignment is on its way. Please find a solution as quickly as possible. The task should be self-explanatory." She flings her hands outward, and the code whirls onto our infotabs. I peer closely at it. Tinks seems to have given us some sort of bug finder, with whole sections of code missing. It feels like cheating to insert the missing code from my memory, but I do it anyway.

Even though I'm finished long before anyone else, I wait. No need to appear too freakish. I watch my classmates' progress from the corner of my eye. Arah's face is scrunched in concentration. Lee's tongue hangs from the corner of his mouth as he stares fixedly at his own infotab. I don't think he realizes he's doing it. Over on the far side, Farr taps at her infotab with bored, languid movements. I pretend to work for a little longer, double-checking the code I've entered at least three more times. It fits. Finally, I press Enter.

The only sign that Lover Tinks has received my entry is the single eyebrow that rises above her left eye. Then a little chat box appears on my infotab.

Tinks: Not bad.

I type a response.

KF: Thanks.

Tinks: Let's see if that was a fluke. Am forwarding something extra to you.

A stream of code floats across my screen, larger than the last one. Another algorithm. I haven't seen the answers to this one, but it doesn't take long to recognize the pattern. Pretty soon I'm sending answers back as fast as Lover Tinks can send problems.

When the buzzer sounds, the whole room stretches as if

waking from a code-induced dream. I press Enter one final time, shooting a tricky surveillance code back to Lover Tinks. Everyone else tumbles out of the room. I stand and do my own stretch, arching my back and shaking my feet to get the blood pumping back through them. I hurry toward the door, anxious not to be the last one out.

"Apprentice Flick," Lover Tinks calls, arresting my escape.

I turn around. "Yes, Lover Tinks?"

"I'd like you to explain your processes here."

"I, uh . . . I need to get to Elite Axioms, Lover Tinks."

My instructor waves a dismissive hand at my words as the last few people leave the room.

"I'm guessing you could already cite every Axiom and sub-clause and explanatory paragraph right down to the thousand pages of rubric. Couldn't you, Apprentice Flick?"

I think about pretending, but I wilt under her stare.

"Thought so," Lover Tinks says. "So tell me. How did you find the answer to my code so quickly?"

"I just see the patterns, Lover Tinks."

"Huh. Well, I know it's early days, but you've just completed a group of problems we don't address until second year specialist. I'd recommend you to start tomorrow in the Coders cadre if I could."

"Thank you, Lover Tinks, but I'm not sure I want to be a Coder," I reply.

"Really? Why? You have a natural aptitude."

"I want to be a Watcher."

Lover Tinks's eyes narrow at me. "That's a big call, Apprentice."

"I know."

"I'm not sure you know what you're asking for."

"I think I can do it."

"We'll see. But if you ever change your mind, I'll put in a word for you with the Coders. Okay?"

"Okay." I smile, but inside I'm thinking, *There's no way I'm ever going to need that. I'm going to be a Watcher.*

17

Nursery Induction Manual
Catechesis volume 2, page 93.
    Q: Second only to Haters, what is the greatest hindrance
    to effective life in the Collective?
        A: Lazy Apprentices are dangerous Apprentices.

THE ELITE AXIOMS ROOM IS LOCATED along the side of a long, straight hallway on the third floor. My feet skid to a halt at the doorway. Normally the door is propped open by a thin steel doorstop. Today, it's shut tight.

I fight back a momentary jolt of panic. If they've already started, I could be in trouble. But I'm sure Lover Kalis will be okay if I explain. Lover Tinks wanted to talk to me about my plans for the future. When a Lover wants to talk, you talk. Lover Kalis can complain to Lover Tinks later.

I take a second to wipe my sweaty palm down my shirt before I reach out for the doorknob. In my mind, I rehearse the conversation I'm going to have with Lover Kalis.

"Sorry, Lover Kalis, but Lover Tinks—" The words die before they reach my lips. The door handle won't budge. I jiggle the handle back and forth, but nothing happens. When I swipe at the ID panel beside the door, the panel makes a loud beep and emits a red, flashing light.

Strange. That's never happened before.

I wonder what to do next. The classroom door is heavy, built soundproof to shield lessons from hallway noise. It's a long shot, but I knock, timidly at first, then louder and louder. When nobody answers, I bang my fists on the solid steel until my hand is throbbing with the effort.

A small rectangle of glass sits in the door above my head. I extend myself upward, standing on my toes and craning my neck to see inside. My view is somewhat obscured by a secondary glass door, which is also closed.

That's never happened before, either.

Beyond the "airlock" of doors, the class is gathered in a semicircle facing the front lectern. Lover Kalis is speaking, moving her arms with energetic vigor. It's like watching a mime artist. She makes a grand gesture, and the class erupts in silent laughter.

I wave and jump, hoping the movement will get Sif's attention. In the front row beside Chu, she leans down to look at something on his infotab. When she smiles up at him, her eyes light up in a way I've never seen before. Normally, I'd think it was cute. But not right now when I need her to focus.

My jumps and waves take on the jerky movements of a crazy person. Everyone else is too busy listening to Lover Kalis. All except Zin, that is. Her eyes dart away from the instructor's face and alight on me. I frown back, giving in to a flash of irritation. Zin mimes an expression of mock surprise, followed by an exaggerated pout. Slowly, with deliberate care, she makes the same gun-firing motion with her fingers pointed at me. Lover Kalis sees her then, and Zin quickly morphs the movement into a quick scratch of her head. She gives Lover Kalis such an innocent look that Carell Hummer would be proud.

Zin's mime tells me everything I need I know about the locked door. She's waited for her chance, and now she's trying to get her revenge. Rage overwhelms me. I whip out my infotab, flicking it over to the messaging app. I bring up Sif's avatar and fire off a quick message:

Help. Zin locked me out of room. Open door. Quick!!!!!!

A red dialogue box pops up on my screen.

Lesson mode activated. Apprentice messaging disabled.

Of course it is. Anything I send will be bounced until class is finished, which will be way too late. Still. Sif should notice that I'm missing. Why isn't she looking out for me? I try Lover Kalis:

Dear Lover Kalis, I am so sorry, but Lover Tinks kept me back at the end of Coding. Could you please unlock the door for me? Thank you!

I tap Send and stand back on my toes to peer through the door. Lover Kalis stands in the middle of the room, gesticulating toward the ceiling. The class laughs again. Any moment now, the message will ding, and she'll see the notification and then come and get me.

Hope soars when Lover Kalis turns back toward the lectern. As she steps toward it, Zin's hand shoots in the air, and Lover Kalis's head snaps up. Zin's face is a perfect mask of polite interest as she speaks. Lover Kalis nods. Then she starts what seems to be a long and earnest explanation of something. With growing horror I watch as, still talking, Kalis flicks a switch on her lectern, and the console goes dead.

"Gah!" I slump down in frustration against the door, defeated. What happens to Apprentices who skip class? Here in Elite Academy, it doesn't seem possible that anyone would even want to.

I cross my arms over my knees and drop my head down, wishing I could evaporate. Cold from the floor tiles seeps up through my uniform. Perhaps I should run back to Lover Tinks, since this was all her doing. I flick open my Elite timetable, searching for some clue to her location.

Footsteps echo in the distance. Heavy footsteps. Shoving my infotab into my bag, I scramble to my feet and stand to attention. My dignity is in tatters on the floor, and it's not like there's anywhere to hide, so this is all I've got. Out of the corner of my eye, a figure in a Lover's uniform emerges at the end of the corridor from around the corner. The figure lets out a familiar snort of derisive laughter, and my heart sinks.

Please, no.

The heavy footsteps slow as they approach me. My heart starts to race.

"Well, well, well. What have we here, Apprentice?" Lover Fuschious smiles at me like a Squad officer who just busted a wounded Hater.

I swallow hard, schooling my face to a mask of stillness. "Locked out, Lover Fuschious," I reply, trying to squash the nerves out of my voice.

"Why does that not surprise me?" Lover Fuschious purrs.

I have to wrestle down the flash of indignation that brings hot, angry words to my lips. It takes visible effort.

"Lover Tinks—"

"I don't want to hear your whiny excuses, Flick. You keep your mouth shut unless I specifically ask you a question. Do you hear me?"

I nod.

"Do you hear me?" Lover Fuschious repeats, and his voice has lowered to a vicious growl. He towers over me, his face threateningly close to my own.

"Yes, Lover Fuschious," I say in my most polite voice. I do not meet his eyes.

"I've been waiting for this for a long time, Apprentice. Knew you'd get too cocky for your boots before the year was out."

"Not cocky, Lover Fuschious. Just—"

"Watch your attitude, Apprentice. Now come with me."

"But my class . . ."

"I don't care about your class. Of all my new Apprentices, it's you I've been itching to throw into Realignment. You and that weird parrot brain of yours. Now you march behind me without a word, or so help me, I'll throw you in solitary and lose the key. Understood?"

I nod.

"Understood?"

"Yes, Lover Fuschious."

"Good. Now march."

I'VE SEEN THE WAY LOVE SQUAD OFFICERS march Haters into their trials. Backs straight. Eyes front. Legs moving with crisp, efficient speed. Lover Fuschious is doing that to me now. His arms are as straight as broom handles, and they rise and fall like a judge's gavel with every step he takes. The longer we march, the more I fight back angry tears.

Every step sounds like the drum beat of an Embracement Squad, and my imagination starts to go a little wild. Any moment now, I'm sure we're going to round a corner into a Haters' Pavilion packed with jeering app monkeys, all baying for my blood. Carell Hummer will welcome me with that wide smile. He'll announce my punishment for everyone's viewing pleasure. I can't see Lover Fuschious's face ahead, but from the proud set of his shoulders, he seems pretty pleased with himself.

It's not fair.

"Lover Fuschious?" I call, the fast pace making me sound breathless and weak. I wish I had one of those deep, sonorous voices like Rook or Arah. Compared to them, my voice sounds small and reedy.

Lover Fuschious's shoulders stiffen. Other than that, he gives no sign that he has heard me.

"Lover Fuschious? Sir?" I call again. "I know you said—"

"Shut it."

"But Lover Fuschious, if you check with Lover Tinks, you'd—"

His turn toward me is so swift and violent that I shrink against the wall. His glare is as hot as a furnace, and the unblinking fury he aims at me makes me start to sweat.

"You got too much nerve, Apprentice," he snarls. When he jabs his thick finger into my collarbone, it's as solid as a Love Squad baton, bruising and painful. "Listen well, since you're obviously a bit slow. The Love Collective don't abide people who step outta line. Got that?"

"Oh, I get it," I say, voice dripping with sarcasm.

Fuschious's hand comes out of nowhere, swift and unexpected, and cuffs me across the side of my face. The slap knocks me sideways. I reel against the wall, struggling to keep my balance. It takes every ounce of my self-control not to cry out.

The instructor leans closer, so close I can smell the faint whiff of coffee on his breath. My cheek stings.

"Now, as I said before," he continues, a dark flicker in his expression. "I don't want your whiny excuses. You could tell me Dorm Leader Akela sent you to that spot, and I wouldn't give two flying . . ."

"I sent who where?" croons a strong, steady voice from somewhere behind Fuschious's shoulder.

It's a cause of immense satisfaction to me that Fuschious's face freezes into a particularly sour expression. Only for a moment, though. He pastes an insincere smile across his face as he turns.

"Dorm Leader Akela." Lover Fuschious snaps to attention, his voice unnaturally smooth and light.

"Ah, Fuschious. Thanks be to you for your presence." The edge of Akela's mouth twitches.

Fuschious quickly collects himself. "Harrumph. Yes. Ah. May you reach your dreams and find yourself in the universe,

Dorm Leader Akela. My apologies," he mutters, flushing pink around the back of his neck.

I could laugh if it weren't for the searing pain across my cheek.

"Likewise, Fuschious. A pleasant surprise to see you." The woman smiles, although the warmth doesn't reach her eyes. "I heard my name as I was leaving a meeting. What seems to be the problem?"

"Transferring a truant to Realignment, Dorm Leader," Fuschious replies. Dorm Leader Akela casts an appraising glance over me. Shame drops my gaze to the floor.

"Really?" Akela says, her voice even and unreadable. All I can see are her expensive shoes pointed toward Lover Fuschious's boots. "Did she give an explanation for her truancy?"

"Her presence outside the classroom was enough of an explanation, Dorm Leader."

Silence stretches out for a moment, and I risk a glance upward. A deep frown creases Dorm Leader Akela's face. She catches my eye, and her gaze is steady. Concerned. Her eyes flit toward my cheek and back again.

"Apprentice Flick?"

"Yes, Dorm Leader?"

"Can you explain your absence?"

I raise myself up, straightening my shoulders. "Lover Tinks wanted to speak to me after Coding, Dorm Leader. She kept me in for quite some time, and when I arrived at my next class, the door was locked. I tried to message Lover Kalis, but I think she had her infotab switched off. I was waiting outside the room when Lover Fuschious found me."

"Ah."

I refuse to look directly at Lover Fuschious, but his movements beside me are agitated.

He gives an exaggerated snort. "She's lying."

"Well, her story can easily be checked," Dorm Leader Akela says lightly.

"She should be in Realignment," Fuschious snaps.

"Possibly. But perhaps, Lover Fuschious, it will be better if I take this matter to hand." I could be imagining it, but I think she emphasizes the word "hand" on purpose.

Lover Fuschious gives a stiff nod. "As you wish, Dorm Leader Akela."

"If her story is a lie, as you suggest, I will take her to Realignment myself. You know the Love Collective takes a dim view of rule breakers." Dorm Leader's gaze never leaves Fuschious's face.

He swallows nervously, then straightens himself beneath her glare. "Yes, Dorm Leader."

"Thank you for your . . . diligence, Lover Fuschious."

Lover Fuschious snaps a salute toward Dorm Leader Akela and then marches back the way we have come. She watches him leave, waiting until he has disappeared through a door at the far end of the corridor. Then she turns to me.

"Right, Apprentice Flick. Follow me."

I obey. Somehow I have been rescued from a furnace only to be thrown into the sun.

18

Nursery Induction Manual
Catechesis volume 1, page 16.

> *Q: Who are your Lovers?*
>
> *A: Your Lovers have been specially appointed to be your guardians. They are entrusted with your care and always have your best interests at heart. Trust them.*

THE PROBLEM WITH HAVING A MEMORY LIKE mine is that the old memories keep rewriting themselves over my new experiences. Like right now. I'm supposed to be walking down the hall beside Akela. But her last words to me from the infirmary play in my head like a vidscreen recording.

"Lies disappoint me more than failure, Apprentice. Remember that."

It's more than just the sound too. I can smell the disinfectant, hear the hitch of sadness in her voice. I can even remember the way her words cut me as if they were knives. The memory paints itself over the empty corridor I'm walking now.

"I am sorry, Dorm Leader Akela," I say quietly.

She turns toward me, surprised. "Sorry for what, my child?"

"Sorry to be inconveniencing you like this."

Akela laughs softly. "Only apologize if you have done something that needs apology, Apprentice."

"Yes, Dorm Leader."

Our footsteps make hollow echoes.

Lies disappoint me more than failure, Apprentice.

"I . . . I wasn't lying, Dorm Leader." I risk a glance sideways.

Dorm Leader Akela has clamped her mouth in a tight line of disapproval. "Lover Tinks will no doubt confirm your story, my child."

"I mean about everything. I'm sorry. I'm not lying."

"You haven't told me the whole story, either."

"I am sorry, Dorm Leader."

"You say that a lot."

"Sorry."

"See?" Dorm Leader's mouth twitches.

"Sor— Oh yeah."

She stops in the middle of the corridor, whirling to face me. I stop too. Her eyes search my face.

"K–Apprentice Flick, I know that you have had a . . . variable . . . experience with some of the instructors here." She nods back in the direction we have come, and Lover Fuschious's angry face flashes back across my memory. "But I want you to know that you can speak to me about anything that troubles you. I am not as unapproachable as some."

Again, there are soft crinkles at the corners of her eyes. She looks nothing like the kind of fearsome leader I'd expect in the Elite Academy. Come to think of it, I don't remember any adult ever looking at me with that mixture of acceptance and care.

"Thank you," I say, swallowing a whole search engine full of questions.

She gives me a small nod. The silence stretches out around us, and I begin to think that perhaps it isn't such a bad idea to speak to her after all. I take a deep breath. "Dorm Leader, I—"

My words disappear under the sound of a loud buzzer. As if

someone has turned on a tap, streams of Apprentices flow from the classrooms along the hall, surrounding and passing us by. A few make respectful bows to the Dorm Leader.

Akela sighs. "Right." She pulls a miniature infotab from her pocket and flicks her finger across the screen. Her face resumes its distant, regal look. "Lover Tinks is going to meet us in Lover Kalis's classroom. I wasn't planning on it, but I have decided to summon Lover Fuschious back too."

"Yes, Dorm Leader."

The older woman turns away from me, and I fall into step behind her. Her braids hang down her back, swaying hypnotically as she walks. I'm back to being the delinquent Apprentice who was caught out of class when she should have been listening to Elite Axioms.

A few familiar faces head in our direction, released now from the class I couldn't reach. Zin sees me walking behind Dorm Leader Akela and ducks her head, suddenly fascinated by her feet. Lee and Pim are right behind her.

"Flick! Where were you!" Pim calls out, jumping across the hall toward me.

"I have to stay with Dorm Leader," I reply, nodding forward to where Akela is disappearing into the crowd.

Pim shrinks back. "Oh, sorry." She glances at the Dorm Leader with uncertainty.

"What happened?" Sif steps up beside Pim, concern etched on her face.

"Tell you later," I say.

Her eyes question but she gives me a swift nod.

I quicken my steps to catch up. Dorm Leader turns into the Elite Axioms classroom, and I follow. As we sweep into the room, Lover Kalis looks surprised to see us.

She salutes. "Thanks be to you for your presence," she says.

Dorm Leader waves back. "May you reach your dreams and

find yourself in the universe. Thanks for meeting me here. We are just waiting for Lover Tinks, I think," Akela says.

"Here, as requested," Lover Tinks calls, entering the room.

Lover Fuschious darkens the doorway behind her. I avoid looking at him.

"Thank you all for being here," Dorm Leader Akela addresses them. "This should be a simple matter."

Lover Kalis looks from face to face, confusion written across her expression. "To what do I owe this honor, Dorm Leader?" she says.

Dorm Leader turns to me. "Apprentice Flick, you were found loitering outside Lover Kalis's classroom. Is that correct?"

"She was," Lover Fuschious growls.

Dorm Leader Akela holds up a hand to silence him. "I believe I asked the Apprentice the question, Lover Fuschious. Thank you. Apprentice?"

"I was, Dorm Leader."

"And can you tell me why you were not in your classroom, Apprentice Flick?"

"I was locked out," I reply, trying to ignore the way Fuschious's mouth twists into a murderous scowl.

Surprise flashes across Lover Kalis's face. "Really? But I don't lock my doors."

"I sent you a message, Lover Kalis," I say. She fumbles with her infotab, turning it back on. Seconds stretch out in awkward silence.

"So you did," she admits. Her cheeks turn almost as red as her hair.

"I should claim responsibility here." Lover Tinks raises her hand. "I'm sorry, Lover Kalis, but I'm afraid I was trying to recruit Apprentice Flick here into our Coding cadre. She showed exceptional skill in the previous class, you see, and I just couldn't wait until a study period to ask her about it. Her methods and her code were just incredible, and I—"

"Thank you, Lover Tinks," Dorm Leader Akela interrupts. "Lover Fuschious, I believe we have an answer to your concerns, do we not?"

Lover Fuschious's jaw is set like stone. He glares at Akela with a look that could wither grass, and gives her a nod so small it's nearly invisible.

"Good. You are dismissed, Lover Fuschious," Dorm Leader Akela says as she turns to Lover Kalis. Lover Fuschious gives a stiff salute, then marches with exaggerated aggression out of the room. "Now, Lover Kalis, you said that you don't usually lock the door. Was there a reason why this happened today, do you know?"

The redheaded instructor shakes her head, biting her lip in thought. "The only explanation I can give is that perhaps one of the students locked it accidentally. It is only a push-button lock on the inside." She turns to me. "I am sorry, Apprentice Flick. I can see by this message that you were quite distressed to have been locked out."

"You do not usually turn off your infotab in class, do you Lover Kalis?" Dorm Leader says. "You know that we need to be able to contact you at all times?"

Lover Kalis's eyes drop to the floor. "I am sorry, Dorm Leader. The students had many questions today, and I felt it was important to—"

"You did not notice Apprentice Flick's absence?"

"Apprentice Zin told me she was ill." Lover Kalis's face gets more and more miserable.

"And you didn't check the Apprentice's statement on the student welfare system?" Lover Tinks says, incredulous.

"Interesting." Akela purses her lips, displeased. She turns away from the glum figure of Lover Kalis and looks at me. "Apprentice Flick, your Lovers must confer on this matter for now. We will inform you of our disciplinary decision via message. Understood?"

"But Dorm Leader—"

"You know better than that, Apprentice. State Hater Recognition Sign 1.1."

"Haters question what they are given," I say, my gaze pushed to the floor by a container-load of shame.

"Correct. Dismissed."

I stand to attention, then turn and march out the door with brisk, angry steps. After the drama of this morning, this is how they treat me? It's not fair!

I storm down to the cafeteria, my mind brimming with frustration. First Lover Tinks keeps me in after class. Then Lover Kalis shuts me out without any reason. Then Lover Fuschious goes off like a firecracker for no reason. And after everything, they shut me out as if I'm completely irrelevant!

I'm still fuming when I pick up my green slop at the servery and catch up with Sif at our usual table. Her eyes widen in surprise when she sees the expression on my face. Pim and Chu surround her on one side, and Cam sits alone on the other side of the bench. Out of the corner of my eye, I see Zin look up from a bench a few rows away. Her whole body stiffens when she sees me, and then she bows her head low over her food.

I slam the tray down on the table, directly in front of Sif. Cam flinches out of the way, and I plonk myself down on the bench beside him.

"What's got you?" Lee asks, mouth full of lunch.

"These Lovers are crazy," I growl.

"I got your message. A bit late, sorry." Sif's eyes are full of apology.

"Yeah, well, it wouldn't have mattered anyway. Lover Fuschious went off at me, and then I ended up in a meeting with Dorm Leader."

"What?" Pim's eyes nearly bug out with shock.

"What happened?" Cam asks. He turns sideways beside me, worried.

I explain, leaving out nothing. When I get to the slap from Lover Fuschious, Pim lets out a gasp.

"He did what?!" Sif's knuckles whiten on her food tray.

Cam looks shocked. "We have to do something."

"Do what? If Dorm Leader Akela hadn't come along, it would be my word against his."

"But he's sick." Cam's fists clench and unclench.

Sif is fuming now too. "I always knew he was a psychopath."

"How did you get the Dorm Leader to take your side?" Pim leans in, curious.

"She turned up right as Fuschious was about to drag me into Realignment," I say. "You should have seen his face!"

Cam's agitated movements stop, and his eyes gleam. "I bet he wasn't happy to be outranked."

"You'll have a target on your back now," Chu points out.

I give him my best withering look to cover the nervous dread that his comment causes.

"He'll have to get through Cam and me first," Sif vows.

Pim nods, twirling a knife in her fingers. The movement is slow and menacing. "Me too." She looks at me with grim determination.

"Thanks everyone. I'll just have to wait and see what Dorm Leader says."

I keep my worries about Zin to myself.

19

Hater Recognition Signs: A Primer for the Young
   4. Allegiance
         Haters cannot ally themselves with the good
         and kind reign of the Love Collective.
         Haters wish to tear down our peace and
         prosperity.

"YOU HAVE TO REPORT HER." SIF IS ADAMANT as she kicks at a small patch of dirt at the side of the grassy field. In the distance, a group of Apprentices kicks a ball around, chasing each other away from the goals.

I shake my head. "No way."

A shout from under a tree near the corner of the field draws my attention. Far away, Cam leaps from the pack, ball clasped to his chest. When he's sprinted in front of the crowd, he turns toward us and waves the ball above his head, whooping in wild joy. Behind him, Rook sneaks up with stealthy steps. I open my mouth to call out, but it's too late. Rook takes Cam down with a sudden thump, ripping the ball out of his hands and dancing over Cam's collapsed form.

"But the love points you'll get. I mean what she did crossed so many boundaries it isn't funny," Sif argues. "Locking you out of the classroom. She can't get away with it."

"If I report her, she'll report me back. And those reports are more pain than I need right now."

"You been reported?" Sif's head snaps up and she gives me a sharp look, full of suspicion.

"False report. Long story."

"I got time." She shifts away from me ever so slightly, and a familiar old nausea grips my stomach. All of the sensations of that horrible day come rushing back to me like I am still there. The sterile office. The quiet hum of the ancient air conditioner on the wall. The triumphant grin on Fedge's face as the Lovers marched me in.

"There were these three guys at Nursery Dorm who always had it in for me."

"Why?"

"My memory, I guess. I made them look bad, so they wanted to put me in my place. Anyway, one day they decided to try and get me removed. So they made up some story about how I'd supposedly said Supreme Lover was a Hater, and—"

"Wha-at?" Sif gasps. "That's the dumbest accusation I've ever heard!"

"I know. They weren't very clever. But we still ended up in the Lover's office for hours." I stare off into the distance, fighting against the tide of unwanted memory.

"Now see here, Apprentice Flick," Lover Zink says. *"Lovers don't make up accusations. You must have said something to make them think—"*

"I didn't say it, Lover Zink!" I wail. *"I love Supreme Lover Midgate. I would never say . . . that!"*

"What happened?" Sif asks.

"Huh?" I am still trapped in a fog of recollection.

"What happened to the accusation?"

My head clears. "Eventually the boys' story fell apart. They couldn't even agree on where I'd supposedly said this horrible thing or what I was doing at the time. Bez swore I said it on the drill fields, and Myk claimed I was in the dining hall, and Fedge . . . well anyway, the Lovers realized that they were making it all up, and they had to let me go. But only after three hours of interrogation."

"What happened to the boys?"

"Not much, really. They had a few Love Points docked. I think the Lovers were too embarrassed because they had believed the boys so many times before. It would have been awkward to go back and reinvestigate all their old accusations."

"I still think you've got a case against Zin. She tried to get you sent to Realignment," Sif says.

"She failed."

"So she's going to keep on trying until she succeeds."

"Nah. I think seeing me at lunch has scared the vengeance out of her."

Sif gives a derisive snort. "Wish I had your confidence."

"It will be fine."

A loud cheer erupts on the playing field. Cam is running in circles, arms out like wings. Chu bounds over to clasp him in a tight hug, lifting him off the ground. While they do a complex victory dance, Rook and Arah stand dejected, heads bowed and feet kicking into the grass.

"Just watch your back, okay?" Sif gives me a worried look. "I know we're all Elites here, but Zin is . . . well, I just don't trust her."

"I've got nothing to hide," I say with false confidence. It's the biggest lie I've ever told. But even Sif would report me if she knew how much the nightmares are invading my daily thoughts. They're getting more violent and painful too. So painful that I don't think I'm going to be able to keep them secret much longer.

THE SUMMONS COMES LATER THAT
afternoon while we are walking from VR practice back to the
drill yard. I'm freaking out about how I'm going to survive
Lover Fuschious's wrath when my infotab buzzes. A message
notification flashes on the screen, setting my heartbeat racing:

Apprentice Flick,

Please come to my office at your earliest opportunity.

Signed,

Dorm Leader Akela
Love All. Be All.

"I gotta go." I hate the way my voice has gone all shaky, so I
make a weak cough to cover it.

Sif's eyes get wide when I show her the message. She
nods, pale.

Cam pokes his head over my shoulder to look. His face goes
all serious, as if he's just heard someone died.

"It's been nice knowing you all," I say as I turn back the
way we've come, following the GPS directions in the message.
Back in the assembly atrium is a set of elevators. I jump into
the nearest one and wave my wrist over the access panel. A
small message appears on the elevator screen: *access granted.*
My stomach is full of butterflies again.

Why am I worried? It's not like I did anything wrong.

I pass through a series of sliding glass doors into a wide,

carpeted hallway. It would be a peaceful place if I wasn't so scared. The doors are made of warm-colored wood. The plush burgundy carpet is soft and bouncy under my feet. The cacophony of Apprentice crowds has vanished, replaced by a serene silence.

I take a few faltering steps forward. Glass-fronted doors along the corridor give me glimpses of important-looking offices. Unfamiliar Lovers are hard at work inside, peering over infotabs and consoles. Something tells me I'm heading to the far end of the hall, to the enormous oak doors carved with a familiar water-flow pattern.

When I get there, I wave my ID over a glowing green console beside the door. There's a soft buzz.

"Yes?" a brusque male voice whines through the intercom. The unfriendliness is so thick I can almost feel it oozing out toward me.

I take a deep breath. "I'm here to see Dorm Leader Akela," I say.

"I wasn't aware that she was meeting anyone today."

"She sent me a message. I can show you my infotab."

"Dorm Leader is exceptionally busy. She can't—"

The male voice cuts off suddenly. I'm left standing for a few awkward seconds, hearing nothing and knowing even less. Then the doors curve inward, and Dorm Leader Akela steps out into the hall.

She smiles down at me. "Ah, Apprentice Flick. Glad you could make it."

She beckons me to follow her, and I scurry into a plush-carpeted reception room. My cheeks get hot. The boy from the train station sits behind a large walnut desk. His hair is cropped in regulation style, and his fingers are a blur over the keyboard of his console.

"Don't mind Wil," Akela says, leaning toward me with a wink. "He's just doing his job."

I nod, confused. Wil gives a resigned little shrug, then flashes a smile so dazzling I'm sure it gets him out of trouble every time. I frown. When he turns his green eyes on me, I turn away. I'm not some quivering fangirl.

"Wil, could you hold my calls for a while?"

"Yes, Dorm Leader."

The Dorm Leader waves her hand over another console, and an inner set of double oak doors swings open. I gasp, staring into a room both familiar and completely new.

Sunlight pours in through floor-to-ceiling windows, making dazzling rectangles on deep-red carpet. My feet draw me toward the view. Beyond the windows, the entire Elite Academy stretches out, a huge white circle of a building enclosing green drill fields, gardens, and a small forest of trees. A small group of people move around one of the drill fields, as big as grains of rice.

"Whoa," I breathe, letting my gaze sweep around the room. Behind a mahogany desk, a bookshelf runs the length of the room from floor to ceiling. I've never seen a real book before, but I've seen this bookshelf. In my dream, Dorm Leader Akela was sitting right there in front of it.

"Beautiful, isn't it?" Akela smiles, seeing my gaga expression.

"Sorry, Dorm Leader Akela," I say, ashamed. "I did not mean to forget myself. May you reach your dreams and find yourself in the universe, Dorm Leader Akela."

Akela nods, a slight crook at the corner of her mouth. "Thank you, Apprentice Flick. Please sit down."

She points to a stuffed armchair set in front of the antique desk. I sit as directed, hands folded neatly in my lap, waiting for the axe to fall. My mouth goes dry.

Dorm Leader circles behind her desk, sitting in a high-backed, black leather chair. She watches me from a dignified distance for a few moments while I twist and untwist my mouth at the corners.

Then she leans toward me. "How are you?"

"I am fine, thank you, Dorm Leader."

"I trust Lover Fuschious's . . . treatment . . . has left no lasting scars?"

"I . . . uh . . . no, Dorm Leader. Although I'm sure he will try and regain some face when I'm next in his class."

"After today, he won't be taking your group anymore. Do not fret."

I smile. I had already been dreading my next drill class. "Thank you, Dorm Leader."

"So how are you *really*?" she asks again. Concern radiates toward me from her gaze.

I think back over my Elite Axioms. *Elites are always on duty. Elites are never sloppy. Elites show no weakness.* I lift my chin, keeping my gaze cool and controlled.

"Doing my best to be worthy of the title Elite, Dorm Leader."

She waves a dismissive hand. "Don't give me that. I don't want to hear what you think you should be saying. Say what you really think."

"I . . ." I splutter. "What is my punishment?"

Akela smiles. "You are not being punished, Apprentice. You did everything you were supposed to do, except for going back to Lover Tinks. The matter is being dealt with elsewhere for now."

"Oh. Then why . . . ?"

Dorm Leader watches me across the table like she's trying to make her mind up about something. She taps her bottom lip. "This is a welfare check, Apprentice. A few anomalies in your records have come to my attention, and I wanted to see for myself what was going on."

She fidgets with her fingers, turning them over and twining them around each other. I wait for her to explain what she means by "welfare check," but all she does is twirl her fingers and look at me. Her expression becomes increasingly frustrated.

"I'm not sure what you mean," I say.

Dorm Leader's shoulders droop just a little. But she quickly covers with a friendly smile. "You must know that we are aware of your . . . gift," she says, smoothing out an imaginary wrinkle on the table. "Your memory is something we have never seen, even in Elite dorms. During the short time you have been here, your Lovers have frequently been astounded by the detail of your recall."

You've failed, Memory Freak.

The vision of Fedge leaning over me is so vivid that I squeeze my eyes shut.

"I'm sorry," I say, wiping a shaky hand across my forehead. "I can't help it."

"Again with the apologizing."

I open my mouth, but Dorm Leader holds up a hand to silence me. "Before you apologize again, stop. You are in the opposite of trouble, Apprentice Flick. I've seen your Nursery Dorm test results, and I've been following your early progress here with a great deal of interest. To be honest, I wanted to see for myself how good your memory really was."

"Oh."

"I had even begun to hope—but no, it's not the time for that." Dorm Leader straightens in her chair. "There are some things I need to know first. Call it a little test."

20

Nursery Induction Manual
Catechesis volume 2, page 42.
> *Q: How are Haters removed?*
>> *A: The Collective is compassionate and kind. It will do everything in its power to remove hate without inconvenience to its citizens. Lovers will always be safe.*

I SIT FOR WHAT SEEMS LIKE HOURS, answering Dorm Leader's questions about my memory: How many drills did we complete yesterday? What was Supreme Lover's speech two weeks past? What are the first thirty-seven Hater Recognition Signs? As time passes, her questions get more specific and further back in time.

"What were my first words to you?"

I reel off her entire speech from that first night on the train platform. She nods, impressed. Then she flicks open her infotab and begins scrolling through something I can't see.

"Day 66, two years ago," she reads. "Describe your day."

I cast my mind back, scrolling through the memory tape. Then I begin counting things off on my fingers: Hater Recognition lesson. Prep lesson. Drill. Food.

"Good. Let's try for something a little trickier. How about Day 247, eight years ago?"

It takes a little longer to scroll back. I use the year markers to help me rewind to the right day. When I do, the memory floats in my mind's eye like a ghostly movie.

"Breakfast of vitamin juice and protein meal. Drill practice—butterfly pattern, followed by net form. Apprentice Koah stumbled on the second-last turn, but she managed to avoid a discipline for it. Then Prep class. Lover Zink handed out the class info tabs and taught us how to vote on the Haters' Pavilion Show."

"Who were the contestants?" Dorm Leader Akela asks. The sharpness in her voice makes me lift my head.

I gulp, nervous. "Hater One had committed high treason against the Supreme Executive. Hater Two was reported by a brave neighbor. The neighbor got an entry ticket into the Hall of Love lottery for their loyalty. And Hater Three was a suspected spy for the Haterman's forces beyond the border. Lover Zink's words were, 'Vote as you see fit, children.' We all knew he wanted us to vote for Hater One because they did something so hateful that he couldn't even talk about it. He just spat into the rubbish bin after he said the words 'high treason.'"

A shadow passes across Dorm Leader Akela's face. "Do you remember anything else from that day?"

"Well, after lunch we revised Hater Recognition Sign 9.37, and then we had another drill practice of the butterfly formation with a parade march. After dinner and showers, we were allowed to watch the elimination round of the Haters' Pavilion Show for the first time. Lover Zink said, 'You have all done so well, my Lovelies, that I think you are mature enough to watch the ending this time.' Myk was so excited he did a running backflip into his seat, which Bez punched him for, and then Rip had to step in and—"

"I get the picture. What do you remember of the show?"

"Not much. I think I spent most of my time watching through my fingers because of the blood. Fedge called me a 'weenie' for it. I kind of focused on what the other Apprentices were doing. They were cheering and shouting at the Haters, and when Hater One was eliminated at the end, you should have heard the roar. It made my ears ring."

"What were the contestants' names?"

"They didn't say."

"No, but their names were printed on the sides of their collars."

"Oh, um . . ." Dread seeps into my gut, as if I was seeing the gore and violence for the first time.

"I know it might be hard, but tell me what you see," Dorm Leader commands. I close my eyes, suddenly back in the Nursery Dorm assembly hall watching the floor-to-ceiling image of the Haters' Pavilion Show.

In my memory, Supreme Lover Midgate gives her nightly lecture, and then the arena anthem plays, and a hush falls over the crowd. We watch the general interviews and Carell Hummer's monologue. Then the stadium lights up. Three crouched figures stand at one end of the wide arena, their arms bound and faces obscured behind twisted, angry Haterman masks. At the other end of the stadium stand two Love Squad officers, each holding a pack of baying dogs. One of the masked people makes a sudden dash away from the dogs, and the camera zooms in to the sides of their faces. The embroidery shimmers, a faint red streak along the side of the black prison uniform.

"Hater Three was a man named Harald Glover," I say. I let the movie play in my head for a bit more, jumping to another point where the camera zoomed in close. I try and pause the image in my head to focus on the Hater's name. A laser sword slices through Hater Two's shoulder, and the Nursery hall erupts in laughter and cheers while the man staggers around in pain. It makes me want to gag.

"Hater . . . Two was . . . ugh . . . Dar Revell. I don't think I got the other one—oh, wait." A brief flash. The most hated contestant lost her mask. A stream of blood flows down the side of her face. She looks surprisingly normal for someone who committed treason. A huge Love Squad solder rains down his fists. She reels under each blow but pushes herself back to her feet. After one particularly heavy slap, the camera zooms in to show the damage in ultra-high definition. That's when I see her collar, tinged with blood.

"Angelica. Hater One's name was Angelica Williams," I say, glowing with a flash of triumph. The glow fades as soon as I get a glimpse of Dorm Leader's expression.

Her face has gone deathly pale, and she stares at me openmouthed. "That certainly is a very detailed memory."

My cheeks get warm. "Thank you."

"Do you remember anything else about that night?"

"Well, there was a broken globe five rows along, up on the hall ceiling, and . . ."

"You have an amazing eye for detail, I'll give you that. No, what I'm wondering is if there was anything you noticed about the people you saw on the screen? Anything that might have . . . triggered . . . something?"

"No. Why?"

Akela doesn't answer straightaway. She seems to be fighting an internal battle I can't see. Finally, she stands and walks back toward the oversized bookshelf behind her desk. She lifts out a small volume from a high shelf. Clasping the book against her chest, she returns to the desk. She leans across the desk, opening the book wide enough that I can see a small silver pendant dangling between two pages. A small figure hangs within a laser-cut circle: a silhouette of a tree and a human figure. When I see the design, a lightning bolt of pain stabs across my temple.

FLASHES OF LIGHT FILL MY VISION, LIKE ripples of lightning across the surface of water. Dark clouds roll across a moonlit landscape. My skull throbs in pain.

"Cadence? Cadence!"

Someone's pounding on a door. Yelling. Heavy boots thump down the hall.

My nose tickles with the smell of dust and old clothes mixed with mothballs and damp carpet. I can't move. My cheek is pressed against something soft and warm. I'm rocked back and forth with fervent intensity. Folds of fabric cocoon us.

Us. There's someone here. But who? A silver pendant dangles in front of my eyes, catching tiny glimmers of light. Something crushes me against a soft warmth that rises and falls with panicked breaths. Urgent whispers flutter into my ears.

"Cadence, these people want you to forget. Never forget him, Cadence."

Pain shatters the darkness, splitting my head into a million tiny pieces. All is searing light and pain. Screams fade into silence. A rush of a billion confusing images flickers across my vision. Then nothing. Somewhere beyond my splintering skull, a distant siren wails.

LIKE A CAMERA SLOWLY COMING INTO focus, I become aware of the room again. I have clamped my mouth shut so tightly that my teeth hurt.

"You remember this, don't you?" Dorm Leader Akela asks, face eager.

"No, I . . ." I mumble, rubbing at my forehead to calm the spikes of pain. "I don't think I've ever seen it before."

Dorm Leader's face falls. "Hmm." Turning her back to me, she returns the book, caressing the spine as she places it back on the shelf.

"Apprentice, have you been experiencing any . . . mental episodes?"

"Pardon?"

"Any strange dreams?"

As a matter of fact, yes. I've been slowly going insane for months now. Why do you ask?

I smooth my face down, opening my eyes in faked innocence. "I don't know what you mean."

"Let's cut the act, Kerr."

Attacked by a vicious stab of guilt, I duck my head, unable to look her in the eyes. Of course she can see through me. I'm going to Realignment for sure.

"Is there something important about that pendant?" I ask, grasping at any slim chance to change the subject.

"If you don't already know, I can't tell you." Dorm Leader Akela sits back in her chair.

"Why not?"

"Only Haters question the Love Collective, Apprentice Flick." I might be imagining it, but there sounds like a hint of sarcasm in Dorm Leader's tone.

"I need to know."

"And I need to know about this." Akela lifts her infotab and points it toward me. There on the screen is surveillance footage of the VR classroom. The date stamp at the top of the video proclaims it as the day I collapsed and ended up in the infirmary. A horrible, sick nausea gurgles in my stomach, but I can't look away.

In the video, a buzzer sounds. I am frozen like a statue.

Until I start flailing my arms, that is. With a wild shudder, surveillance-video me lets out a loud shout:

"Cadence!"

The surveillance video freezes, and I stare down at the floor, ashamed. It's no wonder Dorm Leader is frustrated with me. My shaky lies and excuses can't even begin to explain this.

"If you can't be honest with me, Apprentice Flick, then I'm afraid I can't help you."

"Am I going to Realignment?" My voice trembles.

Akela's eyes widen in surprise. "What? No. I just need to know what happened. The truth this time, not what you think I want to hear."

So I tell her. From the nightmare weeks before Fitness to Proceed, to the dream on the train, to every instance of the waking hallucinations I've been experiencing in Elite Academy. There's no point denying it. The evidence is there, as obvious as the freeze-framed figure lying in a twisted heap on the VR room floor, headset still covering her eyes.

After I have finished spilling my guts, Akela just stares into the distance, deep in thought. There's an ocean of words behind her eyes—years full of unspeakable and untold secrets. But her eyes soften, and I begin to see something else, something I've never seen in a Lover's eyes before: hope.

"You're not going crazy, Apprentice."

"But these dreams. I have to be going insane. They're . . ."

"They're not dreams."

"Hallucinations, then."

She just shakes her head at me, and all the lights go on in my head, like I've just woken up. I'm not dreaming. Not hallucinating. That leaves only one glaring explanation for what's been going on for these past months.

"Am I . . . remembering something?" The words tremble as they come out of my mouth, and as I speak them, I know with relief and exhilaration that they are truth. Dorm Leader lets out a long sigh and seems to be struggling to keep her face controlled. When she finally speaks, her voice is unnaturally loud.

"The Dorms are your life, Kerr. You know that." She reaches across her desk and touches something on her console screen. The door behind me opens.

"Wait. What?" I splutter, glancing into the front office. Wil stands to attention, waiting for me. "You're *dismissing* me?" Indignation flows hot through my veins. My hands tighten on the armrests of my chair.

"Love all, be all, Apprentice." Dorm Leader gives me a stern stare.

For a second too long I stare at her like a stunned fish, mouth opening and closing. Then I stand, formal and brusque. "Love all, be all, Dorm Leader."

With the practiced obedience of a decade of drills, I snap my hands to my sides, make an about turn, and march stiffly out of the room. Memories swirl around in my head, dipped in a cold fury. I am not crazy. I am remembering. But what are these cold, dark, fear-soaked fragments that keep interrupting my days? What happened to me?

Whatever it is, Dorm Leader won't tell me. And that is the most infuriating thing of all.

I stride through the doors, and they close noiselessly behind me.

Wil stands in the reception room, his hands clasped behind his back. When he sees the look on my face, he raises an eyebrow. "How did it go?"

I pause mid-step, confused by the sincere concern in his tone. I scowl. "Why do you care?" I say. I fold my arms and give him my best Elite Lover Team Six impression, just for good measure. Elite Lover Nissa would be proud.

"I might know more than you think." Wil gives me a lopsided smile.

"I thought Dorm Leader would . . . but she didn't . . . and

then . . ." Words desert me, and I just shrug, all of my rage dissolving into a riot of sad helplessness. My shoulders slump.

"Seems like you need to get back to your drills," he says, taking a step sideways. He holds his hand out toward me, ready to give it a perfunctory shake goodbye.

"Okay, then." I sigh, looking down. Of course he wouldn't want to keep talking with me. I make no sense with all the jabbering and the scowling. And Dorm Leader has dismissed me, so my time here is done. I take his hand. As I do, I feel the unmistakable smoothness of paper being thrust into my palm. Surprised, I look straight into his eyes.

"Wha—?" I begin.

He gives a slight shake of his head. "Your access permissions have been modified. If you have any more questions for Dorm Leader, you may return here to this office at a later date."

"But I have questions now, and I—"

"Love all, be all, Flick," he says, and my surprise deepens that he knows my name.

Against my will, I smile. "Love all, be all, Apprentice," I reply, holding his gaze a second more.

Heat passes between our clasped hands. Then he drops his and takes a step back. Clutching the paper in my fingers, I nod and march out of the room. I walk back past the opulent top-level offices, waiting until the solitude of the elevator to risk opening my hand. The paper is no wider than my fingernail, rolled up into a tiny scroll. I unroll it, finding hope written in letters too small to be read by a surveillance camera:

Obstacle course bend 3,
1945 hours.

21

Hater Recognition Signs: A Primer for the Young
  1. Doubt.
      Haters question what they are given.
      Haters do not understand the privilege they have
      to live in the Love Collective.

WHEN THE ELEVATOR DOORS OPEN ON
the waterfall atrium, I spot my friends straightaway. Cam
sprawls across one of the orange lounges, an arm draped across
his face. On a lounge beside him, Lee and Pim face each other,
a game of infotab chess lying between them. Across the aisle,
Chu is snuggled in beside Sif. Their heads are nearly touching,
and they both stare at Chu's screen.

As I approach, Sif glances up. "How'd it go?"

"Fine," I lie. "Just fine."

"You in trouble?"

"Nope. She just wanted to test my memory."

"I'm guessing you passed."

"More than." I glance over at Cam. "What's up with him?"

"Ha!" Lee exclaims at his infotab, jumping with triumph in
his seat. His elation fades when he notices Sif staring at him.
"Sorry. Carry on."

Sif turns back to me, giving a little shake of her head. "Fuschious was in a *bad* mood, so Cam's traumatized."

"Lover F was super mad when you didn't show," Chu speaks, eyes fixated on his screen. The only response from Cam is a low, pained groan.

"Sorry," I say.

"No you're not," Cam's voice comes out in a muffled whine from beneath his arm.

"Well, he won't be taking any more drill classes, so don't worry."

"What?" Cam yells.

"Sorry."

"You'd definitely be sorry if you were there," Chu says. "Forty laps of the obstacle course, followed by two hours of reps. We had to—"

"Make him stop!" Cam groans.

"Shh, you're traumatizing the poor boy." Sif gives Chu a gentle pat on the knee. Chu gives her a mock scowl but takes the opportunity to let his arm fall around her shoulder. Sif's cheeks dimple.

"You two are getting on well," I observe.

"Shut up." Sif's voice is gruff, but she's hiding a smile.

"You see what I have to deal with?" Cam throws his arm up in the air. "I'm in more pain than I've ever been in my life, and they're so busy canoodling that I can't get a shred of sympathy."

"We aren't canoodling." Sif shifts away from Chu just a fraction. "You know Elites can't fraternize."

"Then stop canoodling all night, canoodlers." Cam pokes his tongue out at them like a little kid.

Chu throws himself across the gap, landing on Cam. They're soon pummeling each other, falling off the couch and rolling around the floor.

"For a guy who's supposedly traumatized, you don't look too badly hurt," I say to Cam, as he rolls on top of Chu, pinning him down. He raises his hands and lets off a whoop of triumph, only to be tackled down to the ground by a sudden lurch from his opponent.

"Oof!" Cam exclaims as the wind is knocked out of him. "Not . . . my . . . fault . . . I was attacked . . . for no . . . reason!"

"You get him, Chu." Sif's eyes get a faraway look. "Man, I'm so hungry right now I could eat forty-seven burgers without chewing any of 'em."

"Burgers? Since when have you had a burger?" Pim scoffs.

"One day I'll get a burger. When I'm in the Pleasure Tribe and I can afford anything I want with my well-earned riches, I'll eat a burger a day. With fries and extra hot sauce on the side."

"Yeah, well, that habit will cost you more than an apartment," Lee tells her. "You'd be out on the streets and starving for a protein meal."

Sif's face screws up in disgust. "Ugh. You *need* to be starving to stomach that stuff."

"At least it keeps us alive," I try to find the bright side.

"I guess. Better get it over with." Sif stands up and brushes imaginary dust off her knees. "When you two work it out, we'll be downstairs. It's Haters' Pavilion night, remember?"

I had forgotten.

Lee glances up from his game. "Who's up for elimination?"

"Two 'failure to use approved lexicons' and one 'suspicious anti-love activities,'" Pim answers, flicking her finger over the chessboard. She grins at Lee. "Checkmate."

"What? No!" Lee throws his hands in the air, shock and disbelief written across his face. "How do you always do that?"

Pim gives him an enigmatic smile.

"Who are you voting for?" I ask Sif.

"Dunno. They're all low-level Haters this time, so I don't really care."

"You're getting soft," Chu calls from the carpet where he's busy trying to get Cam in a headlock.

"Call me soft again and I'll be down there helping Cam beat you senseless."

"Ooh! Lovers' tiff!" Cam crows. He's silenced by a sudden thump from his assailant.

"Don't encourage them," I say to Sif. "Let's go and get some food."

AS WE WALK THROUGH THE DINING HALL, I keep seeing Dorm Leader's office in my mind, as vivid as if I was still there. Sunlight plays over the desk in warm streaks. Wil's serious stare as he holds out his hand. The curve of his fingers resting over mine. The memory brings the same rush of heat to my cheeks. In my mind I see those spindly black letters—an invitation I am still struggling to comprehend.

Obstacle course bend 3,
1945 hours.

1945 is right when the Haters' Pavilion Show gets cranking. Somehow, I have to meet Wil in the middle of it. But how? I'd be questioned before I could even leave the building. How on this wide earth could he think that I would escape in the middle of our compulsory entertainment?

The internal battle rages in my head all through dinner. I snap at Chu's jokes. He gives me a funny look, but I can't help it. I have a chance to see Wil later, as long as I'm willing to break all the rules.

How is that even possible?

MEMORY DATE: CE 2272.01 (9 YEARS AGO)
Memory location: Nursery Dorm 492, assembly hall

Memory time: 0903 hours

"Apprentices always obey orders!" yells the tubby Lover at the front of the room. He says his name is Chief Lover Comb. We cower down on the floor, foreheads pressed against the cool white tiles. It's impossible to block out the whimpering that follows each thump of a white stick. I can't see anything but floor, so I don't know why the Apprentices are being chastised. The room around me is filled with quiet weeping.

MEMORY DATE: CE 2286.362 (5 YEARS AGO)

Memory location: Nursery Dorm 492, assembly hall
Memory time: 0917 hours

"Apprentices always obey orders!" screeches Lover Zink. His face is a vivid shade of red, and Bez cowers in front of him, legs quivering. The entire classroom is hushed. Fear has kidnapped our voices.

"I'm . . . I'm . . . I'm sorry, Lover Zink," Bez blubbers. Tears stream down his cheeks in wet lines. "It . . . it won't h-happen a-a-again . . ."

The white stick in Lover Zink's hand hovers above Bez's head like an antenna. I shut my eyes tight before I can see what's next. But I can't shut out the noise.

"ARE YOU OKAY?" CAM'S BROWN EYES ARE full of concern.

I give Cam an apologetic grimace. "Sorry. Not good company tonight, I guess."

"Wanna talk about it?"

"Don't think I can."

Cam's face closes down. "Sure." Staring down at his plate, he pushes the last couple remnants of food around, making green ribbons across the white. His eyes won't meet mine.

"Cam, it's just . . . I'll be fine. I think I'm just tired after today."

"You don't need to explain, Kerr." The green streaks stretch out across his plate like window bars.

"We've got a lot of work, you know—"

"I get it."

Far at the other end of the dining hall, the large digital clock on the wall blares out the time in vivid red: *1807*.

I don't need the reminder. Wil has given me an impossible choice. On the one hand, I can't disobey orders. But there's something going on. Something that Wil might be offering to share with me.

After the meal, a sea of grey uniforms makes its way to the large lecture theatre for the Haters' Pavilion Show. Outside the entrance, Sif is pulled aside by a linen-clad Lover. Cam and I flow into the room with the crowds. I let him go first so I can sit on the end of a row. Finally seated, I check the clock on my fitness tracker for the millionth time.

"What's up?" Cam whispers into my ear as I sit beside him. His face is so full of worry that for a second, I could tell him everything. But I don't. Something tells me that he wouldn't understand. What could I say, anyway? *Yeah, uh Cam, there's this guy who just asked me to a secret meeting, and . . .*

"I'm not feeling all that well," I lie, patting my stomach. "Might need to make a dash for the facilities, if you know what I mean."

Cam leans away from me. "Well, don't share that around."

I laugh. Ha ha. How jovial we are this evening, my facial expression says. All the while my brain is a whirling mess. In the middle of my internal torment, Sif bursts into the theatre and stomps up the stairs with barely restrained fury. She shoves past our knees and drops into the empty seat beside Cam, glowering and sullen. Cam gives me a look full of questions, and I give him an "I have no idea" shrug back.

1859. The lights in the lecture theatre dim. I mentally replay the floorplan of this part of the Elite facility, trying to map out an escape route. The bathrooms are three doors down. Beyond them lie three sets of empty hallways until the exit door. Too far. But Wil would know that. Wouldn't he?

1905, says my clock. Supreme Lover Midgate's lecture begins. As usual, our leader sits in her white chair in the white room, her silver hair cascading around her face like a helmet.

"My Lovelies, you can be *anything* the Love Collective wants you to be!" Her voice is warm, but her face is like ice.

Perhaps this is a loyalty test. Perhaps Lovers are waiting for me outside in case I try to escape. I said some pretty dangerous things up in Akela's office. Maybe Akela is mad, and she's using Wil to get me sent to Realignment. But then, why the secrecy? I'm sure Wil's too nice to do anything that twisted.

1915. Carell Hummer breezes onto the stage, arms open wide, basking in the wild cheering of the crowd. He makes a few jokes, and the whole lecture room lights up with laughter. I laugh a little too loud. Cam gives me a weird look.

1920. Hummer starts to introduce tonight's Haters, and the crowd responds with loud jeers and shouts. My nerves thrum, making my legs all jittery. I can tell by the groans that Hater Three is tonight's worst. It's hard to concentrate.

1935. I lean over to Cam. "Gotta take a bathroom break," I whisper.

He swivels toward me in surprise. "Now? They're just getting warmed up."

I hold my stomach and shrug an apology.

Understanding dawns on his face. "Ugh. Go."

Up on the screen, Hater Two screams as a hot poker hovers near her arm.

"You can tell me what I miss," I say. I'm out of my seat before he can say anything else, glad that for once I won't have another bloodstained memory. Unbidden, visions of hundreds of other shows begin replaying like movies.

MEMORY DATE: CE 2281.075

Memory location: Nursery Dorm 492, assembly hall
Memory time: 1947 hours
Three Haters try to find their way through a boobytrapped maze. As the camera zooms in on one contestant, a panel of spikes flicks out of the wall, impaling him.

MEMORY DATE: CE 2278.317

Memory location: Nursery Dorm 492, assembly hall
Memory time: 2006 hours
One Hater has made it to the end of a brutal obstacle course. They are bleeding from their head, legs, and abdomen. As they emerge from the exit, panting and exhausted, a Love Squad soldier throws his electric net. The Hater writhes on the ground, leaving red streaks across the floor.

MEMORY DATE: . . .

I PUSH INTO THE CLOSEST BATHROOM, wrapping my hands around the cool porcelain of a sink. My pale face stares back from the mirrored wall in front of me. Dark stains form deep crescents under my eyes. My hair frizzes out like a fuzzy halo around my head.

"What do I do now?" I say to my reflection. The only answer is the hollowness of my voice echoing off the tiles. I turn on the tap. Splash cool water over my skin. Drink.

1940. Time is running out. No matter what I do now, I lose. Go, and I'm breaking the rules. Stay, and I'll never find out what's behind my nightmares.

1943. The door of the bathroom opens, and Sif enters the room, a little out of breath. "What's wrong with *you?*" Her eyes scan my face.

A deep, rushing sigh escapes my lips.

"You've been as cagey as a Hater all evening," she says.

"I'm fine."

"Liar."

"So report me."

"Not even if my life depended on it." Sif's tone is sincere. "But someone else might if you keep this up." Her nod up at the ceiling is subtle, but it's impossible to miss her meaning.

I cast a glance around the room. The familiar black eye of the camera sits in one corner of the roof. I can't tell where it's looking. It's everywhere and nowhere all at once.

When she speaks again, Sif's lips barely move. "Smile for the camera, sweetie."

I shrug and plaster a vapid smile across my face. The smile wobbles around the edges. Before it can fade, I lean forward and splash my face with water again.

"It was just a stomach ache. I'll be fine," I assure her. The sound of my voice disappears down the plug hole along with my plans.

"Right answer." Sif smiles back. She gives me a little pat on the back and leans forward to whisper in my ear. "You're never not being watched. Did you know that? Never."

Her tone is brittle. I wonder what the Lover said to her that has gotten her so riled up. Then it hits me. A cold fear prickles the hair on the back of my neck.

I lower my voice. "You got in trouble for Chu, didn't you?"

"Let's go back to the show." She cocks her head to the door beside us, and my heart sinks. There's no way I'll get out of here now, not with Sif watching. I've missed my deadline and lost the truth. I can't shake this feeling that I've just made the worst mistake of my life.

22

Tonight on the Haters' Pavilion Show . . .
Actual wild beasts, here to tame our beastly Haters!
Who will triumph? Love or animal hate?
Vote for the worst Hater, and win a trip to the Love
City lifestyle!

MORNING ALARM. I ROLL OUT OF BED AS usual. I put on my uniform and wash my face as usual. As usual, I walk down to the dining hall and take my place in the line, obediently accepting the tray of food they offer. I sit at the table and talk to my friends. But a deep, crushing disappointment has settled over me, and I can't shake it.

I made a big mistake. One I'm going to regret forever.

The good news is I am not going crazy. The bad news is I am remembering things from before I woke up in the dorms. Nightmare things. Something awful and terrifying that hurts my head every time I think of it. Or try to think of it. But no matter how much I try, I can't get past the pain and the screaming.

"You're so stupid," I mutter to myself.

Sitting directly across the table from me, Cam looks up from his breakfast, startled. "Huh?" he asks with a mouth full of protein goop.

"Sorry. Not you. Never mind," I reply, pushing my food away.

Cam shrugs and goes back to his food, scooping it up eagerly.

My dark mood deepens. All I can think of now is how stupid I am. I should have followed Wil's instructions. Should have run out of that bathroom before Sif came to get me. Should have raced to the obstacle course before I could think myself out of it.

My usual morning routine is ruined beyond repair. I answer people's questions with sullen grunts, going through the motions with limbs as heavy as lead. On the outside, I'm a normal Elite Apprentice, heading for the day's lessons with her classmates. Inside, I'm screaming.

One choice is all it takes to ruin a life. One stupid, ridiculous, weak, and watery choice.

Sif walks the hallway beside me, silent and brooding. The whole world could be bathed in vivid rainbow lights and we'd be two little black rainclouds in the middle of it, each trapped in our own deluge of pain. She should be bouncing around, celebrating her new thing with Chu. Not scuffing her feet along the tiles, glancing up at every surveillance camera with an expression of murderous hatred.

"EVERY TIME I THINK ELITE HEROES IS JUST fiction, something like this happens," Sif whispers, waving her arm at the scene in front of us. I just nod, my words evaporating in the face of what looks exactly like the infotab set. Then I turn around, just to make sure Elite Lover Hu isn't behind us.

"Welcome to the Engine Room." Lover Herz smiles.

The lights in the VR simulation are dim. Long black glass tables set in semicircular tiers lead down to the floor where Lover Herz waits in front of a large blank wall. It's like a cave. A soft hum vibrates from row upon row of equipment.

She waves us toward the tables. We sit, waiting for some kind of show.

"What is the responsibility of Engine Roomers?" she asks. Hands shoot up all around me. Lover Herz nods at Arah.

"Logistics, Personnel, Health, and Containment," Arah says, listing off the summary we have all read. I managed to memorize the whole first chapter, but even I couldn't stop yawning. It's about as interesting as watching a clock tick.

With a satisfied nod, Lover Herz waves her ID against a console on the lower wall. Everyone gasps as the wall lights up in a series of boxes. In one rectangle, rows and rows of names and numbers scroll up, almost faster than we can comprehend. A central panel blooms into a large set of circles. At the opposite side of the wall, another long list of incomprehensible letters sits beside percentage points. One of them—WSP: 1%—blinks red.

"This is an Engine Room simulation," Lover Herz explains. "Next week we'll look at the Health stream, but for now, we're going to focus on Logistics. You'll be responsible for coordinating food and supplies for our Love Squads in the blue zone. If one of the supplies drops to dangerous levels"—she waves her hand at the WSP: 1%—"you could seriously compromise our operations. If you were working a real Engine Room, the lives of millions of Love Collective citizens would be in your hands. So work together."

The electronic hum rises in frequency, and our glass desks flicker into life. Rook and Arah jolt backward as a large green map revolves into existence below their elbows. Zin wiggles her fingers at a panel of dials and buttons. Lee and Pim's table seems to consist of a group of truck icons, surrounded by various cartoon buildings. I can't read any of the labels on their desk, but Lee and Pim are both jiggling with excitement. Buff and Dona shake their heads in wonder.

"What is this?" whispers Sif in my ear.

Distracted by the reactions of my classmates, I hadn't even

noticed our own desk. I balk. Below our fingertips, a table lists troop numbers and other military equipment. Coded icons float around a large square map.

"We're running the Love Squad," I say.

"Great. No pressure." Sif gives a despondent sigh.

"All right," Lover Herz continues. "You'll notice that you are working in pairs. Each pair has a different responsibility, but you need to work out how to cooperate. Flick and Grohns, for example, you will need to work with the transport group when you want to move your troops. Forerunner teams—that's you boys—will need to set up engineering and camp facilities if your troops are going to settle for any length of time. They need food. Sanitation. Medics. Even a little Pleasure Tribe now and then. Agriculture, warehousing, public sanitation teams are all going to need help from the Love Squad to protect their facilities. Haters are everywhere, people, and we won't let them win. Am I right?"

"Yes, Lover Herz!" we chant.

She clicks her fingers, and the simulation flickers into life.

Farr raises her arm in the air. "Lover Herz, I need some help. What are those things over there?" Her voice is plaintive as she points to her right.

"Best way to learn is by doing, Apprentice," Lover Herz replies with a grin. "Since you're the one in charge of utilities, you better get to it or you're going to run out of water."

"What? Where? How do I do anything?" Farr shrieks. With panicked movements she swipes at her desk, turning a few knobs and flicking some switches. The display on the wall lights up with a whole series of flashing warning lights. WSP: 1% becomes a flashing red rectangle, and an alarm sounds in time with the pulsing light on the screen. Farr lets out a screech.

"I can't do this!" she cries. "We're all gonna die!"

"How did you even get into this program?" Zin snaps at her partner, exasperated. She leans over Farr and soothes the knobs into place again. The panicked whooping of the alarm shuts off, and a few of the flashing lights wink out.

"That was . . . special," Rook comments.

"She's Engine Room material for sure," agrees Arah. They both laugh.

Ignoring the twins, Sif's head is bent over our shared display. "Hey Flick, what do you think this is?" she asks, pointing at a glowing list.

I lean over to get a better look. "Looks like Love Squad deployments," I say with a wry smile. "That's what the heading says, see? 'Love Squad deployments.'"

"Duh." Sif rolls her eyes. "No, I was talking about this. I understand all these codes. You've got the border forces, city watch, the guard defenses, and all of that stuff. They link with the map over here. But this entry—I just can't get my head around it."

Her finger rests beside an entry code. NURSERY DA. It lists a hundred soldiers under its command.

"Look," she says, tapping at her display. "You tap in to the border force entry, and it gives you a breakdown of where they all are and what they're doing. Same with city watch. You've got the Eastside patrols here, river patrol here, and all the little local precincts. But this? Look."

Sif taps the mysterious entry, and a list of locations scrolls up. Five patrols are sprinkled around the blue sector in what seem to be residential areas. As we watch, one of the patrols' indicators changes to IN TRANSIT. A small display appears: PACKAGES: 12.

My hand shoots up, and Lover Herz nods at me.

"Lover Herz, we've found something we don't understand here. Could you help us, please?" I say.

She glides over toward us and peers over our shoulders.

I point at the mystery code. "We don't know what this one is, Lover Herz."

"Hm." Lover Herz frowns. "What's that doing there? I didn't . . . Forget about that one." Lover Herz's voice hardens. "Leave it alone."

"But why? Surely we've got to keep them supplied too?" Sif persists.

"It must be a glitch in the system. Just look after all the rest, and I'll follow that up later."

"But—" I begin, but Lover Herz's sharp tone cuts my words off before I can go any further.

"Drop it, Apprentice Flick. Do you hear me?"

The level of hostility in Lover Herz's voice shocks me. She's always been the calm instructor. I nod, mute, and Lover Herz stalks back to the front of the room. Displeasure creases her face. There's something else in the instructor's expression too. A hint of fear at the corner of her eyes.

Sif raises her eyebrow at me. "What was that?" she mouths. I shrug.

We turn our attention back to troop numbers. Moving the Love Squad around is like an intricate ballet with string puppets. It's exhausting. But we also keep checking back with the mysterious NURSERY DA. Over the course of the hour, every patrol flicks back to being in transit. All of them have varying numbers of packages listed as they travel.

"Maybe they're the mail squad," I joke.

"Can't be. Mail's over on this screen. Besides, if it was just mail, Herz wouldn't be so worried," Sif whispers.

"Prisoners?"

"Not sure. The patrols and guard forces all list prisoners properly here. See? 'Hater Transport.' If I didn't know better"— Sif leans in close to my ear—"I'd think they were hiding something."

Even as she speaks, the status of one of the mysterious squads changes. Sif gasps. Startled, I follow her gaze. No longer in transit, one of the squads' indicators now reads: DELIVERY LOCATION: ND57.

I look at her. "What?"

"It can't be," she gasps, hands shaking violently over the console. Sif's whole body is trembling.

"Oi! Love Squad!" Arah calls out. "Why did you send a guard squadron out into the river patrol? You're spooking the citizens!"

Sif gives herself a little shake. "Sorry!" she responds with a clipped kind of cheerfulness. "My hand slipped!"

"Not a good habit," Lover Herz says sternly.

"I'm so sorry, Lover Herz. It won't happen again, Lover Herz." Sif ducks her head low, a good imitation of an apology.

"It had better not," Lover Herz informs her. "Mistakes can be fatal."

There's something in our instructor's warning that sends a chill right down my spine.

WHEN CLASS IS OVER, SIF WRENCHES her VR headset off with a violence that surprises me.

"What?" I ask.

She doesn't answer. Instead, she pushes her way out of the room, bumping past Rook so hard that he teeters off balance. His angry expression gives way to surprise when he sees that it is the tiny Sif barging past. He shrugs at his twin, and they saunter out of the room behind her.

I hurriedly squash my VR equipment into my bag and run after her.

"Are you okay?" I reach over to touch her shoulder.

She flinches away from my hand. "Something's going on here, and I don't like it." Sif strides down the corridor, face livid with fury. She brushes past two older Elites, and they stare back at her in surprise. I shrug an apology to them.

"What do you mean? The cameras?" I say.

Sif spins to face me, eyes blazing. "Why were the Love Squad taking packages from random residential areas to my Nursery Dorm? They're not Engine Room personnel. They're armed to the teeth! And why did Lover Herz get so antsy about it?"

"Your Nursery Dorm?"

"Didn't you see that label? ND57? That's *my* old dorm. It was in the right sector and everything."

"How do you know which sector . . ."

"I just know, okay?"

"So what?"

Sif looks up and down the corridor, then pulls me closer. "Think about it, Kerr. You're smart. Residential areas. Homes. Driving packages from homes to a Nursery Dorm. Why would they do that? It's not like they're getting protein cereal from a warehouse. Why homes? Why Love Squad?"

I shrug, dumbfounded. I'm struggling to follow Sif's line of thought here. It's a no-brainer to see that she's really worked up about it. She lets out a frustrated gasp. Her eyes blaze.

"You know what I think?" Her forehead is so close to mine, it's almost touching. She speaks in an angry whisper. "You might play dumb, but I know there's something big going on in this here Collective. And I mean to find out what that is."

She storms off, leaving me staring at her back.

23

A MONTH FLIES BY, AND THE WINTER RAINS begin to set in. Our drill classes move to the large atrium, where our marching practice booms around the open space in echoes loud enough to make my ears hurt. When we're not working on the precise Elite versions of Apprentice marches, we're in the enormous gym, running on treadmills and working out until our legs turn to jelly and our arms ache.

Life settles into a more familiar routine. We go to class. We do our drills. We listen to Supreme Lover Midgate's evening lectures, then we yell enthusiastically at the screen while more Haters are paraded before us. All systems normal, or so it seems.

But things aren't normal. My nightmares return nearly every night, with a few unwelcome additions. I'm still dreaming of the darkness and screaming, but Wil is there, standing beside Dorm Leader Akela.

"You failed, Apprentice," Akela sighs. "There's no way you'll be a Watcher now."

"I thought you were going to be my friend," Wil says, morphing into a Love Squad soldier holding a baton above his head.

I try to turn my head, but I can't. Someone is crushing me to their chest. I can't see their face. Just hints of the silvery pendant hanging around their neck—a tree with a human figure in front of it. I turn my head to the side as they start whispering, but the whispers transform into the voice of my friend Sif.

"Never forget him, Cadence."

". . .You're never not being watched. Did you know that? Never."

"These people want you to forget . . ."

"There's something big going on in this here Collective. And I mean to find out what that is."

The whispers get louder until I can't hear sirens or shattering glass or screams or anything. Only these nightmare phrases repeated over and over in my head. I wake, feeling as if I should be caked in blood but instead am drenched with sweat. The answers are just out of my reach.

Sif's fury has calmed down to a low simmer, but that doesn't mean she's over it. My closest friend disappears from our conversations at dinner, leaving Cam and Chu and me to make awkward small talk. One night when she doesn't even touch her food, I decide to follow her. Giving her a small head start, I stand to leave. Cam gives me a curious look, but I just point at Sif's disappearing back, and he understands.

From a distance, I watch as Sif heads with purposeful steps up to the study zone. By the time I get there, she's already found a spot in one of the small isolation cubicles, head bent low over her infotab. I wander up to the cubicle and tap on the glass. She is so engrossed in her study that she doesn't notice I'm there. I start doing a crazy dance to get her to notice me, waving my hands around in the air. She waves me away and goes back to reading her screen. I tap on the glass again, and she opens the door with an impatient huffing sound.

"What?"

"Are you okay?"

"Fine."

"Anything you want to share?"

"I'll tell you when I find something."

With that, she closes the cubicle door and flicks the lock, shutting me out.

A FEW DAYS LATER, WE WALK OUTDOORS into a cloudy day, our VR suits on and headsets dangling around our wrists. The cold air wraps over my face like an icy cloak.

"Got your rig?" Cam jogs up behind us, looking worried.

"Don't tell me you forgot yours," Sif scoffs.

"Course not. I just had to run back and get it, that's all."

"Idiot." She rolls her eyes. Her breath makes misty clouds in the air.

"This is a bit different, isn't it?" I say, trying to sound excited.

"We get fresh air. I'm good." Lee stretches his arms high above his head.

"Cold, though." Chu wraps his arms across his torso, shivering.

"I don't care as long as I'm out of that building," Pim says. "Do you ever get the feeling we're doomed to live forever in a white box?"

"No way. No matter what cadre they put me in, I'm going to be out under the sky as much as I can," Lee replies, turning his face to the grey sky.

"Don't be a Coder, then." Sif grunts. "You'll have your head bent over an infotab for the rest of your life."

"I'd rather be in the Love Squad, anyway. They get guns and nets and cool utility belts." Lee's mouth widens in a wicked smile.

"And we look good in black," says Pim with a cheeky wink at her friend.

Lover Kalis waits for us just beyond the entrance. Her red hair curls around her head in glossy waves that just won't obey regulation style.

"Ah, good to see you've arrived," she says. "Who's up for some combat training?"

"Bring it on," Rook and Arah declare in unison. The two boys shake out their arms, flexing their muscles and stretching. I make a mental note to try and get on their team.

"Fall in!" Lover Kalis bellows.

We obey like a machine, organizing ourselves into neat lines of equally spaced Apprentices without a second thought. With a nod of her head, she leads us on a jog down tree-lined paths toward a grassy compound. As we go, she starts up one of the Elite chants.

"Ain't gonna be no Haterman."

"Ain't gonna be no Haterman," we all shout after her.

"We're Elite Apprentices, understand."

"We're Elite Apprentices, understand."

"Hate don't have no hold on me."

"Hate don't have no hold on me."

"In the Love Collective, we are free."

"In the Love Collective, we are free."

"Sound off . . ."

I risk a glance sideways at Sif. With every repetition of the chant, the lines around her downturned mouth deepen. By the time we're at the compound, she's modified the chant. She's muttering under her breath, but it doesn't take a Watcher to work out what she's saying.

"We are *not* free . . ."

A canopy of logs announces the entrance, and with excited grins, we line up at the course boundary. Tall timber structures stand in each corner of the compound. They look a little bit like miniature skyscrapers, with small holes at random places up three of the walls. A maze of timber barriers and poles is planted in the hard dirt surface between them, like incomplete fence posts. The air smells of dirt and wet grass.

"Headsets on!" Lover Kalis commands. As we fit our VR headsets over our heads, she lifts her infotab and presses something on the screen. Visors drop down in front of our eyes. They fade to transparent, and the compound lies before us unchanged.

"What's going on?" Rook calls. "The VR isn't working."

"That's because you're in AR today." Kalis smiles. She touches the infotab, and a heads-up display appears around the edge of my vision.

I stand in stunned silence, but Cam lets out a soft, "Augmented Reality? Ooh."

"Right now, you're all seeing a simulation of the Love Squad helmets," Lover Kalis continues. "With a few differences. Put your hand up if your display is red."

Rook, Arah, Buff, and Dona all raise their hands.

Lover Kalis nods at them, then looks around at the rest of us. "Okay, who's got purple?"

Lee, Pim, Chu, and Zin raise their hands. Farr looks crestfallen.

Lover Kalis nods again. "And the rest of you are blue. In a moment, one member of each team will have a flag appear in their display. They're the targets. Your team's mission is to get another team's target while defending your own. If you eliminate a target, you receive 100 points. But if you can capture them and bring them back to your base, your score will rise to 100,000 points. You'll also receive points for hits against the opposing team. Any questions?"

"Where are our bases?" Lee calls out.

"Look around you," Lover Kalis responds. Thanks to the AR app, three glass fortresses rise high above the compound like points on a large triangle. Different colored banners wave boldly from the fortress rooftops, one for each team. A junkyard lies in between the fortresses, littered with rusted cars, high stone walls, and discarded rubbish. Sif lifts her hand and points to where a vivid blue flag waves above one fortress.

"There's us . . ." she starts, but I'm too busy grabbing her wrist.

"Look at your hand!" I gasp.

Sif looks down at the same time I look at my own hands. Golden orbs glow over our palms. I turn my hand over, looking in wonder.

"I see you've found your weapons," Lover Kalis says.

"How do we use them?" asks Lee.

Lover Kalis turns toward a large car laid between the blue and red bases. She holds her hand out in front of her and then jerks it backward. A stream of laser light shoots out from her hand, exploding in a golden cloud. The car rocks and then returns to its original place.

"Awesome!" Chu shouts, mimicking Lover Kalis's shooting movement. When nothing happens, he looks down in disappointment at his hand. "What the—?"

"You aren't activated yet," Lover Kalis tells him. "Get to your bases."

We jog away, heading for the blue-flagged fortress. Sif scuffs her feet along the ground behind us.

Cam squints across the field. "This is going to be so easy. Quick run; dodge the bullets. Done."

"Who's the target?" I ask.

"Not me!" Cam says, bouncing from foot to foot.

Farr raises her hand. "That will be me."

I look over at Farr, who's been separated from her bestie. She looks like she just swallowed something sour.

"You going to be okay?" I ask.

Farr shrugs.

"Why don't you take defense up in the tower?" I offer, trying to be helpful.

She shrugs again, rolling her eyes as if I asked her to do the most boring thing in the universe. "Whatev."

"She's gonna be fun," Sif mutters under her breath.

About as fun as you would be, I think. I paste on a smile, though.

"I'll keep watch, Sif. You don't have to hang around. If you go with Cam, you can work together to capture a target."

We come up to the oddly shimmering fortress. The blue banner waves above our heads, out of reach.

"They're going to send their biggest team members to get Farr, so watch out for the twins," I say, scanning the field.

"That shouldn't be a problem." Cam grins. "I'm gonna be too busy capturing the purple target to bother with defense."

As he speaks, a wall of fire erupts along the line of junk and ruined metal. Cam's mouth drops open.

"Well that changes things a little," Sif says.

Cam gives himself a little shake. "Bring it on," he growls. "It's not real." He reaches out toward a flame flickering on a nearby wall and runs his fingers through it.

"Ow!" he cries, snatching his hand back. He freezes, his face taking on the expression of a lost puppy. "Oh."

"What?" Sif asks.

"Just lost twenty health points," Cam mumbles, dejected.

"You had to be the idiot, didn't you?" Sif retorts, then turns to me. "Kerr, you all right to defend here with Farr?"

"Sure. You good with that, Farr?" She acts like I haven't said anything. I shake my head. "Guess I'll be defending alone."

Sif and Cam give me sympathetic looks.

A loud siren wails. Cam sprints away toward one of the gaps in the defensive walls, Sif at his heels. The field descends into an eerie silence. I stare at the simulated flames, wishing they were as warm as they look.

Farr turns her sulky expression out toward the maze. I do an exploratory lap around the base of our fortress and discover a small door at the back. Opening it, I climb a few steps to a hidden landing. Some of the windows give a better view of the junkyard. I climb up a little higher and risk a look. The AR flames make the view difficult, but I can see a couple of heads bobbing around obstacles in the distance.

"Rook's coming," I say, more to myself than Farr. Rook's head bounces along just out of reach behind an old truck. When I stare long enough at his head, a target appears. It flashes red, and the word *Lock* blinks briefly. I raise my hand, pointing it through the window. With a quick push forward, a golden beam of light flashes toward him. It curves over the top of the truck and then explodes in a flash. Rook disappears.

There's another shout in the distance, and a red light flashes in my heads-up display. Cam is down.

"Great. Just great."

"This better be over soon," Farr huffs below me.

I glare down at where she's still leaning against the wall.

More shouts echo over the walls. It sounds like a massive disturbance in front of the purple fortress. Against my better judgement, I climb down from my vantage point.

"Where are you going?" Farr demands.

"Just don't get taken."

"I'm not stupid."

I run, hunched over so that my head doesn't extend above

the barrier. Stopping at every junction, I look around, hands ready to shoot at any attackers. The course is deserted.

The shouts grow louder near the purple fortress. I reach the source of the disturbance when I round the back of a rusted truck. A small circle has formed. Rook and Arah are holding back Cam and Chu, their muscles bulging against the two shorter boys. Chu's face is a mask of agony. When Cam's worried glance catches my eye, he mouths one urgent word at me,

"Help!"

I reach the edge of the small crowd, and my heart sinks. Zin is flat on her back in the middle of the circle, dark hair spreading out into the dust. A stream of blood trickles from her nose and across her cheek. Sif is straddling the slender girl, pinning her arms to the ground with her knees. My friend's fists rain down with a fury I have never seen before. It's all Zin can do to turn her head so that Sif's fists hit her cheeks instead of her eyes.

"That's . . . for . . . ratting . . . on . . . Kerr. And . . . that's . . . for being . . . a lousy . . . cheat . . ."

I dive in, pulling her fists back. She lets out a guttural shriek and nearly turns on me before recognition dawns in her eyes. A conflicting ball of emotions flashes across her face: guilt, fury, despair. As I drag her away, Buff swoops in to help. Zin shakes Buff's hands away, turning her sullen glare on everyone. Stiff and slow, she stands, brushing dust off her pants.

"What are you doing?" I hiss at Sif, ignoring the jeering around me.

"Let her go!" Rook yells.

"That was just getting good!" Arah adds.

"She cheated." Sif lunges back at Zin, who is dabbing the blood on her face with the back of her hand.

Seeing Sif flying at her, Zin ducks. I grab Sif by the waist and hoist her back a few steps.

Sif roughly pulls her arms out of my grip. "Why are

you stopping me? She tried to get you sent to Realignment. She's a leech!"

"You don't have to do this," I say, trying to keep the fearful tremor out of my voice.

Chu and Cam place themselves between Sif and Zin, watching us with wary expressions.

"What happened?" I ask them.

Cam sighs, looking shaken. A purple lump swells above his left eye. "Zin used a plank to take me out," he says. "Sif thought that was against the rules. Zin taunted her about"—he glances sideways and lowers his voice—"about Chu, and . . . well, that was like throwing gas on a fire. We tried to stop them, but the twins . . ."

"You're dead!" Zin screeches, lunging away from Buff and toward Sif.

Chu steps between the two girls and forces Sif back. Sif looks up at him, adoration and grief mingling with her fury.

At that moment, the AR disappears from the course, leaving us back in a bare timber compound. The group goes silent. Lover Kalis steps forward, Farr trailing behind her like a lost puppy.

"What is going on here?" Lover Kalis's voice is cold and hard. Everyone in the group is suddenly staring at the ground.

Everyone except Zin, that is. "*She* attacked me for no reason," Zin spits, blood and bruises turning her face into an ugly specter.

Lover Kalis frowns at Sif. "Explain."

"Why? You're part of the conspiracy too. Don't pretend you weren't watching every second of that."

Kalis holds her hand up. "I don't know what you're insinuating, Apprentice Grohns, but—"

"You saw what happened. You must have. But you let her cheat anyway. Why didn't you stop her? We're all just puppets in one big game. You just—"

Lover Kalis stops Sif mid-sentence. "Grohns. To my office. Now."

"No."

When the single word comes out of my friend's mouth, it's as if the whole world forgets to turn on its axis. My mouth drops open in horror. Even Lover Kalis's face is a mask of shock.

She covers quickly, and her words come out in a seething, furious hiss. "Nobody refuses a Lover's order, Apprentice. My office. Now."

Sif returns her stare, arms folded, hip jutting sideways in one monumental display of sass. "No."

And that's how my best friend ended up in Realignment.

24

Hater Recognition Signs: A Primer for the Young
Haters cannot take our society forward into the future.

FOR THE FIRST FEW DAYS, I WAIT AND HOPE
that Sif comes back quickly. When a week passes, I'm alarmed
that they've kept her away for so long. After two weeks, my
alarm settles down into a deep, heavy grief.

Even grief, it seems, can't stop Elite Academy life from
marching on. News of the impending Filtering exam bursts
into our Apprenticeship like a bomb rips through a bus. Dorm
Leader makes the announcement to our group after drill
practice one day. Sweaty and panting, we stand to attention
while she walks onto a low platform at the front of the field. Her
dark braids are wrapped in an intricate arrangement around the
back of her head, and her uniform flows in pristine linen folds.

"I hope you are all feeling more at home here in Elite
Academy," she says. Her eyes flick over me. "But it's nearly time
for you to begin your specialized training."

I check out my classmates from the corner of my eye. They're
all standing at attention, so it's impossible to tell what they're
thinking.

Dorm Leader places her hands behind her back and
continues with her speech. "The Orientation period is short

for a reason. We want you to spend as much time as possible honing your skills and preparing for your future in your cadres. So in a month, we'll be putting you through the Filtering exam."

The only sign of surprise is a small ripple of movement across the group. I hold myself still.

"After the exam, you'll remain in your accommodation and share drills and meals with each other, but you will begin to separate into specialist training sessions. I know you may be worried, but do not fear. We just want to help you to become the Love Collective citizens you were meant to be. Are there any questions?"

Can Sif come back? The thought floats through my mind, but I keep my mouth shut. Dorm Leader dismisses us, and my mind reels beneath a riot of unanswered questions.

The news of Filtering has a strange effect on all of us. Cam and Chu walk around like mourners at a funeral, still hung up on Sif's absence. Zin and Farr . . . well, Zin's face for a while is a vivid reminder of Sif's fury, all puffy, yellow-green bruises. But the bruises can't hide her crowing triumph or constant comments about how Sif will probably miss the exam. Lee and Pim stop talking to all of us and form a high-pressure study group of two. So it's just me. Me and my unanswered questions.

I'M SUPPOSED TO BE STUDYING FOR Coding, but I can't concentrate. I mean, it probably doesn't matter, since Lover Tinks thinks I'll get 100 percent anyway. But right now I'm sitting alone in a concentration pod in the study center, staring at a blank wall. Too many thoughts to think. Too many memories. Too many days Sif has been locked in Realignment.

Why did I dream about Akela before I'd even seen her face?

What happened to me all those years ago? Am I going crazy? I didn't think I was crazy, but if I'm hearing voices, my doom is inevitable. How on earth am I going to make it to Watcher if I have all of these crazy dreams all the time?

Nothing makes sense.

Cocooned in my study capsule, I flick open the LC app on my infotab. I ignore the social domains, since nobody's speaking to each other anyway. I don't feel like being entertained, so I shut off the movies and Haters' Pavilion replays. I search into the "About Us" domain. The onscreen globe transforms into a pristine white gallery topped with the Love Collective flag. Images sit on the gallery walls like canvases in an art show. I go straight to the headshot of Supreme Lover Midgate, which sits alone on its own wall at the front of the room. Her blue eyes stare at me, as piercing and incisive as I remember from Fitness to Proceed.

"Greetings, Apprentice Flick," the portrait of Lover Midgate says in her soothing tones. "Thanks be to you for your presence."

"May you reach your dreams and find yourself in the universe, Supreme Lover Midgate," I stammer. I know this is an AI, but using approved lexicon is a hard habit to break.

"Welcome to the Love Collective information zone, Apprentice Flick. What would you like to know today?"

"Please tell me about the origin of the Love Collective, Supreme Lover," I ask. It's a question the Lovers answered for us many times in Nursery Dorm, so I'm not quite sure why I'm asking again. Maybe I'm just desperate. Maybe there's something I missed every other time I've watched the orientation documentary. Something that will help me understand why I'm so messed up.

On my screen, the pixelated portrait of Supreme Lover gives me a pleased smile.

"What a lovely request, Apprentice Flick," she says. "Any

student who devotes themselves to understanding love is certainly going to go far." Her portrait fades, replaced by an image full of dark shadows. Supreme Lover Midgate's voice begins to narrate.

"In the beginning was hate: a world full of people who hated themselves and hated each other. And the Haterman ruled them all."

The screen fills with flames, replaced by ruined buildings and disturbing images of slums. Emaciated children stare at me with haunted, pleading eyes.

"Life under the Haterman was miserable and desperate. Millions of citizens died without enough food or shelter. Millions more threw themselves at the walls of the Haterman's citadel, sacrificing their lives for the sake of hate and its children. Darkness reigned. Rivers of blood flowed without end."

The flames rise, fading to reveal a city street broken and covered in trash. Groups of masked protestors emerge from side streets, walking and shouting toward a high black wall. They throw flaming bottles and missiles at the wall, which then erupts in more flames.

"Until the day when one woman sought to bring peace. Instead of an iron fist, she created a Collective. Instead of hate and fear, she ruled with love. She gathered about herself a group of Lovers who would fight hate by any means necessary to bring prosperity for all. That woman's name was Supreme Lover Midgate."

The flames part, and the smiling face of a much-younger Supreme Lover steps forward into the gap. She holds up her hand in a powerful salute, and a group of people step up behind her, arms folded or resting on their hips. The Supreme Executive, looking young and strong and beautiful. Our superheroes.

"With the help of her small band of Love Collective loyalists,

Midgate brought down the evil regime of the Haterman. Her Love Squad became a force for good."

Supreme Lover stands before one of the emaciated children from the earlier pictures. She holds out a flower, and the child runs to embrace her. Supreme Lover smiles.

"Many years passed, and many battles were waged by the Haterman's evil Haters. They despised the goodness and light that the Love Collective offered. They dispensed lies about Midgate's true identity. They resisted peace. Haterman's lying armies killed friends and enemies alike, blaming the disappearances on Midgate's innocent friends."

The caricatured Haterman snarls from his podium, spit flying from his mouth. He raises his fist, and hordes of red-uniformed soldiers swarm from behind him to attack a white-clad, unarmed mob. Supreme Lover steps forward, looking sad. She points. Love Squad soldiers form a barrier between the attackers and citizens. The screen quickly fades to white.

"Through great cost, peace finally reigned. The Love Collective nation was born. The Collective committee that served Midgate so well now became the Supreme Executive of our blessed and happy land."

The Hall of Love rises out of the city landscape, its flag flying proudly atop the highest tower. Flowers and light and party decorations fly through the air in swirling celebration.

"Thanks to Supreme Lover Midgate's foresight, every Love Collective citizen was given a home, from least to most important. Everyone was given employment. Everyone was guaranteed love and entertainment. Everyone had enough to eat."

Supreme Lover Midgate appears in various situations: handing food packages to dirty, starving people; turning the key to a house's front door and welcoming a family inside; shaking hands of factory workers while wearing a bright-yellow hardhat. She always smiles.

"But there are still those who seek to bring chaos and disorder where Midgate desires only peace. Haters walk among us. They look like us. They talk like us. They live where we live. They work where we work."

Several scenes pass: uniformed factory workers lean over a conveyor belt. One man looks up, and his face transforms into the Haterman mask. In an open-plan office, Lovers in white linen suits work at consoles. The camera pans into one cubicle, and a worker turns to show that they are also wearing a Haterman mask.

"Haters would destroy everything the Love Collective sought to build. They refuse to listen to the pleas for peace. So only one solution remains: to Embrace them, exposing their lies and hatred."

Supreme Lover Midgate stands on a plinth looking somber but determined. She points sideways, and a group of Haters walks through the door of a white building. Behind them, a crowd of Lovers cheers and claps at Supreme Lover's actions.

"Love will always succeed. The very citizens of the Love Collective themselves rise up in defense of our beloved way of life. No matter how many people try to tear down our utopia with hate, love will always win."

The movie finishes with a final image of the Love Collective flag fluttering in the breeze. Then the portrait shrinks back to its original size, and Supreme Lover's face smiles at me again.

"Thank you, Supreme Lover," I say, my voice shaking.

"My pleasure, Apprentice Flick. Did you find everything you needed today, or would you like to research some more?"

"No, thank you, Supreme Lover. I think I should go and study for my Filtering exam."

"Very well. Love all, be all, Apprentice Flick."

"Love all, be all, Supreme Lover."

I switch off the screen and storm out of the study cubicle,

shoving the infotab into my bag as I go. I came looking for answers. I'm leaving certain that I'll never find them in that app.

"Embraced by love?" I mutter under my breath. "What a load of garbage."

NOTHING FITS. THE TRIUMPHANT, GLOSSY propaganda of Midgate's victory seems too good to be true. Nobody could smile that much all the time. And the Haterman? His face was more like a cartoon than a real human. Why would so many people follow a cartoon like that?

I need answers. And even though I've let him down, there's only one person I know who can even begin to give them to me.

I make my way up to the executive level, stomach churning with nausea and anxiety. Silence surrounds the noisy raging of my thoughts. I haven't spoken to Wil since I stood him up, but I can't avoid this anymore.

As the elevator swishes open on the top floor, I step into quiet, opulent settings again. A trickle of sweat falls down the back of my neck. When I reach Dorm Leader's office, I swipe my wrist over the ID panel without thinking. There's a soft beep, and a familiar voice crackles out of the intercom.

"Yes?" Wil says. The anxious, fluttery feeling in my stomach turns into a riot at the sound of his voice.

"I have to come in."

"Can I ask why?"

"Let me in, and I'll explain."

"Suit yourself."

The doors swing open. From his place behind the desk, Wil waves me toward a plush, leather armchair in the waiting room.

Ignoring his gesture, I stride over to him, leaning across the desk. "I need to know," I say, almost losing my nerve at the way he looks straight into my eyes.

"What do you think you are—"

"I need to know."

His mouth tightens. His eyes don't leave mine, and I am frozen beneath his gaze. Then, with slow and deliberate movements, he tilts his chin toward the ceiling behind me. His eyes flick upward and back, signaling something. I follow his direction, and turn to see a familiar black eye, pointing at me from the corner of the office. Fear nearly knocks the strength out of my knees.

Cameras. Duh.

I take a step back. Clear my throat. "I am sorry I missed my previous appointment," I say in a loud, formal tone. "I was wondering if I could make another time to discuss that matter."

Wil's shoulders relax, and a hint of that dazzling smile plays at the corner of his mouth. "Dorm Leader is busy right now, but if you could come back later . . . ?"

I nearly fall for it. But my impatience wins. "Not later. Now."

His smile freezes again. "That's not possible," he says through gritted teeth.

"I can wait."

"You'll be waiting a long time."

"Don't care."

I flop down into the chair Wil indicated earlier, my arms crossed and face sullen. Wil rubs his eyes with his hand, sighs, and turns back to his console. All hints of smile have gone.

Minutes tick away. The high window casts a rectangular patch of sunlight onto the warm carpet. I watch the rectangle creep toward me as time flows toward night. Out of the corner of my eye, I watch Wil at work. He keeps his face turned away, as if I don't exist.

"Hmph," I snort. Two can play at that game.

Wil gives me a curious look. "Are you okay?" All his former

hostility has melted away. Now, his face is so open and gorgeous that I want to blurt out everything.

I shrug instead, dragging my eyes away from his and down to the floor, certain that my face has flushed bright red.

"You don't look okay," Wil says.

"I'm not. But you wouldn't want to know what I have to say."

"Try me."

"I just . . . I think I let you down, and I wanted to apologize and . . ." *And ask for help.* I don't say that bit, though. "My best friend has been sent to Realignment, and she's been paranoid that . . ." My breath hiccups. I glance up in the direction of the ever-present camera. "Anyway, I was watching a Collective documentary, and I wanted to see what you—what Dorm Leader thought about it all, and I thought that maybe since she had a lot of books she might have one that could help me, and . . ."

"That's a lot to have on your mind."

"You have no idea."

"I might have more of an idea than you think." He grins, and the butterflies set off a riot in my stomach again.

I'm about to ask him to tell me what he knows when the large doors swing open, and Dorm Leader marches in.

I stand, darting toward her. "Dorm Leader, I'm so glad you're back, I—"

The words run dry in my mouth as a man with slate-grey hair sweeps into the waiting room behind her. He is tall, broad-shouldered, and clad in the crisp, gold-trimmed linen suit of the Supreme Executive. He turns his wrinkled face toward me, surprise and hostility mixing in his glance. I stop dead. Every hair on my arms rises in alarm. I've just seen this man's face in a documentary. He's on my vidscreen every night for the Love Collective anthem. What is Executive Lover Crucible, Minister for Educational Intelligence, doing in Dorm Leader's office?

"Forgive me, Dorm Leader." I salute stiffly, standing to attention.

Akela's mouth turns down in disapproval.

"Who is this young upstart?" the old man's voice is cracked and rasps like crumpled paper.

I straighten my posture, too scared to look at him.

"Executive Lover Crucible, this is one of my first-year Apprentices. Please excuse her. Although we have high hopes for her future, she has not properly learned the protocol, it appears. Apprentice Flick, you have forgotten yourself. And before a member of the Supreme Executive, no less."

"Love all, be all, sir!" I salute, shame and guilt heating my cheeks. I bow low. "I Embrace myself in penitence, sir."

Executive Lover's smile is mirthless. "It's a good thing I have seen a tight ship so far, Apprentice. Otherwise I would be forced to be very disappointed."

I bow again, too ashamed to speak.

"Well then, Dorm Leader, shall we continue with our inspection?"

"Of course, Executive Lover. Come to my office, and I will turn over the records." It's impossible to miss the note of mortified misery in Dorm Leader's reply.

I have shamed her. I should be shot.

I remain motionless while the pair exits into Dorm Leader's office. When Akela's inner door closes and the adults are out of sight, I let out my breath in a long, slow sigh. My legs are shaking.

"Well, that was unexpected," Wil quips, but the glance he casts at the door to Akela's inner office is fearful.

"Might be best if I come back another day," I say weakly. My throat has gone dry.

"Yes. Might be best." Wil's mouth is in a tight line. "If we're still here."

"Tell Dorm Leader I am truly sorry," I mumble. Then I turn and walk out, trying as hard as I can to stop my knees from buckling beneath me.

25

Memory location: Love Collective History lesson, Nursery Dorm 492, Room 37, Row 5, Seat 4

Memory time: Approx. 1100 (uncertain)

Lover Zink says this vision happened long before we were born. On the vidscreen, the Hall of Love gleams so brightly that it makes my eyes hurt. High on the tallest tower, a large balcony stretches like a wide-open mouth. It is empty. Far below, a sea of citizens screams and waves and shouts. Every few minutes the cameras zoom in on a Love Collective citizen to show us how excited they are. Some of them jump up and down. Some of them are crying with happiness. They all wave little LC flags.

The vision zooms back on the empty balcony. Five figures march out of the darkness, and the crowd erupts in a deafening roar. Four men and one woman—all clad in bright, white linen— smile and wave. Supreme Lover raises her hand in a salute and steps forward to the edge of the balcony. She looks younger than she does in her nightly lectures.

"My Lovelies, it is my pleasure to announce that you have elected a new Supreme Executive to lead us into our brilliant future. Executive Lover Munsch"—a tall, thin man with jet-black hair and steel-rimmed glasses gives the crowd a smiling nod—"has been elected for a tenth time to be our Engine Room Executive. Executive Lover Worthing is likewise reelected without opposition into the office of Collective Messenger."

A wide-waisted man with a pronounced paunch and reddened cheeks lifts his hand to wave at the crowd below.

"Executive Lover Crucible continues his role of Minister of Educational Intelligence."

Executive Lover Crucible nods, a supercilious expression on his face.

Supreme Lover Midgate continues to smile and wave at the crowds below. "And finally, our Science and Technology Minister, Executive Lover Fareyn. I remain, as always, your Supreme Lover. First among equals, and director of the Collective."

The crowd erupts in wild shouts and screams again. Supreme Lover holds her hand up, and the screaming dies down.

"But this good news is not all we have to share. For today, dear friends, today marks the final nail in the coffin of hate. So in the spirit of the Love Collective, we are instituting a new and wonderful event. The Triumph of Love! Every year on this day, our Love Collective will begin a week of celebration. Carnivals. Parades. The most Exciting of Excitements!"

At this announcement, the crowd below erupts in a roar even more deafening than before. Until cascades of fireworks explode on the roof of the tower in a hail of crackles and bangs. The vidscreen fades, and Lover Zink steps up from behind his desk.

I raise my hand.

"Yes, Apprentice Flick?" Lover Zink says, looking annoyed.

"When do we get to go to the Triumph of Love?"

"When you are old enough to do the work of the Love Collective. And not a moment before."

"How will we know we are old enough to do the work of the Collective?"

"Oh, we will tell you. So until then, you need to work hard and be the best Apprentice you can be."

"Yes, Lover Zink."

I HURTLE DOWN THE ELEVATOR, DASHING out of the atrium and into the sunshine outside as if I'm being chased by hounds. My friends—at least, the ones who aren't in Realignment—are walking out toward our regular drill practice. I come up beside Cam, who raises one quizzical eyebrow at me as I huff and puff into place. I can't speak. What would I even say?

Drill practice is the usual rows of marching and chants. I know them all so well that my mind has plenty of time to keep punishing me for what I just did. I have failed Dorm Leader in front of an Executive Lover. Failed Sif. Failed Wil. Failed, failed, failed.

By the end of drill practice, it's a relief to let my friends chatter around me. But Cam has other ideas.

"So, the Filtering exam. Where do you want to go?" Cam asks me, his footsteps ringing out on the wide concrete path back to the building.

I raise an eyebrow at him. "You should know by now."

Cam has the good manners to look embarrassed. "Still set on being a Watcher, then?"

"I was. But after today, I am pretty sure that idea is dead." I duck my head to avoid the curious expression Cam shoots my way. "What about you?"

"I think I'd make a good Engine Roomer." He squints up at the Academy, and his eyes rest on the Engine Room sector.

"You'd be the best Engine Roomer, Cam. You keep track of things really well."

"Cam thinks he can shuffle trucks better than anyone." Lee smirks as he comes up beside us.

Pim gives him a little shove. "Cut it out, Lee. You're just

jealous because you'll be all alone with the twins in the Love Squad while Cam and I move you around."

"Buff and Dona will be there too," Lee replies. "Anyway, it's better than all that Pleasure Tribe twisty-body stuff."

"Careful. Sif wants to be Pleasure Tribe," Pim says.

Cam looks glum. "Are they even going to let her out in time for the exam?"

I cast a glance over at Chu, who's scuffing his feet along the path as if his shoes are concrete blocks. Falling back, I shuffle into step with him. We walk together in silence for a few minutes. As we reach the tree-lined avenue that leads back to the entrance, he finally speaks.

"It's my fault, Kerr."

"Chu, you couldn't have predicted—"

"Is she going to miss exams?"

"I don't know. I hope not, but who knows how long they're going to keep her?"

"What if we never . . . never see her again?"

I look into Chu's eyes in time to see the flicker of pain. "You really care about her, don't you?" I say.

He lets out a ragged breath. "Not allowed. But I can't . . . I can't just stand around out here and let her . . ."

"Then let's go and find out when she'll be back."

"What?"

"Come with me."

With a quick glance at the back of my other friends' heads, I grab Chu's hand and hoist him away from the path. He doesn't protest. We cross the open fields, passing the combat training grounds.

"Where are we going?" Chu asks.

"To get some answers."

At the playing fields we take a sudden right and head back toward the building. The door I'm looking for is a nondescript glass rectangle set into the curving wall just outside the

Introductory wing. Glass doors glide open as we approach, and we step into the cool, sterile air of an empty white hall. White tiles glisten on the floor. White walls gleam all the way to the far end where a white security desk with a tall counter stands in front of a white door. A white embossed sign, barely visible over the door, confirms my hopes and sends a thrill of fear across my chest: Realignment Chambers.

I slow down, uncertain. I'd been so determined to talk to someone about Sif that I hadn't thought this far ahead.

"What do we do now?" Chu asks.

"This all worked out better in my head."

"What did?"

"I thought we'd find a security person and just ask them when Sif was coming back."

"You thought we'd just walk in here and *ask someone*?!" Chu splutters.

"Well, yes," I admit. "'Can I help you?' the person would say, and I'd say, 'Yes, thank you. Do you know when Apprentice Sif will be let out?' and they'd say—"

"We need to get out of here now." Chu looks wildly around.

I pull him forward. We reach the security desk, and I peek over the tall counter. No one is there. There's a wall of vidscreens behind the counter, a long-forgotten coffee cup, and an empty chair. But no human.

I take a few tentative steps around the counter.

Chu hisses at me in panic. "Kerr! What are you doing?"

"Whoa. Chu, look at this." I beckon to him. He hesitates, glances around the room with furtive looks. I smile, reassuring. "Oh, you need to see this. Come on."

Chu swallows nervously, but he does as I ask. When he sees where I'm pointing, he freezes. "What the—?"

Security cameras cover every inch of the Realignment chambers, or so it seems. Every twenty seconds, the screens shift. We get an ever-changing view of the area, from the path, the entrance, and deep into the chambers behind the door.

"We don't need to get inside," I whisper. "We can see everything from here."

On the screens, white-coated medics wander through the chamber, clutching infotabs and looking purposeful. Multiple hallways lead away from a central control desk. In the center of a circle of consoles and chairs, other medics sit and stare at their screens. Like the infirmary, glass-fronted rooms open onto the halls. Each room contains a therapy bed. Wires and tubes tether unconscious Apprentices to small medical consoles beside their heads.

"Look!" exclaims Chu, pointing at one of the screens in front of us. I gasp. There, lying immobile on a clinical bed, is Sif. Her hair is hidden beneath a halo of wires and electrodes. Her arms are strapped to her side by wide silver manacles. Her body is covered by a white sheet. She looks as if she's asleep, but it's hard to tell with the thick plastic tube that protrudes from her mouth. A drip snakes up from the back of her left hand.

"What are they doing to her?" I breathe.

"We gotta get her out of there." Chu makes a dash toward the door, but I grab his wrist and wrench him back to me.

"Don't be stupid. How in the love are you going to do that?"

He tries to pull away from me. "I'll think of something."

"Like how to get through the impossible security door? And that's before you even think about what to do with all those medics." I confront him, eyes blazing.

He wilts. "But she's . . . she's . . ." He gestures at the security screens. Agony creases his face.

"I'm sorry, Chu. If I'd known this was what we'd find, I never would have brought you here. We should go."

He stares again at the screens. "It's a bit late for that." His voice is flat. A trembling finger points to one of the screens. "We're dead."

The vision has flicked to a series of cameras set outside the building, and two figures march toward us. Lover Fuschious stamps down the path toward the entrance. About thirty meters behind him, Dorm Leader Akela glides along, looking for all the world like she's out for a stroll. But she keeps her eyes fixed to Fuschious's back, and it's obvious she's heading for this hallway too.

"Haterman in a basket of Haters," I spit.

Chu's whisper is frantic. "What do we do?"

"Get down!" I pull at his elbow, dragging him under the desk. We cram our bodies up against the solid wall, scrunching our knees against our chests to try and make ourselves as small as possible.

"We're dead." Chu drops his head into his hands.

"On the bright side, at least we won't have to walk far when they drag us into Realignment."

That gets Chu's attention. He looks at me, scandalized. "Not funny."

"Sorry."

There's a quiet whoosh at the end of the hall, followed by those unmistakable heavy boot steps. I hold my breath. Chu tenses as Fuschious's steps approach our hiding place. I fight back an overwhelming panic. It doesn't help that the nightmare memories of Fuschious's slap start replaying in my brain. The Lover is only a few meters from our hiding place when the doors open for a second time. Lighter, softer footsteps enter the hall.

"Lover Fuschious?"

The heavy boots stop right on the other side of the desk. There's a small squeak that I guess is Fuschious swiveling on the tiles.

"Dorm Leader."

"Thanks be to you for your presence."

"May you follow your dreams and find yourself in the universe. What do you want?"

"I need to speak to you about the Realignment subjects."

"Go ahead."

"As you know, Executive Crucible was here yesterday for an inspection."

"Really?"

"Yes. It seems *someone* suggested to him that there might be some . . . untoward activity . . . happening in the Elite Academy."

"Surely not."

"You are a bad actor, Lover Fuschious."

"Well, we all know you are the worst Dorm Leader this Academy has ever seen. Too soft, for a start."

"Executive Crucible did not seem to agree with you."

"Well." I never knew it was possible for one word to hold so much venom. Somehow, Fuschious manages it.

"So you still answer to me for the time being."

"Yes, Dorm Leader." Lover Fuschious's voice sounds as if he's speaking through clenched teeth.

"Tell me about the subjects."

"They are all proceeding according to plan, Dorm Leader."

"What exactly *is* the plan, Lover Fuschious? Did you receive direct orders from Crucible to be so extreme in your treatments?"

"No, but . . ."

"So you just took it upon yourself to use heavy cerebral measures in the discipline of Apprentices?"

"I am doing what is best for the Collective, Dorm Leader."

"Realignment was supposed to be a mild corrective, not a wholesale recalibration and memory wipe."

Memory wipe? I mouth the words to Chu. Chu's eyes go wide and he covers his mouth to stifle a horrified gasp.

"Executive Crucible didn't seem to disagree with that aspect of my treatment, Dorm Leader. Or are you setting yourself up against the Executive so quickly after they've left the building?"

"Not at all."

"I said it before. You are too soft to be Dorm Leader."

"You are too hard." Akela's voice is strong with emotion.

"If it is for the good of the Collective, then no harm is done."

"Except to those brilliant young minds."

"They should have thought more carefully before disobeying Love Collective directives."

"Realignment is not Embracement, Fuschious. We do not dispose of Haters here."

"Prevention is better than cure."

There's a small beep, and the security door near our heads opens with a click and burst of air, like opening an airlock.

"Consider this a spot inspection, Fuschious. If I find one hint of harm to any of my Apprentices, you will be demoted to a Nursery Dorm janitor so fast you won't even have time to blink. If I can remove you from drill practice, I can remove you from this too."

"As you wish, Dorm Leader." I've heard Lover Fuschious sound displeased before, but not like this. His words bubble through a seething cauldron of hate.

As their footsteps pass our hiding place, both of us cram ourselves further back, clinging to the shadows. The security door makes a soft beep, and the footsteps pass from the hallway into the next room. There's a hiss and click, and the door closes again.

When there is no further sound, I let out a long breath that I didn't realize I was holding. Beside me, Chu trembles.

"She's . . . she won't even know who I am," he says, disbelief and shock etched across his brow.

I pat him on the shoulder. "Dorm Leader won't let that happen. You heard her."

"What if it already has?" He looks up at me, and tears fill his eyes.

"She won't forget you."

The promise is empty, and Chu and I both know it. He pulls his knees tightly against his chest, burying his face against them.

I hoist myself into a kneeling position. On one of the security screens, Lover Fuschious and Akela have walked to the circle of desks, and Akela is leaning over a console while a medic talks. Fuschious stands behind them, arms folded and a stony frown carved into his face.

"We've got to go," I say.

Chu rises beside me. "I want to see what happens."

"We can't. If they catch us here, we'll be Realigned for sure."

Chu's eyes brim with tears. "Maybe I should let them catch me. Then I could forget her too."

26

Nursery Induction Manual
Catechesis volume 1, page 12.

> *Q: Who is our Supreme Leader?*
>
> > *A: Supreme Lover Midgate is our leader and friend.*
>
> *Q: What is the role of our Supreme Leader?*
>
> > *A: Supreme Lover Midgate is our Carer. She is the protector of our peace. The guardian of our safety. The source of our life and light. Without our Supreme Lover, we are lost in chaos, hate, and darkness.*

CHU WITHDRAWS EVEN FURTHER INTO himself after that. I throw myself into Filtering study, filling as much of my waking time with revision as I can. I search my infotab library for any hints on how to become a Watcher, but details are sketchy. The mystery around the Watchers' cadre just deepens with every search. I find brief descriptions of them in an article titled "Hall of Love Hall of Fame," but apart from the fact that they are very wealthy and very secretive, there are no hints on how I can get in. Hodge's words keep rattling around in my head: *Forget the last one. It's too hard to get into.*

I'm too stubborn to let Hodge be right.

Three days later, Sif returns. We're gathered in the assembly atrium after morning announcements. She approaches us from a side hall, arms wide and a huge grin on her face.

"I'm here! Didja miss me?"

We all shout and crowd in around her, giving her big hugs and high fives. She laps it up, the familiar old Sif smile lighting up her face.

"We were so worried about you," I say, looking into her eyes for any signs of damage.

She stares at me for half a second too long, and I see a flicker of something I can't define. Her smile is just a little too bright. Her face is just a little too . . . too . . . I can't quite put my finger on what it is.

"I'm fine. Glad to be with you guys again." She beams at us.

"Tell us everything!" Pim says as Lee knocks her aside to crowd in beside me.

"Did they suck your brain out and put it back again?" Lee is staring at Sif, seemingly searching for zombie evidence.

"Don't be an idiot, Lee." Cam gives Lee a withering look. "I'm sure Sif doesn't want to talk about Realignment. Not when she's got much better things to think about. Like exams!"

"Exams? Ugh." Sif makes a disgusted face.

"But it's the Filtering exam!" Cam exclaims. "The big one that gets you choosing where you're going to spend the rest of your career!"

"It will be fine, Cam. I've got it all up here." Sif taps her forehead. "Never felt better."

I give her a little reassuring pat on the shoulder. "We were worried you wouldn't make it back in time. Lover Tinks has been cramming our heads with more code than you can imagine and—"

"Don't worry about me, Kerr. I'll be fine. You don't need to know how to code in the Love Squad."

"Wait. Love Squad? I thought you were heading for Pleasure Tribe. You were so good at the gymnastic drills, and you said—"

"I was always going to be in the Love Squad, Kerr." Sif's tone is so harsh that our whole group freezes in shock. I catch Cam's alarmed expression across the circle. Pim gives a nervous little giggle.

Stupidly, I press ahead. "But you said you felt like a bird flying up there on the trapeze. You were—"

She turns to me, eyes flashing. "I don't care what you think I said. Listen to what I'm saying now. The Love Squad is where I fit best. You aren't trying to distract me from serving the Love Collective where I fit best, are you?"

I open and close my mouth like a goldfish. The sudden flip in Sif's expression and tone has knocked all the words out of me.

Lee steps into the awkward silence. "You do you, Sif. Whatever gets you excited to get out of bed in the morning," he says. "Besides, I'll be glad to have someone other than the twins to train with."

"Elites focus on the goal, not the game, Lee."

Lee gives a half-mocking salute. "Yes, Apprentice Sif."

For a tense moment, we all share side glances. Sif's face is like stone. She captures each one of us in turn with a steely, penetrating stare. When the tension doesn't seem like it can get any worse, she erupts in a loud laugh.

"Gotcha!" she crows, poking Lee in the stomach. "You thought I was going to report you as a Hater, didn't you?" She gives Pim an exaggerated wink.

Lee hesitates for a moment, uncertainty etched across his face. "Oh, you got me! Good one. And we thought Realignment was going to turn you into a monster," Lee replies with an edge in his voice. We laugh—tense and uncertain.

"But it did," Sif deadpans. Like the flick of a switch, our laughter stops. Then she cocks her fingers at us all. "Huh?

Huh? Gotcha again! Come on. Haven't we got a class to be in or something?"

We turn toward the hallway, and I finally see him. Chu is leaning against a wall, clasping and unclasping his hands in front of him. He starts up toward Sif, but she sweeps past him as blindly as if he was a janitor. Chu visibly wilts, and my heart goes out to him. I let the rest of the group go ahead. He clears his throat.

"S-she doesn't remember," he stammers.

"Give her time, Chu. She's been in Realignment for weeks. I'm sure deep down she knows."

"Something's off. The way she looks at everyone, it's . . . it's just weird."

"She'll come around," I say with more confidence than I feel. I give him a little pat on the back.

Chu opens his mouth as if he's about to say something, but he closes it again. A hopeless heaviness seems to weigh down his shoulders. "Thanks, I guess."

He gives a deep sigh, and we wander to class behind everyone else. I make sure we keep extra distance between us and Sif's determined march.

SOMEONE'S POUNDING ON A DOOR. Yelling. The nightmare is back again. Why can't I wake up?

"Cadence? Cadence!"

Sharp pain stabs my temple. A silver tree pendant dangles in front of my eyes, catching tiny glimmers of light from a crack in the door. Someone is holding me in their arms, crushing me against the soft, warm surface of their clothing. Their chest rises and falls with panicked breaths. Urgent whispers flutter into my ears.

"Cadence, these people want you to forget. Never forget him, Cadence."

Pain shatters the darkness, splitting my head into a million tiny pieces. Rough, gloved hands are pulling me away. Searchlights burn into my eyes. Thundering shouts fill the hallway, barked commands through the upper floor of a suburban home. A child's cry echoes into the sky.

"Target acquired. Bedroom one."

"Roger. Transportation protocol: go."

"No, no, *no!*"

Screams fade into quiet sobs, tearing my heart with panic and pain. I kick my feet and writhe with every muscle in my body. I'll never be safe if they get me. My feet connect with something solid, and then everything goes black.

Somewhere beyond my splintering skull, a distant siren wails.

THE WARNING FLASHES ON MY INFOTAB in the middle of a Pleasure Tribe lesson.

> *Apprentice Kerr Flick,*
> *Proceed to Dorm Leader's office immediately.*

My heart sinks. I'd been dreading this moment since I ran from her office. After embarrassing Akela in front of Executive Lover Crucible, I was sure I'd be expelled on the spot. For some weird reason Dorm Leader left me alone. But apparently she didn't forget.

Seeing my infotab display, Lover Weekes waves me out the door before I can ask. Sif glances expressionless at me from the corner where she's retreated all lesson. I give her a quick

grimace and head up to the executive level. The outer door to
Dorm Leader's office swings open even before I move my wrist
over the ID scanner, and my mood drops even further.

Wil is not in his usual spot behind the reception desk, but
Akela's door is wide open. I shuffle forward, hoping that this is
not going to be my final moment of freedom before Realignment.
Dark thoughts of doom flitter across my imagination: Akela
will banish me for the dreadful sin of humiliation in front
of the Supreme Executive. She'll say, "Wanted to see what
Realignment looked like, did you? Well, now you'll experience
it for yourself!" The whole Academy will line up to laugh me out
the door as I head back to my Nursery Dorm and eternal shame.

The glass walls of her office reveal a gloomy, cloudy
afternoon. Foggy patterns of grey and white battle each other
in swirling formations across the sky. Dorm Leader sits behind
her desk, waiting for me with hands folded on the table and
a solemn expression on her face. She makes a small gesture
across her console, and the doors slam shut behind me.

"Thanks be to you for your presence, Dorm Leader." I snap
my feet together in salute.

Dorm Leader motions me forward without the approved
lexicon reply. "Sit."

"Yes, Dorm Leader." Heart pounding I obey. My hands
tremble, and I grasp the arms of the chair until my knuckles
turn white.

"You have some explaining to do."

My mouth goes dry. I lean forward, hands clasped in
supplication. "I-I am sorry, Dorm Leader. I forgot myself, and I
apologize for shaming you, and it was—"

"The matter regarding Crucible was dealt with, and Wil
explained your plight."

I start to wonder what Wil could possibly have said to Dorm
Leader about my so-called "plight," but I don't get much of a
chance. Dorm Leader keeps talking.

"Kerr, you were foolish, and in the normal run of events I would be forced to order a strict course of discipline for your abhorrent behavior. But right now, I want you to explain to me what on earth possessed you to go to the very entrance of the Realignment chambers."

I try and totally fail to keep embarrassment and confusion away from my face. My mouth still drops open. "How—"

"Oh come on, Apprentice. Do you really think that anything you do in this dorm can escape the attention of the Dorm Leader? I thought you were smarter than that."

I hang my head, staring at my knees. "I embrace myself in penitence, Dorm Leader."

"Embracement is precisely the thing I am trying to avoid, Apprentice," she snaps. Something in her voice seems out of place.

I look back at her face, but all I see is a smooth mask of disapproval.

"What were you doing with Apprentice Chu in the hallway leading to the Realignment chamber?" Akela asks.

I become fascinated with my knees again, picking absently at a nonexistent blemish in the fabric of my uniform. "Sif was in Realignment for a long time. Weeks. We were . . ." I trail off. Chu's devastated face appears in my memory again. His pain is in every corner of his eyes and in every muscle around his downturned mouth. I feel a strange sense of warmth toward him. He's wounded. I need to protect him, not betray him. "She was away for too long. *I* wanted to find out when she would be back."

"That is all?"

"Yes, Dorm Leader. I was just curious."

"There is an ancient saying, Apprentice: curiosity killed the cat."

"I do not understand, Dorm Leader. What is a cat?"

Dorm Leader's face crumples. She turns away with a

swiftness that surprises me, and steps up to the library behind
her desk. Her fingers travel toward the book she produced at
our last meeting but refrain from touching it. Instead, she leans
both hands against one of the shelves, her back to me.

"Did I say something wrong?" I ask.

"A cat . . ." Dorm Leader's voice is low and agitated. "A
simple cat . . ."

"I am sorry, Dorm Leader."

When Dorm Leader turns back to me, she leans against the
bookshelf as if needing it to hold her upright.

"Kerr, the Realignment chambers are under the command
of Lover Fuschious. Did you know that?"

"Yes, Dorm Leader."

Pushing herself away from the books, she steps back to her
chair and sits down. "Then you would also be aware that he is
no particular fan of yours?"

"Yes, Dorm Leader, although I don't know why he—"

"Fuschious does not like to look bad in front of Apprentices.
You humiliated him in your first lesson."

"Oh." The look on Fuschious's face back at the drill fields
was already burned into my mind. I knew I shouldn't have said
anything, but Memory Freak just had to open her big mouth . . .

"He would love nothing better than to make an example
of you, Apprentice. If I hadn't happened on you that morning
in the hallway, he most certainly would have hauled you into
Realignment on some trumped-up truancy charge. Yet instead
of staying away from him, you walk right into his spider's web
wearing a 'Pick me!' sign. You are incredibly fortunate to still
have a brain!"

Sif's strange, hostile expression wafts across my thoughts,
along with a stab of grief. Against my will, my mind gives
me an unwanted image of me being forced into one of those
Realignment beds until I look just like my best friend. I shake
my head to try and dislodge the thought.

"But you're the Dorm Leader," I blurt. "Aren't you in charge?"

"Apprentice, you know the precepts and rules of Elite Academy. There are corners of this place where even I cannot overrule. If you were recorded as a rule breaker, then by Love Collective precept you are automatically out of my jurisdiction."

"Oh," I say, feeling incredibly small.

"Promise me." Dorm Leader's voice is laced with something I can't quite make out. "Promise me you will never go to that hallway again. Ever."

Her fierce gaze bores into mine.

"I promise, Dorm Leader."

"You must never go there, Apprentice. Do you hear me?"

I nod, struck dumb by the veil of tears brimming in her eyes.

27

Filtering Exam
Rationale

> *1.3 All Elites are superior, having a particular set of competencies and skills that set them above the general population. The Elite Academy shall filter Apprentices into specialized cadres at the earliest opportunity while not neglecting the broad education required for a truly well-rounded citizen.*

EXAM SCHEDULES ARE POSTED TO OUR infotabs, and within a week I've had enough of the reminders.

Five days to Filtering exam.

Four days to Filtering exam.

Three days to Filtering exam . . .

When the final reminder arrives—*Filtering exam today*—I wish I had more daily reminders left. I still haven't the faintest idea of how to get into the Watchers.

The walk to the VR chamber is long and tense. Rook and Arah lead the way, marching as if they're already in a drill line. Dona and Buff follow, unsmiling. Farr's the only one in the mood to talk. Her high-pitched chatter echoes around the hallway.

"I am *so* nervous, I think I'm going to faint!" she exclaims, looking healthier and stronger than I've ever seen her. Zin walks beside her, sullen and silent. As usual, Farr doesn't seem to notice. "I just know I'm going to fail the exam. I haven't done *nearly* enough study. Did you do the Pleasure Tribe practice? I kept getting stuck on question forty-seven. What answer did you get? The trajectory angles just didn't seem to match up no matter how many times I tried it. Although I don't know why we need to do such advanced theory calculations when—"

"Does she ever shut up?" Sif mutters. "First to Embracement, if I had the choice."

"Sif!" I say, shocked. "That's a horrible thing to say."

Sif just shrugs and keeps glaring at the back of Farr's head.

"Did you look at the Coding protocols?" Farr prattles. "I'm sure I've forgotten half of them already. But do you remember what they said in the third chapter of our manual? Argh! I'm so tense, I can't handle it! I was wondering—"

I glance back to see how the rest of my friends are doing. I catch Chu's worried expression, which is directed at Sif. He heard her, and like me, he's freaked out about it. I grimace. "What?" Sif is now looking my way. "What's that for?"

"Nothing." I try to neutralize my face. "You feeling okay about the exam?"

"Never better." She goes back to shooting imaginary lasers out of her eyes at Farr's head. The fact that she doesn't ask me how I'm feeling unsettles me. The old Sif would at least have pretended to care.

No, that's not right. The old Sif would have actually cared. I've seen Sif angry before, but never like this. It's as if all of her former fiery passion has been sucked out and replaced with cold, unrelenting steel.

Sif, what have they done to you? my heart cries.

"APPRENTICES MOUNT."

We step into our VR rigs as Lover Herz commands, even though we know the drill so well that most of us could follow her orders in our sleep.

"Headsets on."

The only sound our obedience makes is a quiet rustle across the room. A flutter of nervous coughs. The solid thud of my own heartbeat in my ears. This part we've all done before. What comes next, none of us knows.

My hands tremble as I fit my goggles on top of my head. It's hard to focus. I can't shake this ominous sense that I'm about to lose something really important.

"Good luck," whispers Cam from the neighboring station.

I give him a cheesy grin and a thumbs-up, pretending I'm not a complete wreck. He gives me a thumbs-up in return. His eyes look oversized through the transparent screen of his goggles. I turn back to the VR wall, butterflies doing drill marches in my stomach.

Everything is going to change from here. Filtering will send us into different specialties. We won't travel in the same group to the same lessons every morning, learning the same stuff together. From today, we move into our cadres for the rest of our lives. I'm sure at first we'll try and keep it together. But it won't be long, and we'll be too busy doing our own things to notice.

The realization lands on me like a sucker punch. On the other side of the room, Sif's back is turned to me. She stands perfectly still in the middle of her circle, like a powered-down drone. Pim fidgets with her helmet. Lee is doing a good impression of someone who doesn't care, even though I can tell he's nervous by the twitch in his hand. Beyond Cam, Chu seems a little more alive. He jumps from foot to foot, shaking his hands down by his sides.

"Cam?"

"Yeah, what?"

"Will you still talk to me when we're not in the same cadre?" I ask.

He blinks, surprised. "Why ask that? You gonna forget we exist?"

"Never."

"Then stop worrying. We're friends, all right? That's all there is to it."

I nod and smile, enveloped by a little warm glow. Cam gives me another thumbs-up and then turns back to his VR station. His words rattle around in my head. *We're friends, all right?* Not "Stay away, Memory Freak," or "You're weird, Memory Freak."

It's not so hard to put my VR headset on this time. No matter what changes are ahead, at least I'll have this one, precious jewel of a memory to replay.

A soft ding signals the countdown to the exam, and anxiety bubbles up in a torrent of unanswered questions. Is it going to be like Fitness to Proceed all over again? Or like combat practice? Am I going to fail this time? If I'm going to be a Watcher, what exactly do they want to see from me?

"Begin," drones an artificial voice through our speakers. The world spins into a black void.

A STREAM OF CODE FLOWS IN FRONT OF me like a river, never slowing or ceasing. I watch the patterns flow upward and out of sight. It's easy to tell what the code is for. It's beautiful. I'm just not sure whether I'm supposed to contribute or applaud.

After a few minutes, I notice a strange glitch that creates a decaying loop in the program. I reach out with my finger, and the stream of code halts. Fascinated, I give a few experimental finger waggles. The flow of code follows, dancing around in front of me. I start to use my hands to scroll backward, swiping down with large, fluid movements. Eventually, the spot where the glitch first begins hovers in front of my eyes. I hold it in place with my finger, thinking through the next step.

"Now what?" I look around for a virtual keyboard like I had in Fitness to Proceed. Nothing appears. Wiggling my fingers to erase the letters doesn't work; it just jiggles them around.

Using my hand, I pluck a word out of the line, squishing it between my fingers. It explodes with a satisfying *plink*, and a flashing cursor appears beside the empty space in the line.

"Insert code . . ." I say, and the words flow in shining streams from my mouth into the space. I giggle like a little kid. Why was I worried? I could do this all day, and then some.

THE FILTERING EXAM DOESN'T STAY FUN for long.

No sooner have I fixed the code when I am transferred into a large Engine Room. Every nightmare scenario we practiced in class combines into one mutant disaster. A mountain of warning signals flashes with urgent, panic-inducing beeps. Apocalypse looms, and I have to solve it by moving units around like pieces on a chess board.

I never liked chess.

Heart pounding and panic rising, I wrestle dials and buttons and disaster simulations with shaking, sweaty hands. By some miracle I manage to switch off the final alarm, and the exam whisks me into a Pleasure Tribe test. Surrounded by plush pink cushions, I get to spend time identifying some of the more famous members. My answer on Carrell Hummer covers several screens. After that, the exam gives me a few entertainment apps to design, then I am applauded out of the Pleasure Tribe center by a crowd of AI pleasure-seekers.

When the parties and acrobats fade away, the VR snaps me into a wide avenue that I vaguely recognize. As soon as my feet touch the ground, a distant riot of protestors in Haterman masks runs toward me, loud, guttural screams bouncing in nightmarish echoes off skyscraper walls.

"Love City," I murmur. The rioters charge up the hill. Behind me stand the filigreed gates of the Hall of Love. It's just me and a line of Love Squad soldiers standing between order and chaos.

"You're all dead!" screams one Hater as he rips off his mask. His face is twisted in a fearsome rictus of loathing, and his eyes bore into me. In his hands, he brandishes a long, nail-encrusted plank.

I nod, and a red heads-up display materializes in front of my face:

Welcome, Commander Flick.

"It's like that then, is it?" I murmur. I pull up memories of the Love Squad procedure manual. Chapter 18: Riot-Quelling Tactics. Back when we studied it, I thought it was a relic of the old battles against hate. Right now, I'm glad I read it. Memory Freak to the rescue again.

"Awaiting orders, Commander!" yells a soldier beside me. The screaming horde is about a hundred meters away. They fill the street, bearing placards and screaming obscenities. Small, dark projectiles lob up over the heads of the protestors. Those rocks won't kill us, but even in armor, they'll hurt.

"Deploy road shields!" I yell, knowing that the command will be relayed through every helmet. "That'll give us a few extra seconds." On cue, a series of blue-glowing barriers rise from the street. A few projectiles fizzle on the edges of the shields. The riotous crowd surges toward them.

"Countermeasure one! On my mark!" I yell.

As one, the line of soldiers hunches forward. They turn crowd-control cannons toward the shields. A similar cannon materializes in my own VR hands.

"Dissuasion aim, mark!"

We angle the weapons upward, aiming just above the protestors' heads.

"Dissuasion fire!"

The powerful weapons kick back along the line with a satisfying thump. A stream of glowing yellow bundles shoots out over the crowd. Like a blooming fireworks display, electrified nets spread open in the air, forming graceful circles as they descend. Wherever the nets land, Haters fall to the ground in writhing heaps, immobilized by electricity.

"Reload!" I shout. On my command, another row of electric nets soars out. Soon there are hundreds of incapacitated enemies, shuddering in little heaps on the road. Here and there, wherever an unsuspecting rioter steps on a net, they fall down, electrified. The flow of Haterman masks hiccups, then comes again. Angry shouts swirl around us even louder than before.

"Countermeasure two! On my mark!" I scream.

At the command, the line of soldiers loads a series of grenade-style canisters into their cannon. I've read about these steps in my manual, so I know in theory that each countermeasure rises in severity. I just hope it works in practice.

"Immobilization aim, mark!"

This time, we aim a little lower.

"Immobilization fire!"

With a solid thunk, launchers shoot canisters out in front of the rioters. The silver cylinders spin and clatter onto the road in front of the rioters' feet. With a hiss, they release bursts of white cloud up into the faces of the frontrunners. The effect on the riot behind them is chaotic. Choking and spluttering, the leaders collapse, grasping at their faces and necks. Those at the back continue to press forward, unaware of what has happened to their leaders. But those closer to the action begin to turn back, fleeing the fate of those now writhing in front of them. The groups meet in the middle, and scuffling begins to turn to fighting. Shouts directed at the Hall of Love become screams of panic aimed at former allies.

"Let's repeat that one more time," I say. "Immobilization aim, mark!"

The soldiers obey orders, and another round of gas canisters lobs into the confused mob. Scuffling escalates into violence. In their panic, the rioters tear each other apart to get away.

"Awaiting orders, Commander!" repeats the soldier beside me.

"Let them duke it out for a while," I say. "They're doing our job for us at the moment."

Sure enough, the pile of heaving, fighting Haters diminishes, replaced by a growing number of bodies. When there are only a few left standing, I move to the next level of the protocol.

"Send out a clean-up crew to mop up any Haters who try to escape," I say. "Arrest the rest."

The Love Squad fans out down the street toward the Haters. Down the road and behind the mob, large black vans emerge onto the boulevard and spew forth more black-clad soldiers. The riot is over.

As the artificial sunlight dims, I let out a long breath. It's good to have survived the onslaught, but I hope I never have to experience it for real.

"Can the next one be a theory exam, please?" I ask no one in particular.

28

Nursery Induction Manual
Catechesis volume 2, page 77.
    Q: Who are the allies of the Love Collective?
    A: The Allies of the Love Collective are its
    citizens, who live by Love Collective precepts
    and build their lives around loyalty to the
    Supreme Executive.

THE WHITE ROOM IS DAZZLINGLY EMPTY, apart from a single white armchair. At first glance, the tall wingback chair also appears to be empty. Then I notice the feet, crossed primly below the gap at the bottom. Putting on my best drill march, I approach the front of the chair. My stomach lurches. I wheel and snap my feet together, stopping in front of the now-familiar white uniform and piercing blue eyes of Supreme Lover Midgate. I look for the telltale evidence that I am speaking to an AI edition of the Supreme Lover, but I cannot tell. Unlike my clunky VR avatar, she is in pristine, ultra-high definition. I give her the proper level of respect in my bow and salute anyway.

"Thanks be to you for your presence, Supreme Lover Midgate." I keep my focus on a spot just in front of her feet.

"And to you, Apprentice Flick. May you follow your dreams

and find yourself in the universe." Supreme Lover Midgate watches me, letting the moment stretch out until it's just beyond comfortable.

"Well done, Apprentice," she says finally. "You are about to undergo an exam that is tailored specifically to your test scores so far."

"Yes, Supreme Lover."

"What cadre do you wish to enter, Apprentice?"

The back of my throat goes dry, and my next words come out in a strangled croak. Argue my case to the Supreme Lover? Are they mad?

"If it pleases you, Supreme Lover, I wish to be a Watcher."

"And why do you wish to be in that cadre?"

"Because it is the Elite of the Elite, Supreme Lover. I have always wanted to succeed as an Elite. What could be more Elite than a Watcher? They protect the Love Collective from their fortress in the Hall of Love. They are the best of the best."

Supreme Lover's expression does not change in the slightest. "What skills do you believe you possess that would make you an asset?"

"I have a good memory. I follow orders well. I work hard. I score nearly 100 percent on every single test. I am smart. I am loyal. I can fulfill any of the requirements the Watchers cadre may need. I will not let you down."

"Your desire is to be a Watcher?"

Nervous excitement pushes my mouth into a smile. "Yes, Supreme Lover."

"Very well."

As fast as a blink, the scene shifts. We stand in a windowless, darkened room in front of a wall of screens that stretch high above my head. In front of the screens stands a single command console. Supreme Lover waves me toward it, and every screen winks into life.

"Welcome to the Watcher Room," Supreme Lover says.

I hold myself back from giving a little excited squeal. This is it. This is what I've been wanting since I arrived. Not just an Elite, but the Elite of the Elite. Could it be true? Could I really be getting what I've wanted for so long?

I let my eyes rove from one screen to another and realize I'm staring at a wall of surveillance footage. There is the Coding classroom. Up on the top is the dining hall. To the left are the drill fields and obstacle courses. I spot Cam, tall and angular, walking beside Chu down the avenue of trees that leads to the combat arena. In another screen, Lee and Pim march in perfect unison down the center of the drill field. Supreme Lover Midgate stands beside me.

"Find the Hater."

"Yes, Supreme Lover."

I step up to the command console. Controls on the screen allow me to select a screen, zoom in, turn on the sound, or freeze the vision. For a few minutes I flick from screen to screen, enjoying the feel of the controls beneath my fingers. It's even more fun than the Coding exam. I could do this all day, no problem.

Life at the Elite Academy plays out before me in ultra-high definition. Somewhere around my friends should be a figure that doesn't belong. I just have to find it. But as I scan the footage, a disturbing truth begins to invade my contentment.

"There are only my friends here," I stammer.

"Find the Hater."

I take another look at my friends onscreen, confused. Even when the camera flicks to the dining hall in the middle of lunch, all other Apprentices have been erased from the vision. No Lovers, either. Just Lee and Pim, Cam and Chu, Sif and me. Has the Hater been hiding behind a tree somewhere? Maybe I missed it.

As if in answer to my unspoken question, the screens all flick to the drill fields. My friends wheel and stomp along the grass, isolated in a wide open space. Large gaps yawn in the places where our classmates should be. We look weird, spaced out at random. But it's really obvious now, and I begin to feel a little sick.

"One of my friends is a Hater?"

"Find the Hater."

I swallow. Hard. If there are only my friends in this vision, that means . . .

"Hater in a pile of Haters," I mutter.

"Is there a problem, Apprentice?"

"No, Supreme Lover," I lie.

Clutching at my stomach to hold back the desire to vomit, I scan the screens. Memories of thousands of Hater Recognition lessons float back:

The Love Collective's Infallible Signs of a Hateful Non-Citizen:

1. Doubt

2. Chaos

3. Speech

4. Allegiance

5. Appearance

I curse myself for being so stupid. Midgate's simple question has ensnared me more effectively than any Love Squad countermeasure. If I want to be a Watcher, this is the price I have to pay.

A Watcher needs to be able to betray their closest friends.

Directly in front of me, one surveillance cam shows Sif and me in a familiar bathroom. She leans toward me. I don't need to turn on the sound. Her words have repeated themselves over and over in my head since that night.

You're never not being watched.

On the next screen, I see myself chasing Sif out of our Engine Room simulation. It's surreal to watch us standing alone in the hallway. Crowds jostled me that day. Now I see myself moving and jolting at nothing. Every other human has been edited out of the picture.

Hater Recognition Sign 3.6: Haters who cannot control their tongues should have their voices removed.

Sif stands in the combat training compound, staring at the empty space where Lover Kalis had been. The six of us surround her in an abstract arrangement, without the presence of Zin and our other classmates. I'd laugh if my task wasn't so nauseating. Onscreen, Sif's face scrunches into an angry scowl.

"Grohns. To my office. Now," Lover Kalis had said.

The Lover isn't visible here, but it's impossible to mistake the word that spits from Sif's mouth. "No."

Hater Recognition Sign 2.2: Haters do not abide by the good and stable laws enacted by the Supreme Executive.

On a split screen, Sif sits in a research pod beside a screen capture of her infotab. She types search strings that make my heart sink: Surveillance. Love Collective rebellions. Hacking. Ways to escape the Elite Academy.

Hater Recognition Sign 4.2: Haters wish to tear down our peace and prosperity.

I grasp at straws. "Supreme Lover, this is old footage. Realignment—"

"State Hater Recognition Sign 2.5, Apprentice Flick."

It takes everything I have to stop from doubling over and vomiting up the contents of my stomach. Stiff with effort, my words come out in robotic, dead tones.

"Hater Recognition Sign 2.5: Haters cannot learn peace."

The footage flicks on each of the screens, and I scan them over and over, looking for some way out. On every screen, Sif is the key player. Whether I'm present or not, she's doing her best to set herself up for the worst possible fate. The first person to treat me like a human instead of a memory freak. The one who listened to me, walked beside me, defended me when I wasn't in a position to defend myself. She might look like angry alien Sif now. But that doesn't mean she stopped being my best friend.

"Have you found the Hater?"

Sif or Watcher. A simple choice, really: the life of my best friend in exchange for the job of my dreams and riches I can only imagine. I scratch absently at the control panel and send a wave of cameras zooming into the distance. The stress of the decision is too much to bear.

Tendrils of pain begin to play along the sides of my temples, like lightning streaking across a night sky. My forehead blooms with sharp, jagged pain accompanied by the sound of unforgettable screaming . . .

Oh no.

It's all the warning I get before everything goes dark.

MUMMA SAYS THAT WHEN THE BAD PEOPLE *come, we have to hide. She says that I must not cry, and I must not be loud, and I must always, always, always stay small like a mouse. If I stand big and tall, or if they see me out the window, the bad people will get me, Mumma says, and if the bad people get me, then Mumma won't see me again. That would make Mumma very sad.*

"HAVE YOU FOUND THE HATER?" DRONES A soft, lilting voice beside me.

"Wha-what?" I stammer, rubbing at my forehead. I'm in two places at once: a darkened room full of screens, and a strange dwelling with cozy rooms and a smell of fresh soup.

Two women stand beside me. One clad in simple white linen, and the other with a smudge of flour over her forehead and a smile like home. When I close my eyes, Midgate disappears and my mother is all that I see.

IN OUR HIDING PLACE BEHIND THE CLOSET, *Mumma holds me close and hugs me.*

"Can you crouch like a mouse, sweetie?" Mumma says. She shows me how to do it.

"Yes, Mumma. See?"

"Good girl. Now let's see how quiet you can be, my darling. I am going to stand outside and stomp around. And I want to see how quiet you can be when I am stomping. Can you do that?" Mumma looks at me with her serious face.

"I will try, Mumma."

Mumma goes outside, but her stomps are so funny that it makes me laugh.

But then Mumma frowns at me. "Please try. This is not a game!" She starts to cry, and her whole body shivers but not with cold shivers, and I get scared.

I do try to be quiet, but I don't like hiding. I want to be in the sunshine.

MY EYELIDS FLUTTER, AND A WALL OF screens slowly comes into focus again. There's a woman standing beside me, clothed in white. Her face is impassive and cold.

"Have you found the Hater?" she asks.

I stare at the screens, stupid with incomprehension. On the closest screen Sif stomps down a hallway, alone. She glances straight at the camera, and her face twists with fury.

My mind is caught in a whirl. What did I just see?

A house, not a dorm. A house with a hidden closet. Nothing to do with Sif at all. Except . . .

Like floodgates opening, an overwhelming torrent of emotions rushes through me. I stare at the VR screen room, uncomprehending. I had a mumma. A mumma who was trying to get me away from the Collective. A mumma who . . .

"Have you found the Hater?" Supreme Lover repeats.

A slow, consistent alarm tone rings through my headset. Like an automaton, I begin reciting Hater Recognition Signs. In my mind, I'm back in a darkened space. A silver pendant dangles in front of my face while a woman holds me close to her body. My heartbeat begins to race, matching the pace of her panicked breaths. Outside our hiding place, a night bird hoots.

"Hater Recognition Sign 3.6: Haters who cannot control their tongues should have their voices removed."

Darkness. Screams. Mummamummamummamumma . . .

"Have you found the Hater?"

The bank of vidscreens stares back at me in a hundred displays of Sif's disloyalty. It's painfully obvious what I need to do. But I'm paralyzed.

"Hater Recognition Sign 4.3: Haters must be Embraced for the good of our society."

Another stab of memory flutters just beyond my grasp. Something about Mumma's eyes . . .

"Hater Recognition Sign 2.2: Haters do not abide by the good and stable laws enacted by the Supreme Executive."

"These Hater Recognition Signs are good, Apprentice. Are they leading you to find the Hater?"

I don't answer, too busy drowning in a sea of memory. Lyric. The one we sang about. Why did I forget him? Where did he go all these years? Lyric, who appeared to me in a dream and told me to find Akela . . .

Akela. Mumma's eyes. This time, the flood of nausea and memory leaves me gasping for air. A trickle of blood. A woman standing proud under the pounding thumps of a Love Squad soldier. The Haters' Pavilion crowd screaming for her death. Did Dorm Leader know when she was probing my memory that she was asking me to remember the public execution of my own mother?

Of course she did.

I sway on my feet. "Could I have a recess, Supreme Lover?"

Through the fog of emotion and nausea, I try to wrestle my inner world into some sort of logical list:

1. Supreme Lover wants me to report my best friend as a Hater.

2. If I do not report Sif, I will never be a Watcher.

3. My mother was a Hater.

4. I had a mother.

"Time is running out, Apprentice. I need your answer now."

I nod, losing the battle against my tears. My whole world is crashing down around me. I let out my breath in a long, shaking sigh.

"I have found the Hater."

SUPREME LOVER MIDGATE SMILES WITH soft invitation. *It will be all right,* her expression seems to say to me. *Tell me everything, and you will be fine.* Her eyes are as cold as an Arctic iceberg, glittering and calculating.

One little word. It's all I have to say.

I hug my arms around my chest, biting my lip. The wall of images plays on, glowing with its unspoken accusations.

Directly in front of me, a camera zooms in on Sif, snuggling in beside Chu. She smiles a glowing smile, and he grins back at her.

It's obvious what Midgate wants me to do. But I can't. Not at this price. Especially now that I know what made Sif so angry.

"Have you found the Hater?"

"I want to make sure."

The woman beside me says nothing. I can almost feel the judgment radiating off her skin. After all, this shouldn't be a tough decision. I'll be a Watcher. Elite of the Elite. No longer little Memory Freak of Nursery Dorm 492. Richer than I could ever dream.

As many hamburgers as I can eat, Sif would say. The memory brings another wave of aching nausea. That was her dream, not mine. My dreams keep throwing me back into a home I didn't know I had. What future could I possibly have as a Watcher with that secret in my head?

A line of screens blacks out, replaced with a countdown clock. Time counts backward in violent red numbers. Each second is marked with a screeching beep. I shift from foot to foot. Akela knew who my mumma was. She knew, and she didn't tell me. Is that what Wil wanted me to know? Is that the story I missed out on hearing? That I came from a disgraceful family and should be ashamed?

"One minute remaining," Supreme Lover Midgate drones. Sif is on every screen now. Vision taken from a thousand surveillance cams, her rage-filled scowl turned up at every single one of them. Seconds tick away. With hands flapping stupidly in front of me, I let out a panicked squeak.

"I know who the Hater is!"

At my exclamation, the countdown pauses mid-beep.

"Yes?"

"If I do not tell you, then I am a failure, aren't I?" I say, turning to my companion for confirmation.

The Supreme Lover looks at me with that same, soft

invitation. "Either you know the name of the Hater, or you don't."

"I cannot—"

"That is not an acceptable answer, Apprentice."

The beeps resume, and seconds count away. *0:10 . . . 0:09 . . . 0:08 . . .* Fear builds in my chest until I can no longer bear it. My head is a jumbled mess of memories and grief and fear. Mumma. Sif. Pain. Loss. The timer knows none of that and counts me down to failure: *0:05 . . . 0:04 . . . 0:03 . . .*

I let out a strangled yelp, and the words erupt from my mouth.

"The Hater is me!"

Everything goes dark. My self-accusation reverberates around my head in ominous echoes,

The Hater is me.

29

Hater Recognition Signs: A Primer for the Young
   4. Allegiance
        Haters must be Embraced for the good of
        our society.

FILTERING EXAM OVER, EXCITED CHATTER whirls around the hallway. It takes about ten seconds to discover that every student had a custom-made test, tailored to their own skills and interests. That sets off another bout of loud questions and nervous laughter.

"Did you have to do the acrobatics?"

"What about when those supply columns were compromised?"

"I could have died; I was so embarrassed!"

"What was that code supposed to do, anyway?"

"I forgot question thirty-two in the Engine Room theory exam. Did you have to do that?"

I wander through the middle of it, disconnected and miserable. Nobody has been through what I just went through. No one is casting furtive sideways glances at other people the way I am.

"I'm with you." Sif follows my gaze to where Dona and Buff are comparing their Love Squad tests.

My head swivels toward her. "What?" I exclaim, guilt pushing my volume way up.

"Talking about the exam. Waste of time, in my view," Sif adds.

"Oh, ha ha. Yeah. No point talking about it now, ha ha. It's all done and dusted, isn't it?" My arms swing in big arcs, and my shoulders take on a jaunty "Ho, ho, we are jovial today!" kind of bounce.

Sif gives me a suspicious look. "What's with you?"

"Nothing. Nothing at all." I try so hard to make my face look innocent.

She doesn't buy it. "Messed up, did you?"

If only you knew, I think. Heat suffuses my cheeks.

"You didn't . . . *fail,* did you?"

"What? Pfft. No, I just . . ." The words evaporate from the end of my tongue. I shrug, helpless.

"Don't want to talk about it?"

"Nope."

"Fair enough."

Cam bounds up to us, excited and eager. "Hey, what did you do in the Engine Room scenario? I was—"

Sif puts a hand up in front of his face. "We're an exam-free zone," she warns. "You can talk about anything except what went on back there."

He snaps his head back, surprised. "Oh. Okaaay." Hunching his shoulders, Cam falls into step beside us.

We walk along in silence for a few hallways. Nothing but white walls and clean white tiles below our feet. Shortly after, Chu falls into step beside Cam.

"So, how about this weather we're having, huh?" Cam remarks with a gleam in his eye.

"Think you're a comedian, do you?" Sif turns on him as Chu lets out a snort of laughter. She frowns at him. "Don't encourage him. He'll think we want him to keep going."

"Some friend you are." Cam gives her a little nudge.

The word stabs at me like a scalpel, piercing and sharp. "I'm sorry, I think I need to get to the bathroom," I stammer and take off at a run.

I CRASH THROUGH THE SWINGING DOOR, gasping for breath and fighting back stinging tears. The bathroom is cool compared to the hallway outside, but my face is hot. I push my way into a cubicle. With a sudden rush, the contents of my stomach heave into the toilet bowl. I am left sobbing, my knees feeling weak and shaky.

I sit on the floor, letting the cold from the tiles seep up through my clothes. Minutes pass. It's so cold that I begin to shiver. Reluctantly I get back onto my shaky feet and step out from the cubicle to the wall of mirrors. My reflection stares back at me, accusing.

"Idiot," I tell myself. The ever-present black bubble of the surveillance camera hovers on the ceiling like a silent judge. I lean over the basin to steady myself as a familiar wave of nausea washes over me again.

Footsteps echo down the hall outside. The sound of footsteps fades away, disappearing in the direction of the dining room. Nobody comes to check on me, and I don't know whether to feel relieved or rejected. My brain decides to keep both.

Hater, traitor, nightmare, failure.

A warning throb of pain stabs into my forehead. Still clutching at my collar, I heave myself out of the room, back into the corridor. The assembly atrium is just ahead. I stumble up the stairs and bolt across the open space, looking for the exit. A nightmare is coming. I've just got to hold it together long enough to get away from people. Got to—

"Apprentice Flick."

I stand to attention and swivel slowly, clasping my hands into hard-balled fists at my sides. My fingernails dig hard into my palms. The pain in my head increases in intensity. Screams sound in the back of my thoughts like a soundtrack playing through a distant speaker.

Notnownotnownotnownot . . .

Dorm Leader Akela is standing before me. "I have received your exam results."

I just nod, clamping my mouth shut. Sweat breaks out along the back of my neck.

"I would like to see you in my office."

I nod again, lifting a shaking finger to press hard against my temple. "Yes, Dorm Leader. I am . . . I am not feeling well. May I take . . . take a moment to rest . . . ?"

"Do you need to go to the infirmary?"

"No, I think . . . I think I just need a little bit of fresh air." The pain is making me squint.

Dorm Leader's eyes narrow, too, but she seems to be evaluating. Then she nods. "Go. Freshen up as you need to, then come upstairs."

Grateful, I stride out of the doors into the sunshine. The brightness of the warm sun increases the intensity of the pain in my head. Dumb idea to come out here then.

I stagger to the line of trees along the path, collapsing down into a small indentation between large, solid tree roots. The shade blocks out the worst of the brightness, covering me in dappled green.

Hidden from the Elite dorm windows, I lean back against the rough bark and let outdoor noises surround me. The earth hums. Bugs click and snap in the undergrowth. Somewhere overhead, a bird caws into the afternoon sky. My temple throbs in agony.

"Why are you doing this?" I say to my body. "Why can't you just behave like a normal person?"

Elites show no weakness.

Elites show no weakness.

Sweat clams up my palms, and a throbbing headache splits down my forehead like a bolt of lightning. It would be just my luck that after a nightmare of an exam, my brain throws me into another one. The memory of what I have just done won't go away.

I have failed everything an Elite should be. Weak. Unfocused. Disloyal. Hesitant. It's no wonder Dorm Leader wants me in her office. I bet they're preparing to welcome me back at Nursery Dorm 492 already. The welcome of shame and failure. Fit only to do the work of the Love Collective in some garbage dump somewhere.

But then, what else could you expect from the child of a Hater?

MEMORY DATE: UNKNOWN

Memory location: Unknown

Memory time: Unknown

I sit in the darkness, my knees curled up under my chin. Two warm arms fold themselves around my back, hugging me close. Mumma's heartbeat hammers in her chest. She squeezes me, and the prickle of her necklace stabs into my temple.

MY EMOTIONS WHIP UP INTO A SWIRLING tornado of shame and fury. Dorm Leader showed me that necklace. How dare she taunt me like that? Draw me into a trap. Get me to parade my mother's shame just to see if I knew anything. Was she laughing at me? Laughing at the stupid little Hater-spawn who didn't even know who she was. I bet she's happy now that I've confessed myself a Hater. Bet she can't wait to expel the taint on Elite purity.

MEMORY DATE: CE 2273.264 (8 YEARS AGO)

Memory location: Nursery Dorm 492

Memory time: 2037 hours

The Haters' Pavilion crowd bellows with rage. Hater One has lost her Hater mask, and she pulls herself up to a standing position for the fourth time. Despite the trickle of blood at the side of her head, she stares with quiet determination at the Love Squad officer in front of her. A chant begins to reverberate around the arena:

"Kill her now!"

"Kill her now!"

Carrell Hummer stands on his commentator's podium, explaining the scene for all of us.

"As you know, Lovelies, sometimes these Haters just don't know when to quit. So it's time for you to vote. Do we end this little scenario, or should we let this Hater keep showing us her rebellious hatefulness? You decide. The vote is up on your infotabs now!"

"NO. STOP!" I SNARL, SQUEEZING MY EYES shut to try and stop the mental vidscreen running forward. I still remember the pile of Nursery Dorm Apprentices falling over each other to tap their votes on their infotabs. But it's different now, knowing the person behind the screen. Knowing that I—

I push the nightmare memory to the side, gasping for breath. Gaze around me. Let the world flow into my thoughts and push away the darkness.

The sun has travelled toward the horizon, and the trees now cast long, spindly shadows. Gone are the afternoon smells of warm earth and sunshine. The breeze that rustles the leaves now carries a distant hint of the cold night ahead.

Dazed, I lift myself off the ground, brushing stray dust off the back of my uniform. The panic and nausea have finally dissipated, leaving behind a dull, heavy void. It's as if gravity has doubled its force, and every step is twice as hard.

I'm not ready to meet Dorm Leader yet. She betrayed me. Why else would she want me to remember Hater One on the Haters' Pavilion Show eight years ago? Akela played me so well I even betrayed myself. I guess I'll be sharing Mumma's fate after all. What a Haters' Pavilion Show that will be. Elite on the platform, daughter of a Hater? The crowds will bay for my blood.

Hater, traitor, nightmare, failure.

"Time to say goodbye," I sigh. It's not hard to imagine their faces when they learn the truth. Their disappointment will tear my heart in a million pieces, but there's nothing else I can do. Clean myself up. Wash the tears from my face. Then Akela can have me.

My feet shuffle in the direction of my bunk room—the slow march of a condemned prisoner. I argue with myself all the way back. No Hater is allowed to remain in the Elite Academy, let alone be allowed into the Watchers. I've failed my exam, plain and simple.

The Hater is me.

When I reach my room, my arms feel so heavy it becomes a

major effort to lift my wrist high enough to meet the ID panel. I'm shocked when the door slides open and a giggle of happy conversation flows out into the hallway. Bodies crowd the room, older roommates at the front.

Hodge, interrupted in his task of folding his towel, glances my way. "You look like you've seen a ghost," he says.

"Worse," I reply, stumbling past him toward my friends. They're all sitting on their bunks, chatting and joking together.

"There you are!" Pim exclaims. "We were just about to . . ." Her words trail off as she clocks the look on my face.

30

Nursery Induction Manual
Catechesis volume 2, page 49.

Q: What fate awaits a confirmed Hater?
A: A confirmed Hater will receive exactly the penalty they deserve. It is a heinous crime to dissent from the noble goals of the Collective.

IN THE SHELVES BESIDE MY BUNK ARE THE few items I own. I keep them neatly folded in prim regulation fashion: four Elite uniforms, two VR outfits, one formal dress uniform that I've never even worn. Towel. Bathroom items. Backpack with infotab. I sling my VR headset onto the shelf to complete my meager collection.

Not much to leave behind.

I came here to wash my face before leaving, but a heaviness in my limbs drags me down to my bed. I collapse into it with a sigh. I should be in Dorm Leader's office by now—the last march of a condemned Hater. But a deep weariness settles over me. My eyes droop and close, which is a dumb idea because there's nothing to stop the self-loathing from flooding back into to my head.

There's a gentle pressure on the mattress near my feet as someone sits down.

"Do you want to talk about it?" Pim asks from the end of my bunk.

I don't look at her. "I can't."

"It'll be okay." Her voice is gentle.

The snort of laughter is out of my mouth before I can stop it. "You wouldn't say that if you knew." I sigh.

"So try me."

I sit up. Fix her in my depressed stare. "I said I can't."

Pim leans back, offended. "Fine. I was just asking." With a flick of her black hair, she vaults away from me to her own bunk.

I draw my knees up to my chin, hugging my legs against my chest.

Cam bustles in from the bathroom, rubbing at the back of his wet hair with a towel.

"Hey, you," he says with warm affection.

I answer him with silence.

He stops, puts aside his towel, and sits down beside me. "Bad day, huh?"

I hate that I can't stop the tears from trickling out of my eyes. I keep my mouth tight, holding back a sob. All I can do is nod.

Cam's eyes soften. "Do you want to talk about it?" he asks.

From across the aisle, Pim laughs without mirth. "Good luck."

I scrub at my eyes, wiping the moisture across my cheeks, trying to erase any sign that I've lost control even for a second. Gulping back the sob, I give Cam a quick fake grin.

"I'll be fine," I lie. "I may not be here for much longer, but I'll just have to deal with that when the time comes."

Cam's eyes widen. "What? You can't have tanked the exam that bad!"

His shock drags a cynical laugh from my mouth. "You have no idea," I say with bitterness.

"Try me."

I hug my knees again, building up the courage to speak.

"It was all going well until I got to the part with Supreme Lover Midgate," I begin.

"No. Way." Cam's mouth drops open. "Hey Sif, did you meet Midgate in your exam?" he calls out to the room.

"Midgate? Who met Midgate?" Chu ducks his head into our conversation.

"I never saw Midgate." Lee jumps off his bunk. "Who saw Midgate?"

Cam waves toward me, and suddenly I'm in the middle of a huddle of people. Questions fly at me like bullets.

"Thanks for that." I glare at Cam, sarcasm heavy in my tone.

"What? So the Supreme Leader is an exam supervisor now?" Sif stands beside Lee, her arms folded. There's an element of envy in the look she gives me. "Why did you get the favored treatment?"

"It was a test," I reply, misery heavy on my shoulders.

"For someone who just had a brush with fame, you don't look too happy about it."

"That's because I failed." My words come out in a strangled sob.

Sif's snort of derision echoes around the chamber. "Failed? Some Elite you are," she looks at me with derision.

A hot flush of anger pushes me forward. The injustice of it all boils up and out of my mouth before I can stop it. "For your information, Sif, she wanted me to report you."

The shock ripples out across my friends like a stone dropping into a clear pond. Noise shuts off as if someone pressed a mute button. Even Sif looks rattled. Her eyes dart from side to side, but then she straightens her shoulders and glares at me.

"So why didn't you?" Her voice is clipped, defiant. The eyes of everyone in our dormitory room are on her. Their expressions range from horror to fascination and every imaginable combination in between. "If that's what our Supreme Lover wanted, why didn't you obey?"

A dull, heavy ache hits my stomach. "Because you are my friend."

She stares at me as if I hadn't just outed her as a suspected Hater to the whole room. "So friends trump the Love Collective? That's a pretty basic Nursery Dorm error, kid. You should know better than that. What did you say?"

"Nothing. Forget it. You're safe, all right? You're all safe."

Sif lets out an exasperated gasp. "I can't believe it. Supreme Lover is your only hope, Kerr. That's one of the Founding Principles of the Love Collective. It should have been an easy choice."

"Sif," Cam begins, but I talk over the top of him.

"Your life should have been an easy choice for me, Sif? Your *life*? You *wanted* me to sell you out?"

"If I was a Hater, then my life in the Love Collective is forfeit anyway." Her shrug cuts me down more effectively than a chainsaw.

"You already went to Realignment. It's old news. Not worth reporting."

"That's not the point. If Midgate wanted it, then you do it. What did she offer you?"

The depressed cloud hovers above me again. "Watcher."

I hear a shocked gasp from somewhere down the room, but I can't tell who let it out. Everyone is frozen, eyes glued to the two of us.

"Y-you had the chance to get into the Watchers, and you . . . didn't take it?" It's impossible to miss the jealous twist of Sif's mouth this time.

I return her stare, wishing with my entire being that she would understand. "The price was too high."

"Idiot." She stalks away from me toward the bathroom. Chu steps into her path, placing his hand gently on her arm.

"Sif, please, this isn't like you," he begins.

She freezes and then pointedly stares at the place where his hand rests near her shoulder. "Elites don't fraternize, boy." Sif scowls back up at him.

Chu drops his hand quickly but then regains control. Leaning against Lee's bunk, he puts on a dazzling smile. "Come on, Sif. That's not what you said when we were in the atrium that night. Remember?"

I haven't seen him smile like that for about a month. I stand up from my bunk, and his eyes flick toward me. For a split second I see his panic and worry, then they're gone as he turns his confident smile on Sif once more.

"I don't know what you are talking about." She grabs her towel and turns away.

Chu throws his hands up, pleading. "Sif, I don't know what they did to you in Realignment, but this isn't the Sif I know. You were Kerr's friend. *You* were the one who said we were going to be together. You—"

"I would never—*never*—say something like that. How dare you."

The pain is written so vividly across Chu's face that it makes me want to weep. "Y-you don't remember?" His words come out half choked.

"Elites show no weakness, Chu. Pick yourself up, and get over yourself. More important things to do." Sif's voice is cold.

The anger rises in my chest so fast that I jump to my feet. "Wait a second, Sif. You can't say that—" I don't get to finish, because she snarls over her shoulder at me.

"That's exactly what I'd expect to hear from a Hater."

My throat goes dry. "You take that back."

She turns around slowly, closes the distance between us. Fury glitters in her eyes. With a sharp poke of her finger, she prods me in the chest. "You. Don't. Deserve. To. Be. Elite."

Flutters of panic run up my spine. My horror grows as Zin falls in beside her.

"This Hater giving you trouble, Sif?" Zin says. A triumphant gleam fills her face.

"This has nothing to do with you, Zin," I reply through gritted teeth.

"Haters are everyone's responsibility. You know that, Kerr," Zin almost purrs at me. "Supreme Lover said it herself."

A presence approaches along the corridor behind me. Someone tall.

"Cam, back me up here," I say, assuming it's him.

"What's going on?" It's Hodge's voice throwing the question over my shoulder.

I spin around, and every hair stands up on my neck. Cam is way back down the hall, staring at us with horror.

"We're about to report a Hater." At Sif's words, I turn back in time to catch the wide smile on her face.

"You going to stop us?" Zin challenges, one hand on her hip. She's lost a little of her combative edge, however. It's nice that after all this time, Hodge still unsettles her.

"Not at all," he says. "We can only be free to love . . . and all that."

"Good. Shall we take her now, Sif?"

"Sounds like a plan to me, Zin." Sif nods. Hostility is the only emotion I can see in her eyes.

"I am supposed to be meeting Dorm Leader Akela," I protest. "She told me to meet her in her office an hour ago."

"Well, she can come and visit you in Realignment, can't she?" Sif takes a step forward.

Instinctively I step back, right into Hodge's brick wall of a chest.

"You're Fuschious's responsibility now," Sif says.

"As the room leader, what happens in this room is my responsibility, Sif," Hodge says. His heavy hand lands on my shoulder, reinforcing his point with a grip of steel. "If anyone is going to take her in, it should be me."

"But we were the ones who identified her," Sif argues. "We get credit, right?"

"Wait," Cam interrupts. "You're not serious. She hasn't done anything!"

"That's for the Lovers to decide," Zin snaps. "You should know it's a serious offense to interfere with a Hater apprehension operation."

"She's right, Cam," Hodge says.

"We can report you, too, Cam, if you really want." Sif's demeanor has turned her nearly unrecognizable. An alien has taken over my friend's body. A hostile, angry, froth-at-the-mouth kind of alien. She takes a threatening step toward Cam, but Hodge puts up a hand to stop her.

"Thanks for your report, Sif and Zin. I'll take her from here." Hodge's face is unreadable. He's all business, as if someone's asked him to look up the weather on his infotab. "Love all, be all."

"Love all, be all." The girls salute back.

"You'll make sure they know we're the source of the report?" Zin adds.

"They'll know," Hodge assures her.

"This is unbelievable," Chu mutters. But he won't look me in the eye.

"Hater! Hater!" Arah begins a chant, and Rook joins in. Dona's and Buff's faces become cold and angry.

"Apprentice Flick, you need to come with me," Hodge says. With a firm grip, he turns me toward the door.

I know better than to speak, but every inch of my body protests with silent screams. The twins' chant continues behind me.

As we reach the front of the room, Hodge turns and nods to the two bulky Love Squad Apprentices. "Loa and Yip, escort."

The two towers of muscle nod wordlessly, falling into line behind us. I'm hemmed in. There's no way to get a message to Dorm Leader now. My infotab sits neatly on my shelf way back at my bunk. I have no choice but to follow Hodge out of our room and down the corridor.

I don't even get to say goodbye.

31

Haterman, Haterman
Don't hate me.
I'm in the Collective,
Can't you see?

FOUR OF US MARCH DOWN THE HALL IN silence, even though my heart is a dark, swirling cloud of panic and pain. My best friend just sold me out in front of my whole dorm room. Correction: my *ex*-best friend. All the fun and *Sif*-ness is gone, replaced by some kind of Elite drone. Someone who can cry "Hater!" at her closest companions without breaking a sweat.

"Dorm Leader is going to be wondering where I am," I say, loud enough that I'm sure Hodge can hear.

He fiddles with his fitness tracker but apart from that gives no sign that he's heard me.

"It's like talking to a brick," I mutter at his back.

We ascend the stairs into an assembly atrium humming with life. The evening meal is not far away, and Elites mill around in small groups, heading for the dining hall. My stomach rumbles in sympathy, mixing with the stab of shame I feel. I use Loa and Yip as shields, angling my head so that it dips below their shoulders. Nobody can see me like this.

Hodge guides us outside. I can guess our destination; not long ago it was me leading Chu toward that white, sterile hallway. Fuschious is going to think all his dreams have come true when Hodge walks me into that place.

We step out from the protection of the glass walls onto a wide, paved path that leads to the drill fields. When we reach a large tree with boughs hanging over the path, Hodge swivels toward me, bringing us to a sudden halt.

"What—?" I start.

With large, warm fingers he grabs my wrist, holds it in both of his hands. I'm too stunned to struggle. Hidden beneath the palm of one hand, he releases the clasp of my fitness tracker, and it drops neatly into his waiting fingers. Without looking, he passes it to Yip, who flicks it onto her other wrist. She nods at him.

"What . . . what are you doing?" I ask.

"Shh," Hodge says between nearly closed lips. The fear in my heart is rapidly being replaced by confusion.

Still grasping my wrist, he leads me off the path and beneath the trees. "Tell X," he commands over my head. I turn in time to see Loa and Yip nod and melt away into the background. Confusion morphs into a vague sense of alarm.

Hodge marches me along the boundaries between outdoor areas. The obstacle course entrance looms over us. Hodge takes a sudden turn into it, walking me down a path reserved for the Lovers who supervise.

"We're going for some exercise?"

He doesn't answer. The shade of the trees has deepened now, casting dark patches between the trunks like open pits. The air smells like nighttime, damp and cool. Just after the third bend in the course, I stumble over a root, and Hodge catches me.

"Wait just a minute," I say, pushing myself back from his shoulders. "What do you think you are doing?"

Hodge grimaces, and a flush of red climbs from his neck to his cheeks. "Not what you think, obviously." He takes a step backward, putting his hands behind his back.

"Well, it's . . . I didn't . . . I mean, I—but this isn't the way to Realignment," I stammer. I'm sure my face has turned a fluorescent shade of red right now.

Hodge places one finger over his lips. With his other hand, he beckons me to a spot where the path runs beside a thicket. I've run past this point hundreds of times but never paid much attention before. It looks impenetrable.

When I hesitate, he rolls his eyes, exasperated. "Don't worry. Your person is safe in my presence. I won't lay a hand on you."

He ducks under a branch, heading for a dense patch of undergrowth. Following, I step into a miniature jungle. It's a struggle to stay upright, what with branches springing into my face. Hodge boulders his way through. It seems weird that there would be this mess of foliage in the pristine, highly coiffed gardens of Elite Academy.

As we get further into the thicket, the lights of the Academy become hidden behind a wall of trees. My alarm grows. There's no way any surveillance cameras can be watching us here. The branches are woven too closely together. With every step, leaves whip around our faces, and Hodge holds back some larger branches to allow me to pass through. After about ten minutes of our slow, crouching march, we reach an ancient-looking tree, its trunk broad and gnarled with age. Hodge walks straight toward it. Goosebumps prickle along my arms.

"What kind of a place is this?" I look up. The darkening sky forms black holes in the tree's canopy. One or two stars wink at me from above the hazy glow of the Academy's night lights. But there's not even a glimpse of any building.

Without replying, Hodge waves his fitness tracker in front of a knot on the ancient tree's trunk. A dark shadow opens in the bark, and suddenly we're peering into a gaping black hole. Hodge points me toward it.

"Wait. You want me to go in there?" I swallow and take a couple of nervous steps backward. "I can't . . . I can't . . ."

Hodge's face is stern. "You need to go in."

"But bad things happen when I go into dark spaces." There's a tightness in my throat, cutting off the oxygen to my brain.

Hodge leans in toward me. "Either you step in there, or I'll carry you."

Gulping back a little whimper, I nod. Judging by the width of his arms, I reckon he could carry two of me and not break a sweat. "Okay, okay."

With a deep, shaky breath, I step forward, and my foot rings with a hollow metallic sound that echoes downward. What looks like a natural hollow in the tree's trunk turns out to be a carefully constructed entrance, concealing a staircase that descends into the earth. Smooth concrete walls blend into the interior of the tree's natural wood. A breath of cold, stale air wafts up the shaft toward me, smelling of rust and damp and years of disuse. When Hodge follows me from untamed woodland into the narrow stairwell, the space is barely wide enough to fit his shoulders.

"I thought you said you were going to carry me. How would you fit?"

"Didn't say it would be comfortable." Hodge squeezes past me and steps down the staircase with the surefooted confidence of a veteran.

When I take the first step, the door closes behind us, and we're enveloped in utter darkness. All I can hear is the ringing footsteps of our boots on steel and my own heavy, panicked breaths. I calm down a little when a strip of yellow LEDs blinks into existence in a long spiral down the stairwell walls.

"Funny place to put the Haters' prison." I try to put a jaunty chuckle into my words and fail. I sound stupid, like I'm an older Lover who has forgotten how to make a joke.

"It's a bunker from the Haters' War days. Mostly forgotten now," Hodge replies, taking me down the endless spiral.

"So why—?"

"Wait."

"Okay, then. But where—"

"Shh."

"Yes, sir."

After circling down so many times my head is dizzy, we reach a landing. The stairwell continues spiraling into the center of the earth and disappears in a dim yellow haze. Beside the landing, a steel door is built into the concrete wall. The handle contains an ancient-looking lock beside a silvery vintage console. The console is so old it contains a number pad instead of a scanner. Hodge reaches up and enters a number sequence. The console cover flips open, revealing a small recess. He pulls a metal key out of the recess and inserts it into the old lock.

When he turns the metal handle, the heavy door hisses open, releasing a breath of stale, musty air into our faces. Hodge replaces the key in the vintage console, then motions for me to enter ahead of him. My nerves jangle viciously. With an obedient nod, I pass through the doorway into a room that takes my breath away.

"Whoa. What . . . ?" The words die on my lips as I try and take in my new surroundings.

A long wall of bookshelves completely fills the far wall behind a large mahogany desk. Two murals line either side of the room, painted to look like a bank of windows on a bright, sunny blue sky. The floor is bare concrete, and the bunker ceiling with its thick concrete pillars is a reminder that we're not on the executive level. But someone's painted a pretty convincing imitation of the Dorm Leader's office, right down to the sunshine streaming through the windows onto the floor.

I OPEN MY MOUTH TO ASK WHAT THE LOVE I'm doing here when a door opens in the bookshelf. My nerves tense. The bookshelf door opens wider. I get a brief view of a concrete corridor before the doorway is filled by Wil. Shamed, my gaze goes straight to the floor. He doesn't seem to notice and glides around to the front of the desk. Leaning back against the mahogany, he crosses his legs at the ankles. Unaware that my thoughts are a jumble of confusion and self-loathing, Wil turns to Hodge.

"Who turned?" he asks.

"Sif and Zin," Hodge replies. "But you probably already knew that."

"I hoped I was wrong." Wil sighs.

Surprised, I jerk up my head. "Uh . . . What?" I stammer, completely lost.

They keep talking as if I'm on mute.

"Fuschious did a pretty thorough job," Hodge remarks. "When did Realignment start taking six weeks?"

"This year. Part of his grand plan to take over as Dorm Leader. Zed knows but can't stop him. He's got too many friends in high places."

"I couldn't rescue them. I'm sorry." Hodge's shoulders slump a little.

"Not your fault."

"What do we do with them in the meantime?"

"I'll shuffle accommodation. Put something in about a promotion. Zed will understand."

"Is everyone coming tonight?" Hodge asks.

"So far." Wil nods. "Harmony's organizing the tracker hack, so she might miss the start. I ordered countermeasures in case our informants were suspicious. Bell is going to recheck the coding patch and make sure we've got the system blinded. That means most of the team will be late."

"Better late than Realigned." Hodge grimaces.

"Yep."

"What now?" Hodge asks.

Wil pushes himself off the desk and starts to walk around to a small command console behind it. Sitting in the plush executive chair, he starts typing and swiping on the screen. "Zed will need a status update, and then—"

I can't contain myself any longer. "What is going on!"

Wil blinks and looks at me as if he had forgotten I was sitting right there. "Sorry, Kerr. We have to get things sorted."

I shut my eyes, but that doesn't give me any ideas. So I open them again, head swiveling slowly between Wil and Hodge.

Wil gives me a quick smile. "You'll learn."

"Is this Haters' prison?"

When the question comes out of my mouth, Hodge lets out a loud snort of laughter. "Does this look like Haters' prison?" he asks.

"Well, in my exam I said . . . and then my friends . . . and you . . . and now . . ."

Hodge smiles. Wil smiles. I'm sure I've missed a really important part of a joke somewhere.

"Hodge did what he was assigned to do, which is to protect you," Wil states.

"Oh." I look from one to the other again. "What?"

Wil tilts his head back and smacks his forehead. "Oh man. I forgot we hadn't inducted you yet!" he groans.

"You didn't tell her?" Hodge seems incredulous.

Wil looks embarrassed. "She turned down the initial meeting."

"That's gotta be a first," Hodge scoffs.

Wil shrugs. "Yeah, well she came back, and that's when we ran into Executive trouble."

"Executive, as in . . . wait . . . you mean *Executive* Executive?" Disbelief is written across Hodge's face.

Wil looks sheepish. "I . . . I was getting to that . . ."

"Getting to what?" I ask.

Hodge's head sinks into his hands, and he lets out a groan. "Great. Just great."

Wil starts to explain, "Look, she was almost there. I just needed the right time to explain it, but Crucible left us with so many reports and policy upgrades that I couldn't— What are you doing?"

Hodge is fiddling with his fitness tracker again. "This is way over both our heads," he says, poking at the small strip of silicone around his wrist. "You got me to bring an uninducted Apprentice down to headquarters before you work out whether we can even trust her? I'm calling Zed in on this one."

"You don't need to do that." Wil looks a little panicked.

"Too late," Hodge declares.

"Oh man." Wil groans again. "I'm dead."

"What is going on?!" I squeak.

"You were supposed to handle this," Hodge says to Wil, a hint of warning in his tone.

Wil puts on his dashing smile. "I'll handle it. Don't worry. You go start the meeting. I'll brief Kerr here, and we'll be down in no time. Zed won't even need to be here."

Hodge gives Wil a doubtful look. "You sure about that?"

Wil flicks a wink at me, which sends heat straight to my face. I cover my embarrassment with a little cough.

"Come on, Hodge." Wil grins. "When have I ever been wrong?"

Hodge leans over the desk. "There only needs to be one time, and we're done."

"I know what I'm doing," Wil says, stubborn.

"I'll wait. Zed will be here soon anyway, so you won't have time to mess things up." With his arms crossed and drawn to his full height, Hodge looks like a Love Squad guard. A statue carved of sinew and muscle.

Wil must sense something, because he seems to give in. "Suit yourself." He points to one of the chairs in front of the desk. "Kerr, why don't you take a seat?"

"I'm good, thanks." I also cross my arms and stand a little straighter.

"Whatever." Wil shrugs again and leans back in Akela's seat like he owns it.

I rub my face, trying to scrub away the overwhelming sense of confusion. It doesn't work. "Look, this is all very interesting," I say. "But I'm pretty sure I failed my Filtering exam. My ex-best friend reported me as a Hater. I'm supposed to be meeting Dorm Leader in her office, and—"

"I know." Wil has twined his hands behind his head and is looking smug.

"You know?"

He winks at me, and in spite of myself, I smile. Of course Wil would know about Akela's movements. I roll my eyes at my own stupidity.

"Don't worry about the meeting," Wil says. "It's been handled. Tell us about the Filtering exam."

"Why?"

"You told everyone you met Midgate in the exam," Hodge explains. "That means you were up for Watcher."

Wil sits up in the seat. "Only time Midgate ever turns up to Filtering is if someone's up for Watcher." His expression is approving.

"Zed says it's the same test every time." Hodge gives me a sympathetic glance.

"Sell someone out as a Hater, or else," Wil adds.

"Who's Zed?"

"Zed is me," comes a warm, familiar voice from behind the desk. I spin around just in time to see Dorm Leader framed in the doorway. She steps into the room, her expression grim.

32

THE EFFECT OF DORM LEADER'S ARRIVAL IS immediate. Wil leaps out of Akela's chair as if stung and nearly runs to where Hodge is standing. Hodge straightens and gives Akela a salute. I go back to staring from one person to the next, shocked into stunned silence.

"You called?" Akela asks Hodge.

He just nods his head at me. "She hasn't been inducted."

Akela turns to Wil, who looks even more abashed. He opens his mouth, but she silences him with a wave of her hand.

"Right," she says, looking more displeased than I've ever seen her. Wil shoves his hands behind his back, looking for all the world like a Nursery kid caught stealing extra breakfast.

"Let's start from the beginning, then, shall we?" Akela says briskly as she sits herself down behind the desk. "Apprentice Flick, why don't you take a seat?"

"I, uh . . . yes, Dorm Leader." I dance over to the chair, sitting as fast and as gracefully as I can.

"Down here, we don't use that term." Akela flicks a look of annoyance at Wil, then back to me.

"Oh, sorry, Dor . . . ah . . . um . . . Why am I here?" I ask.

She folds her hands in front of her on the desk and gives me a patient smile. "This is a disused emergency bunker. A relic of the old wars against hate. We brought you here because it's the only place in the Academy where you aren't recorded by surveillance cameras."

"So it's not the Haters' prison?"

Wil snorts. "She's pretty slow for someone so clever."

Akela silences him with a warning glance, then turns back to me with a pleasant expression. "No. You are not going to Haters' prison. At least, not as long as I have a say in it."

"But I failed." Tears sting my eyes.

Akela's face softens. "Failed?"

"My Filtering exam. Midgate wanted me to report Sif. I said it was me instead."

Akela looks at me for a long time. "Kerr, perhaps it would be better if I start from the beginning. First of all, I am not testing you on your Collective loyalty here. Anything you say is safe. Okay?"

Automatically, I crane my neck to look at the ceiling. There is no black bubble of a camera anywhere, but it's not reassuring. Dorm Leader's words leave me feeling a little anxious, not comfortable.

"Secondly, your exam results did not condemn you as a Hater."

"Then why am I here?"

"Do you remember the day you first came to my office?"

"Do I remember?" I give her a look laced with "well, duh." *Memory Freak, remember?*

She gives me a wry smile in return. "Of course you do. Silly question. Well, you would certainly remember the invitation Wil offered you at the end."

I nod, shame making me mute.

She goes on, "I was a little disappointed when you didn't arrive."

"You . . . ? But Wil . . ."

"There are certain safety measures I have to take, Apprentice. But the invitation came from me as much as it came from Wil."

"I was scared," I say. "I should have just come, but Sif interrupted me, and then I couldn't do anything. I'm sorry."

"Don't be. I realize that I was asking too much too soon. Nursery Dorms program you to be obedient to the Collective alone. They don't train you to have individual thought. Of course, that makes my job harder, but that's how it is. Love knows I've had to learn patience over the years."

I nod, waiting for her to get to some kind of point.

"It was only a matter of time before you came back anyway," Wil adds.

"I wanted to. I just didn't know how."

Dorm Leader nods. "Understandable. I was asking you to go against ten years of loyalty training, after all. The seeds were there: Your memory was leaking. You knew that they were memories and not hallucinations. When you didn't arrive, I hoped that your memory would return more fully and you'd start to ask questions. It would have solved a lot of things if you knew . . . more about your past."

"I only ever see little fragments, and they're all confused."

"You still try to squash them down, don't you?"

"To be honest, I still think I'm going insane."

Wil coughs behind me. "You're saner than most Lovers," he laughs.

Akela shoots a warning look at him. "Wil is right. There is nothing wrong with you."

"Try telling that to my nightmares." I shudder.

"Memories," Hodge corrects.

"Right." I nod.

Akela continues. "I couldn't reveal the truth until I was sure you could handle it. Not until your final exam confirmed your potential."

"But I said I was a Hater."

"Exactly. What you did was the bravest thing I have seen in quite some time."

Confusion gives way to a small ember of pride. Dorm Leader is . . . pleased?

She smiles at me again. "Most people would have reported a fellow Apprentice without a hint of guilt. But even though you knew they wanted Sif, you held back. Why?"

"I . . . She was my friend." Stammering, I flounder for the words. "I'd rather face the Haters' Pavilion than know I sent her there."

Akela takes a deep breath. "That's a very unusual way of thinking for a Collective citizen."

I hang my head. "Lover Zink always said I would never make it as an Elite." My words stumble over each other.

"You said in your exam that you wanted to be a Watcher. Do you know why?"

I frown, thinking back through painful memory. "I guess I wanted to prove something. Back at my Nursery Dorm, they all laughed at me when I said I wanted to be an Elite. So when I found out the Watchers are the top—the Elite of the Elite—well, I guess I thought . . . if I made Watcher, I'd . . . I'd show them that I really do belong."

Akela presses her lips together, processing what I've just said. "Do you know what the Watchers do?" she inquires.

"I couldn't really find out anything about them. I know they earn a lot of money," I reply, and Wil laughs again.

Akela sighs. "Kerr, you have no idea what a Watcher does, do you?" Her look is one of sympathy, and I start to feel a little foolish. I can't see them, but I am almost certain Hodge and Wil are looking at me like I'm as stupid as I feel.

"I tried to find out." I notice Hodge isn't smiling. "But there's almost no information on Watchers. I just knew they must be important if they work in the Hall of Love, and I—"

"Kerr," Akela interrupts. "The Watchers are the eyes and ears of the Love Collective. They spend their days picking through millions of hours of footage, double-checking the results of surveillance algorithms. They spy on ordinary citizens in order to weed out disloyalty. Their whole job is to report Haters for Embracement."

Her words begin to sink in. My world shifts slightly sideways. "They . . . what?"

"Watchers are spies," Hodge says.

"They're the reason you were there in the Nursery Dorms." Wil walks forward so I can see him without turning.

"So . . ." I stammer.

"So you are totally, 100 percent, absolutely, entirely the wrong kind of person to be one." His grin is wide but not mocking.

Their words sink in a little more. "Did I fail the test?" I say, staring at Akela.

She inclines her head. "Depends on how you look at it," she says. "If I were Supreme Lover Midgate? Yes. Absolutely. You needed to act with unquestioning loyalty without a second thought to condemn your closest associate. In Midgate's eyes, you're not Watcher material at all."

Misery hits me like a bucket of ice water thrown over my head.

Akela smiles. "In my eyes, though, you passed the test with flying colors."

"But I'm still out of the Academy, aren't I?"

"What?" Wil shakes his head vigorously. "No way!"

Akela gets up from her chair and comes around to where I'm sitting. She crouches down in front of me, looking into my eyes with a warmth that I've never seen before.

"My dear, you are so much more special than you realize. All these years, I have never seen anyone do what you did. I've seen a few students take the Watcher test, but never—never—have I seen anyone call themselves a Hater. That is bravery I have not seen since . . ." Akela looks away, her face clouded with pain. "Well, not for a long time, anyway."

"But if I said I'm a Hater, then—"

"You're no Hater."

I look up at Hodge. He leans back against the wall like a Love Squad officer at rest. But his expression is kind.

If I wasn't so emotionally exhausted, I'd probably dissolve into a flood of tears. "I failed the test."

Dorm Leader stands and paces in front of the desk. Her expression is thoughtful, but I notice that she's clasping and unclasping her hands.

"Well . . . that actually depends," she says.

"On what?"

"On whether you want to be inducted or not."

"I don't . . . I don't follow." I look at the boys for some kind of cue. Wil is looking at me as if I'm a Triumph Carnival prize. Hodge still isn't smiling, but he's watching me intently. I look back at Akela. She nods to Wil, who quickly responds.

"Kerr didn't get any of the clues we left her, so I'll have to lay it all out." Akela waves him on and walks back behind her desk to the wall of shelves.

"Clues? What clues?" I haven't seen Wil in weeks. What is he talking about?

"So many." The way he looks at me, he must think I've missed something glaringly obvious.

I bristle. "All I've seen is standard Elite training. Unless you're talking about the note you slipped me."

"Well, that was the biggest one. We've been leaving clues all the way along. Trying to get you to see the lie you've been sold all your life."

"The Love Collective is all there is, Wil. Remember?" I try to mimic Dorm Leader's tone as well as I can.

Wil shakes his head. "Rubbish. You know there's a story the LC isn't telling you. Your memories are proof of that."

"They're proof I'm going crazy."

Wil pinches the bridge of his nose between his fingers. "Oh man. I wish Sif hadn't been Realigned. She was so much better at this than you." He looks back up at me, looking a bit like an adult who's about to explain something to a Nursery Apprentice for the fortieth time. "Do you remember the Engine Room sim where you were in charge of the Love Squad? The one where your friend freaked out?"

"How do you know about that?" My suspicion level rises.

He glances sideways at Akela, then continues. "There was something in that sim that you weren't supposed to see. Wasn't there?"

"The ND mission thing."

"We hacked the sim to show you what a real Engine Room would see. Herz hides the whole picture. Doesn't show Apprentices the dark side of the job until you're 100 percent committed and can't back out. But Sif picked up on what was happening, even if you didn't." While Wil explains, Akela is running her fingers along one of the bookshelves. "The ND patrols are Love Squads sent into homes. Before they arrest the adults, they abduct the kids."

Darkness. Screaming. Boots thundering down the hall . . .

"Nursery Dorms are facilities where children are prepared for what they call 'proper' citizenship," Hodge continues, acknowledging my shocked expression. "But really, they're factories for creating loyal armies of worker bees from the ashes of the homes they burn down and the families they kill."

"The Collective . . . *stole* me?" I manage to squeak out. "But why?"

"What can you remember?" Hodge's hopeful tone is too much for me.

A suspicious little voice goes off in the back of my head: *careful*. I picture standing in the Haters' Pavilion, Wil pointing at me and yelling, "She told us she had *memories*!"

I look at the three of them. Then I look around the ceiling, just to reassure myself that the cameras really aren't there after all.

"I remember . . ." My voice trembles. Darkness and

screaming filter through my thoughts again. I close my eyes. With the rollercoaster of emotion I've been living today, the wall between me and bursting into tears has worn way too thin. I struggle to hold it all back. "It's hard. My head hurts every time I try to go back there."

"Take your time," Hodge says quietly.

"Don't forget him, Cadence. Don't ever forget . . ."

"I can't . . ." I gasp, squinting against the pain.

Wil's face clouds with anger. "Your head hurts because they block out our memories, Kerr. All of us. When they take us to the Nursery Dorms, they give us new names, put us in those sterile prisons, and expect us to grow up feeling thankful for eating protein slop our whole lives."

"Wil," Hodge warns.

Akela steps away from the bookshelf, holding two books. One is a thin, official-looking dossier bearing the Love Collective seal and the title "Operation Cradle." She holds it open toward me.

"Operation Cradle is the official command document for all Love Squads," she explains.

My hand shakes as I take it from her. The pages are yellowing, stiff with age. "This looks like a standard procedure manual for deliveries," I say, reading the stark, ordinary type.

"Typical Collective doublespeak, Kerr. When they talk about 'packages,' they mean 'children.' When they say 'origin,' they mean 'homes,'" Wil says.

I flick to a page headed "Neutralization Procedure" and read the bulleted lists of instructions. My mouth goes dry.

Of primary importance is obtaining unblemished packages that may be prepared in Dormitories with a minimum of medical intervention. Patrols may do whatever is necessary to subdue resistance during the collection of packages, up to and including deadly force.

Like the sudden burst of light exploding from a firework, everything makes sense. The void I couldn't get past. Dark figures in the night. Sif's discovery in the Engine Room simulation. Lover Herz's agitated response.

"I was hiding in a closet. They . . . they found me, and they took . . ."

The policy document falls into my lap, and I look up at my companions in anguish. With a face full of sympathy, Akela pushes another book toward me. It's thicker than the dossier with an old-fashioned red hardcover binding. She points to an open page covered in black, spindly handwriting.

"These records were too sensitive to print, so I had to write them down by hand," she says.

I stare at the writing. It takes a few seconds to focus. When I do, a strangled sob escapes my lips.

Apprentice: Kerr Flick #540/187503
Name: Cadence Elizabeth
Mother: Williams, Angelica.
Father: Williams, Paul.
Residence: . . .

"ANGELICA WILLIAMS . . ." I SAY, VOICE CHOKED with emotion.

"Your name is not Kerr Flick," Akela says, her voice low but tender. "It's Cadence. The Collective tried to erase your memories and start you as a blank slate. But they didn't realize you had a memory that couldn't be tamed."

I caress the letters, letting the names of my parents soak into my memory. Tears begin to stream down my face. "They were Haters . . ."

"That's only what the Collective wants you to think, Cadence," Akela says.

Distant echoes cascade into my memory. I squeeze my eyes shut, letting my fingers flutter to my forehead. A night bird calls somewhere outside the window. But there's no window . . .

"You made me remember my mother's death," I sob, face contorting in pain.

Akela's hand falls on my wrist, gentle but firm. "I hoped that if you saw her face, it would break down the memory walls . . ."

"You made me remember her death!" I spit the words into her face. My scream bounces off the concrete with hollow echoes.

Akela flinches, eyes distraught.

All of the pain and sorrow and tumultuous grief that I had been holding back all these months erupts in shuddering wails. The nightmare floods into my head, and I can't hold it back. I remember the darkness of the closet as Mumma held me, her panicked breaths urging me not to forget. I remember the smell of her perfume. The prickle of her necklace against my face. As if they're in the room, I hear the boots pounding down that hallway to our hiding place. I can still feel the soldiers' grips while they ripped me out of her arms. I remember my screams in the darkness, crying for the woman I wouldn't recognize for years.

My sobs erupt again in soul-crushing grief. Akela's arms enfold me, and I weep against her shoulder, unable to stop memories from piercing me like fresh arrows. I see Angelica—Mumma—standing in front of the Haters' Pavilion. The trickle of blood down her face as she stood proud and unbroken, even as they hurled their insults and fists. Then a sickening memory lurches back and I gasp.

The infotab glass was so smooth beneath my fingers as I watched the Haters' Pavilion Show. Hater One. The worst of them all. My finger poised above the voting screen, adding my voice to the cacophony of condemning shouts. Triumph and jubilation as Carell Hummer pronounced sentence. The victory dance afterward.

My stomach lurches with revulsion and self-loathing.

"I k-killed her." Overwhelming nausea rises in my throat. With a mighty effort I launch myself out of my seat and away from Akela's embrace. Wil and Hodge stand as frozen as the mural around us. I stagger away from them. The contents of my stomach rise up, and I heave them onto the concrete in a far corner of the room.

"I kill-killed Mumma," I sob, sinking to the ground as all my strength seeps from me.

33

WIL DEPARTS ON A MISSION, SENT BY A whispered command from Akela to find something I didn't hear. Hodge runs down the stairs deep into the bunker in search of a mop and bucket. I sit back on the chair facing Akela for what seems like hours, unable to lift my head, thanks to the sorrow weighing me down. A faint, acidic smell wafts across from the far corner of the room. I've blamed myself. I've wept with shame. I've exhausted all my words, and now there's nothing left.

"It's not your fault, Cadence," Akela says kindly, breaking the silence.

I look down at my sleeves, now stained and wet with tears. The cloth she gave me to mop my face is clenched so hard in my fist that my fingers hurt. "How can you say that?"

"It's not your fault."

"But I—"

"It's not your fault." Her voice is more firm and her eyes bore into mine.

A fresh bout of tears wells up in my stinging eyes. "Feels like it." I clench my jaw, holding back a sob. A small tear leaks.

Akela reaches up with another cloth and dabs at my face. I flinch at the unfamiliar sensation. She rocks back on her heels, giving me space.

"The Love Collective did this. Not you," she says, looking me straight in the eye.

"How did I not know? She was right there on the big screen, and I knew nothing. Not even a twitch of an idea that it was her. How? How could they do that?" My voice is thin and tremulous. "What kind of love makes you vote for your own mother's execution?"

Akela pats my knee and then stands. Her braids sway behind her head in a slow, graceful arc. But her face is a warring blend of emotions.

"The question is," she says after she's walked all the way around her desk. "What do you want to do with this knowledge you have?"

"What knowledge? My parents were Haters. Apart from some weird night raid, I know nothing else."

"You know there's more to it than that."

"I can't access it."

"But you know it's there."

"Fat lot of good it does me."

The door to the room swings open, and Hodge enters bearing a clanky old metal bucket and timber-handled mop.

"This is the best I could find," he says. "There's a lot of rust and mold in some of those cupboards."

"Thanks, Hodge. It will do."

He sloshes water from the bucket, wiping away the evidence of my trauma but not the memory of it.

"Sorry," I mumble.

"Don't sweat it. Hodge reacted far worse than that," Akela says, a smile curling at the corner of her lips.

"I may have . . . punched a few holes in some walls," Hodge admits, head bent over his work.

"Wait. They took you too?" I ask, wiping at my nose with the back of my sleeve. I must look like a mess right now.

Hodge pauses, leaning on the mop handle. "Not the way they took you. When I was little, I got sick. My parents took me to a health center for treatment, and the medics just knocked me out. Next thing I'm in Nursery Dorms doing drills. Although I didn't know about the health center thing until . . ." He mimes a punch.

"What happened?"

"Akela helped me through it. Without her, I'd probably have been reported by now." He gives Akela a quick smile and then goes back to wiping my mess off the floor.

"Cadence, it's always traumatic when the memories start to break through," Akela explains. "Traumatic for everyone. But Hodge is proof that it doesn't have to stay that way."

"It hurts," I whimper. "I can't remember her."

Akela reaches out toward me, then draws her hands back again, looking torn. For a moment the tears threaten to erupt again, but I fight them back. With immense effort, I force myself back under control. Out of habit, the old saying wanders into my thoughts: *Elites show no weakness. Elites show no weakness.* The irony of it all drags a bitter laugh out of me, and I shake my head wearily.

"Do you still want to know the real story? Get your memories back?" Akela asks.

"I can't. It's like there's a wall stopping me from getting through. Every time I try and see something else, my head hurts."

"That's what Realignment does. They say they're erasing your memories, but they're only locking them away." Hodge gives me a sympathetic look. "Then they create a conditioning matrix that stops you from wanting to remember."

"So I'm stuck with this pain?"

"There is a way to destroy the Realignment barrier," Akela says. "It's rough, but it will stop your headaches. But I won't let you proceed beyond that until you understand the risks."

"Risks?"

"You can't talk to anyone in public about this. The only reason I am being so frank right now is because we're free of surveillance. Out there is a completely different story." She points upward, beyond the ceiling.

"I understand."

"Sharing this information outside this room could mean your death or the death of others."

A chill settles over me. I swallow. Smooth my face to what I hope is a cool, confident, stare. "I need to know who I am."

Akela steeples her fingers. Thinks for a few silent moments. "There's nothing wrong with waiting a few days," she says.

"Why? I already know my mother was executed as a Hater. What could be worse than that?"

"The process is painful."

"I'm already in pain."

"It may change everything you know."

"Then change it."

"Can you promise me that you will never speak a word of this to anyone outside this bunker?"

"I promise. Absolutely. Not even Sif."

Hodge snorts. "I would hope not!"

Akela stands, steps to the bookcase behind her desk, and pulls on one of the book spines. A panel opens in the wall, revealing a small hallway lined with doors. She beckons, and both Hodge and I follow.

"This will all be okay," Hodge whispers into my ear. "Don't worry."

"I'm not worried," I lie.

The door behind Akela's desk bursts open, and Wil leaps into the room.

"Everything's ready if you are," he says to Akela.

THE HALLWAY CERTAINLY HAS A MILITARY feel about it. Steel doors. Emergency lights. It's like walking through a museum exhibit of the Hater's War. Our footsteps make staccato echoes.

Halfway down the passageway, Akela makes a sudden turn and leads us through an open door. Wil bounds ahead into the room. I gasp when I see where we've come to.

The empty concrete walls speak of years of neglect. Old posters curl away from the wall, yellowed and fading. An old filing cabinet sits empty in a corner, its drawers half open and covered in a thick grey layer of dust. Wil taps away at an ancient console keyboard, which sits on a rusting metal desk. In the middle of the room lies a cracked vinyl treatment bed, surrounded by a small array of medical equipment. There's a hook bearing a medical halo and cables and IV equipment. The same sort of equipment I remember seeing wrapped all over Sif in her Realignment chamber.

"Wait a second. What is this?" I squeak, alarm pushing my voice to a high pitch. I take an involuntary step back, once again colliding with Hodge's chest. He lets out a soft laugh.

Akela lifts the halo into her palm. "I'm not surprised that you would be nervous about this, especially after witnessing your friend's treatment. In the hands of Lovers like Fuschious, it is quite a weapon."

"Why didn't you stop him?" I ask. "You were there. I saw you. Why couldn't you stop him from doing that to all of those Apprentices?"

Hodge's voice beside me is harsh. "Give her a break, Cadence. You've got no idea what she does when you're not looking."

"I wish I could. Believe me." Akela's eyes are sincere. "But I can tell you what would happen if I shut him down. I would be arrested. Another Dorm Leader would be assigned here. And none of you would ever have a chance to know who you really are. At least this way I can save some."

I give a halfhearted nod, still feeling dissatisfied. I may be powerless, but surely she could do . . . something?

"Couldn't you just restore everyone's memories? Why do we all have to live without knowing who we are?"

"Not everyone wants to know the truth."

"I do."

"Your memory is so strong that the past has already broken through. But many of your comrades are so comfortable in their ignorance they just aren't interested. They like being Elite Apprentices. Having app time. Not having to think for themselves. It's easy."

Dorm Leader replaces the halo on its cradle.

"I don't think it's wise to do anything right now, given your uncertainty." She raises a hand, stopping the unspoken protest that she sees forming on my lips. "I want you to have a chance to think through the consequences. This is going to set the course of your life, even more than Fitness to Proceed or the Filtering exam."

"I know I was a bit . . . panicked just then, but I don't need to think about it anymore," I insist. "I need my memories back."

"It's not the memories that I'm worried about, Cadence" Akela's face is somber. "It's what comes afterward that I need you to consider."

"What?"

"All of your life, what has the Love Collective meant to you?"

I pause, scrunching up my face in thought. The Love Collective is all I've known. White, sterile halls and plain, colorless dormitories. Lovers punishing us for disobedience. Drill practice. Hater Recognition Signs and strict lists of approved lexicon. Routine. Education. Discipline. Control. Which up until now has meant only one thing.

"Safety."

Akela nods. "Knowing how you ended up as an Apprentice will shatter that safety. Do you think you're ready for that?"

I bite my lip.

She holds up a palm. "See? You're not ready."

This time it's my turn to raise my hand. Part of me can't believe I'm being so bold. "I disagree. The Love Collective wanted me to report Sif, but I didn't. Correct?"

"Yes, and they would keep expecting it," Hodge replies. "That's how they keep us in line: Report on your neighbors. Tell on your closest friends. That way, nobody ever gains enough power to challenge them."

"That doesn't sound like love to me."

"Well . . ." Dorm Leader's uncertain tone tells me all I need to know.

I straighten my shoulders. Look Akela directly in the eye. "I am prepared to face any consequences of my decision. Put me under. Give me my memory back. I need to know exactly what they've taken from me."

From his seat at the table, Wil gives a little fist pump, lets out a quiet, "Yes!"

Dorm Leader's face carries years of unfathomable mysteries. I wish I could know what she's seen so I could understand why she looks so burdened and weary.

Finally, she nods. "All right. But you have been warned."

With a racing pulse, I step forward to the infirmary bed, hoisting myself up into a sitting position. I kick off my shoes and wait. The screen wobbles as Wil taps out commands on the chunky old keyboard. Dorm Leader glides in front of me, holding aloft the medical halo.

"Hold still for a moment for me, okay?" she says, looking past my eyes at the top of my head. With a graceful movement she scoops my hair into a ponytail, and then sets the halo on my head. The halo fits snugly around my temples, and a pair of earbuds nestle into place. A soft series of beeps emanates from the console where Wil is working.

"Now just lie back gently," she says, all business.

I obey, leaning against the cushioned head of the medical bed and swiveling my legs into place along the mattress.

"In a minute, you will go to sleep," Dorm Leader explains. "It will seem like only a few seconds pass, but this process will most likely take all night."

"Okay. Will I be here alone?"

"No, I will make sure you have company. Hodge will need to get to a meeting shortly, but there will be someone here supervising you until the process is complete."

Akela leans over me and holds my face between her warm hands. "For the last time: are you entirely sure you want to do this?"

"I won't be able to get on with life if my memories keep ambushing me," I say. "I have to know."

"That's the plan," says Wil with bright cheerfulness, still staring at his console screen.

I hold my hand up so Akela can attach a sensor on it.

"You don't have to do this," Hodge says.

"Yes, I do."

Wil makes a few confident taps and then looks up at me. "Okay, we're set to go. Ready?"

"Ready." I give him a thumbs-up.

"Last chance to back out." Hodge waggles his fingers at me.

"I need this, Hodge."

"She's ready at this end," Akela says, prodding the halo gently.

"Alrighty then. Here . . . we . . . go!" Wil calls, pressing a button on his keyboard.

The earbuds begin to hum, and my world whirls into a dark void. This time, I embrace it with my heart soaring, ready to step into a history I never knew I owned.

ACKNOWLEDGMENTS

A book is a long, hard labour of love that cannot be born without the love and support of many others. This book began many years ago, and owes its existence to some really special people.

To Iola Goulton, without whom this book would not have existed. An amazing editor, who suggested that a manuscript 'needed a little backstory'. That turned Book 1 into Book 3, and here we are. Without Iola's keen eye on the story, and her sacrificial Christian love, this may never have found its way into existence. Thank you.

To Steve Laube and Enclave Publishing, who were willing to take a risk on this Aussie author, and who consistently produce fantastic Christian fiction. I feel incredibly blessed that I get to work with such amazing people.

To my little crowd of online cheerleaders, Cecily Paterson, Christine Dillon and Laura Tharion. Thank you. You've been there all the way, encouraging me to pick myself up and persevere. We have laughed together, commiserated together, and spurred each other to keep on writing. Couldn't have gone through this without you.

To John, my love, my cheerleader and the most patient husband. Who didn't complain when I disappeared for hours on end into imaginary worlds. Thank you for our partnership.

To Omega Writers, the group of committed and loving Australian Christian writers, who gave me such a wonderful chance to meet others and to learn from them.

But most of all, I owe my thanks to the real Composer, God our Father. I am so grateful that he gave me the opportunity to be creative in this way. My prayer is that through these stories, we may hear the true song of the Composer, and find his Lyric and the life he offers us all. John 1.

ABOUT THE AUTHOR

Kristen Young is an Aussie children's and youth worker who always has a notebook on hand to catch ideas for her fiction and non-fiction. She loves hanging out with her family, watching movies with subtitles, and chocolate.